"Don't," ___ of her painful memories. "Don't say things you don't really mean."

There was an undertone of something in his voice that made her breath stop. A tightness, an edge, something.

Heat. That, too. In his voice, and in his eyes as he looked at her.

"But I do mean it," she said softly. "I've only just realized I've meant it for a while now."

"Lyss—"

She put a hand on his chest, over his heart, and his words cut off as if her action had sucked the very air out of him. She could feel the thud of his heart, felt a skip in her own heartbeat as his accelerated at her touch.

Dear Reader,

I never grew up with a brother. I had one, but he died as an infant before I was born, so I never had that kind of sibling relationship with a male. Perhaps that's why it fascinates me so. Or perhaps it's because it's so very different from the sister/sister relationship I do know. But my husband had four brothers, and a son and daughter, so I've had great opportunity to observe and learn. And I have a niece and nephew who are playing out that growing up together right now. Right about here is where I should say the story in this book is not a representation of any of those relationships!

If you grew up with brothers, I envy you. It's something I missed, and although I suspect I would not have appreciated it every step of the way, that it intrigues me is obvious since they keep cropping up in my work. And to those of you who would say, "If you'd had one, you wouldn't feel that way!" I can only say I'm the victim (grateful recipient?) of that writer's curse... the words *What if?*

In a previous book *(Operation Reunion)* I explored that brother/sister connection. In this book, it's two very different brothers, one long dead but still affecting the other, in fact shaping his entire life.

I hope you enjoy it!

Justine

OPERATION UNLEASHED

—

Justine Davis

⟨H⟩ **HARLEQUIN**®ROMANTIC SUSPENSE

Recycling programs
for this product may
not exist in your area.

ISBN-13: 978-0-373-27873-2

OPERATION UNLEASHED

H HARLEQUIN®

Printed in U.S.A.

™ www.Harlequin.com

JUSTINE DAVIS

Justine Davis lives on Puget Sound in Washington state, watching big ships and the occasional submarine go by, and sharing the neighborhood with assorted wildlife, including a pair of bald eagles, deer, a bear or two and a tailless raccoon. In the few hours when she's not planning, plotting or writing her next book, her favorite things are photography, knitting her way through a huge yarn stash and driving her restored 1967 Corvette roadster—top down, of course.

Connect with Justine at her website, justinedavis.com, at twitter.com/justine_d_davis, or on Facebook at facebook.com/justinedaredavis.

MAX

I was used to female German Shepherds, so when Mandy died, I immediately sought out another Shepherd. A woman invited me out to see her dogs; she had at least 7 Shepherds. When I got there, I asked, "Which one is mine?" She pointed to a smallish brown and white male dog, with floppy (not pointy) ears. So I said, "What's that?" And she said, "That's Max. He's part Brittany, part Pointer. You can have him." I wanted a Shepherd. Female, not a male mutt. But the thought of having fur to pet and cuddle led me to lead him to the car. By the time I got home, I was in love! Max had eyes the color of sherry, he craved salad, and he was my constant companion and faithful guy for 13 years. The night my mother died, he went into my mother's room and walked around her hospital bed, as if to say, "Goodbye." And less than a year later, Max became suddenly, catastrophically ill—and I was having to say "Goodbye" to him. It is the hardest thing I've ever had to do. He died in 1995, and I still miss him every day. Max the wonderful dog—I still love you.

—Binnie Syril Braunstein

This is the latest in a series of dedications from readers who have shared the pain of the loss of a beloved dog. For more information visit my website at www.justinedavis.com.

Chapter 1

Quinn Foxworth had never really realized just how loud a dog's bark could be. For an instant, when Cutter exploded into earsplitting noise inside the closed vehicle, a vision of distant sands and guard dogs trumpeting a warning of an enemy inside the perimeter shot through his mind.

That hadn't happened for a long time. He consciously eased his muscles, especially his hands, on the steering wheel and instinctively slowed the SUV down.

"Loud when he wants to be, isn't he?"

Quinn looked over at his fiancée, and the last of the memory vanished. He was grateful she hadn't noticed his reaction. And then her gaze locked on his and he saw in her eyes that Hayley hadn't missed a thing. But she had intentionally not prodded.

No wonder he loved her beyond measure.

"Yes," he said belatedly, having to raise his voice just as she had to be heard over the cacophony from the back of the SUV.

"He's not usually like that in the car," she said. "You know he has exquisite manners. Well, except for when that guy tried to reach in."

"Good for him. And lucky for the guy it wasn't me."

She smiled. Yeah, he loved her all right. And their wedding wasn't soon enough to suit him, even though it was less than a month away.

The barking suddenly morphed into a howl, and Cutter clawed at the back hatch of the car.

"Well, that's a new one," Hayley said, wincing at the sound.

"Easy, dog," Quinn said, but the howling continued.

He'd learned by now that ignoring Cutter was never a good idea. They were on a rather narrow lane, headed home from the indulgence of a breakfast out, but they'd passed a park a few yards back. He checked the mirrors, then put the SUV in Reverse. The moment they began to back up, the howling subsided to a mild whine that at least allowed room for thought.

He backed up until he could swing into the small parking area. The whine stopped. But Cutter was clearly still on full alert, ears and tail up, staring out toward the park.

"I suppose he wants out."

"It's raining," Hayley said, "of course he does."

With a sigh, Quinn hit the button that raised the hatch. Before he could even get his door open Cutter was out and running across the wet grass of the park.

"Well, he's thoroughly unleashed now," Quinn muttered as he walked around the back of the car to where Hayley stood, watching the dog go.

"Did that look full of intent to you?" she asked.

Hayley was focused on Cutter. Quinn stole the moment to just look at her again. He never got tired of the little jab of wonder that struck him when he realized she was his, that she would always be by his side.

"Quinn?"

"Sorry," he said, not meaning it in the least. "I was distracted by the view. As usual."

He loved that she still colored up when he said stuff like that.

"Thank you," she said simply. "But…"

She gestured toward the far side of the park, where their rascal of a dog was approaching the child who sat on one of the swings. A blond boy in jeans and a sweatshirt but no jacket, with a small backpack beside him. He was staring at the ground, digging a sneakered toe into the mud.

"If you mean did all that ruckus in the car and then the beeline over there seem very specific, then yes," he said in answer to her original question. "We'd better go rein him in. Don't want the kid getting scared."

She nodded, and they started across the grass. The rain was coming down steadily, but lightly. Cutter was almost there, but the boy hadn't seemed to notice. In fact, he didn't seem to be noticing anything except the way the mud oozed around what looked to be fairly new, once white sneakers.

Cutter had come to a halt about two feet away from the boy. "Maybe he just wants to play," Hayley said. "There haven't been any kids around for him to play with lately, since Brian moved away."

The dog sat. Waited.

"Well, he's not playing," Quinn said. "And the kid doesn't look much like he wants to."

"It is raining."

"When I was that age, I couldn't have cared less if it was raining if there was playing to be done."

Hayley laughed, a light, lovely sound that never failed to expand the warmth he always felt when he was with her.

"Not every boy is a bold adventurer such as yourself," she teased.

"That's what I get for being born before kids became tethered to a video game console."

"Thank goodness."

She turned her gaze back to the pair they were nearing. Cutter had reached out with his nose, and the boy had responded perfectly, holding out his hand, low and slow, for the dog to sniff. Someone had taught him, Quinn thought.

And then the dog rose and went forward, turning sideways to lean against the boy's knees. The boy moved then, reaching to pat the dog. Cutter leaned harder. The boy's fingers burrowed into thick fur. And Cutter leaned even more. They were just close enough to hear the odd sound the boy made before he leaned forward himself, wrapping his arms around the animal's neck as if he were a life preserver. Cutter twisted his head up and back, and swiped his tongue across the boy's cheek. A smile broke through, and only when he saw it did Quinn realize just how downcast the boy had seemed.

"You're right, Cutter isn't acting like he wants to play, either," Hayley finally agreed. "In fact, he looks like…"

Her voice faded away. Quinn nodded. Spoke quietly.

"Yeah. He looks like he's protecting."

"Standing between that boy and the world," she said softly.

Quinn let out a compressed breath. "I knew it had been too quiet these last couple of weeks."

When the boy looked up at them, his expression wary, they stopped a few feet away. Cutter looked at them, his tail wagging in greeting. He made a quiet little whuffing sound, but never moved away from the boy.

Quinn held back slightly, letting Hayley take the lead with the child.

"Hi," she said softly. "That's Cutter, if you were wondering what his name is."

The boy clung to the dog. "Cutter?"

That earned him another swipe of the tongue that made him smile despite his wariness.

"What kind of dog is he? I like how he's black in front and brown in back."

"We're not sure, exactly. He looks like a sheepdog that comes from Europe."

"Oh."

"Are you here by yourself?" Hayley asked.

The boy's expression went back to wary. His gaze flicked to Quinn, then back to Hayley. "I'm not supposed to talk to strangers."

"That's a good plan." Quinn spoke for the first time, gently. "But Cutter's already introduced himself."

"My mom says sometimes bad people use dogs or cats to try and trick kids."

Hayley smiled. "Good for your mom. She's right, and I'm glad she warned you about that. So why don't you take us to her? Then we can talk to her and not be strangers anymore. And she can decide if it's okay for you to get to know Cutter."

The boy sighed. "She'll say no. She's mad again."

"At you?" Quinn asked.

"Sort of. And at my dad."

Hayley glanced at Quinn. He nodded; the boy seemed to talk more easily to her, understandably. "What did your dad do?"

"He said something bad about my father."

Uh-oh, Quinn thought. Already into a domestic situation. Divorce, stepfather, that could get ugly. Except the boy had called him his dad. Did you do that with a stepfather you didn't like? Then again, the kid was very young. Maybe he was just calling him what he was told to call him.

"Your dad and your father don't get along?" Hayley asked, using the boy's terms.

"He's really my uncle. My father's dead."

Hayley blinked again.

"Who's your uncle?" Quinn asked, starting to feel as if he'd stumbled into some kind of comedy skit. But the boy's expression wasn't the least bit amused.

"My dad."

Quinn wasn't much good at guessing ages on kids this young, but he put this one at somewhere in the six to eight range. Six in size, but older in the sadness in his eyes. A kid that young shouldn't be able to look like that. Younger even than the ten he had been when his parents had been killed. But at least this one still had his mother. And… whoever the father figure in his life really was.

"It's my fault," the boy said in a tiny voice.

Hayley moved then, closer. He knew this woman, knew she wouldn't be able to just leave a child who sounded so miserable. He wasn't sure he could walk away himself. Hayley teased him—lovingly—about being a protector to the core. Maybe she was right.

Hayley crouched in front of the boy on the swing. She didn't say any of the things most would, like "I'm sure it's not," or "You must have misunderstood." Instead, she simply asked, "Why is it your fault?"

The boy dug the toe of one sneaker deeper into the mud beneath the swing. "It just is. If I went away, then they'd be happy."

Hayley went very still. Quinn understood. No child should feel that way, but to hear it from one this young was unsettling.

"I'm sure they would miss you terribly," Hayley said softly.

The boy stayed silent then, as if he'd suddenly remembered he was still talking to strangers. Or as if he didn't believe a word of it.

And Quinn suddenly realized Cutter was staring at him. That intense, unsettling gaze was unwavering, and by now Quinn knew all too well what it meant.

Fix it.

He no longer bothered rationalizing it, not even to himself. He'd simply had to accept, by virtue of an undeniable amount of empirical evidence, that the dog knew what he was doing and somehow communicated it to anyone who would pay attention. And he seemed to instinctively know who would get the message, just as he always seemed to know who was in trouble and needed his help.

The problem was Quinn's, not Cutter's. How was he going to explain to a dog that absent genuine abuse, Foxworth never interfered in marital or parent-child situations? But family matter or not, when a boy this young talked about going away, it deserved some intervention. Just not the full force of the Foxworth organization.

On that thought, the dog let out a small sound, a soft but emphatic woof. Then he turned his attention back to the boy. Quinn felt decidedly shrugged off. Cutter had directed "Fix it," and fix it he meant.

"You know," Hayley was saying to the still silent boy, "Cutter's pretty smart. He's not a Bloodhound, but I'll bet he could find your house without you even telling him where it is."

Damn, she was good, Quinn thought. She had the boy's attention now, and she'd managed to focus it on an idea most kids his age would find irresistible. She'd be a great mom.

For an instant his stomach went into free fall. They weren't even married yet and he was thinking about kids? When not so long ago he would have sworn that would never happen, that he would never, ever bring kids into a world so screwed up by the people supposedly running it? But a baby, with Hayley? Their child?

Right, he muttered inwardly. *Just dealing with this kid's got you going sideways. You'd be great with one of your own.*

"Could he?" the boy asked, stroking the dog's head. "Really?"

"Shall we see?"

She glanced at Quinn. He gave her a half shrug. He'd been working with the dog on commands, if you could call it working when the animal seemed to learn everything on the first try. Once he'd come to trust the dog, once they had all accepted him as part of the team, he'd realized it would be best if everybody knew and used the same commands. He'd thought about using a different language, as military and police K-9s did to insure the dog obeyed only their orders, but since Cutter tended to completely ignore anyone he didn't know and trust telling him what to do, it seemed unnecessary.

"We can try," Quinn said. "Just remember Foxworth doesn't do domestic."

Hayley flashed him the smile that never failed to send a shiver down his spine. "It's not me, it's him you have to convince," she said, nodding toward Cutter. She didn't add, "And good luck with that," but it was in her tone anyway.

"Great," he muttered. He'd never met a more stubborn creature than that dog, and that included himself and even Rafe. "Let's go, then."

The boy looked at him somewhat warily. Quinn softened his voice. "Shall we see if he can do it?"

The boy still didn't speak, but slid off the swing.

"Cutter," Quinn said in an entirely different tone, one of command. The dog's head snapped around, those intense eyes fastened on him. Quinn pointed at the boy.

"Backtrack," he ordered.

The dog glanced from Quinn to the boy, then back. And then he whirled on his hindquarters and trotted off toward the tall trees. Quinn watched the boy watch the dog, saw the child's eyes widen when Cutter stopped at the edge of the forest, beside a tall hemlock with a long branch dragging downward, and looked back over his shoulder at them.

"That's my secret path! He does know!"

He took off after the dog at a run.

Quinn and Hayley followed. At least this, Quinn thought, should be quick. Return the kid home, and then they themselves could go home. And he could get back to his thoughts of luring Hayley back to bed for a leisurely afternoon of enjoying the miracle of them together.

He tried to ignore the little voice in his head reminding him that with Cutter, nothing was ever that simple.

Chapter 2

Alyssa Kiley paced because she couldn't be still. Panic was edging its way upward from some low, gut-deep place she hadn't heard from in a long time. Her fingers tightened on the phone she held as she resisted the urge to call the police, the fire department and anyone else she could think of. Drew was on his way. He'd fix all this. He always did. Despite the arguments, despite his sometimes presumptuous manner, he always did.

And her common sense told her he was right, Luke had been missing less than an hour. But she'd checked every place in the house, with some nightmare memory of a murdered child found in her own basement. She'd checked every neighbor on their short, narrow street, and no one had seen him. She'd called his best friend Dylan's house, even knowing they were out of town for the weekend, just in case they'd changed their plans.

She wouldn't be so anxious if it hadn't been for that weird feeling she'd been having lately. It was silly to think someone had been watching her. When she'd mentioned it to Drew he'd naturally wanted details she couldn't provide, because she'd never actually seen anyone. But even his assurances didn't make that crawly feeling at the back of her neck go away.

Now she was wondering if what she'd been feeling was some sort of precognition, a foreshadowing of disaster.

She stared at the stand of trees across the road from the house. Normally, she loved looking at them—tall, strong evergreens, softened by the misty rain. But today that forest had never seemed bigger, or more endless. Even knowing that was silly—that they hadn't changed—didn't help. There was nothing normal about this morning.

It had been a while—quite a while—since she and Drew had argued like they had this morning. But it was Doug's birthday, and that was always a rough day. How did you deal with a man who would just as soon ignore the fact that his younger brother had ever existed?

Luke must have heard them. They were usually careful to avoid that, but this morning it had flared up too quickly. She'd been on edge, knowing what day it was, and all it had taken was one exasperated glance from Drew to set her off.

And now her son was missing. Guilt stabbed through her. This wasn't all Drew's fault, she could have, should have, held it in until Luke was out of earshot. But Drew had a way of—

A noise from across the street, followed quickly by the sight of a dog bounding out of the trees startled her out of her useless musing. God, she was standing around wasting time treading old, tired ground, while Luke was gone.

To her surprise the dog, a large animal with a black head and shoulders shifting to brown over his back and tail, headed straight for her. He didn't seem at all threatening, but she watched him warily. It was a strange dog, after all.

The animal came to an abrupt halt two feet in front of her. And unexpectedly sat, his ears up, his gaze fastened on her. She felt strangely pinned, as if she couldn't move if she'd wanted to. But the dog was sitting so politely she didn't feel the need.

She knew he wasn't from anywhere on the street; there were only two dogs who lived here and they were both the little powder-puff kind of things that seemed as if they'd break if you just looked at them funny.

The dog cocked his head at an angle and made a low, odd sound. If he'd been human, she would have said it held a note of reassurance. But of course he was a dog, so that was silly.

And then he looked over his shoulders, back to where he'd come bursting out of the trees. To where someone else was coming. She could hear the noise of branches pushed aside, rubbing on each other. For an instant she wondered if the dog had in fact been fleeing something bigger and more threatening than he, no matter that something about him made her think he wouldn't be afraid of much. But bears weren't unheard of around here, and—

Her son came through the trees at a dead run.

"Luke!"

She ran for him, sweeping him up before he could say a word. Just the other day she'd been thinking how big he was getting, but now he felt like the slightest of weights, so glad was she to have him back in her arms.

"He knew the way, Mom! I didn't even show him, but he followed the exact way I came."

It took her a moment to realize he meant the dog. And a moment more to realize they weren't alone. Two adults had come along the same path through the trees. A man and a woman, the man carrying what looked like Luke's little backpack, the one Drew had bought him for their hikes and fishing trips. They must be the dog's people, she thought in the moment she spared them before turning back to her son.

"You were at the park?"

He nodded. She felt a twinge of relief; that would have been her next stop, so she would have found him. Somehow that made her feel better. But it wasn't enough to quell the overwhelming relief and the flood of wobbliness after being so frightened.

She wanted to be angry at Luke, to scare him into never, ever doing anything like this again, but she was too glad he was back and safe. She compromised, hugging him fiercely while saying, "Don't you ever do that again. I almost called the police I was so worried."

"Hard, isn't it?"

Alyssa looked up as the woman spoke. The newcomer was a little taller than she was, maybe about five-five, her hair was a rich shade of auburn touched with gold, a shade that Alyssa guessed had to be natural, it had so many layers. Her eyes were lovely, a green that matched the surroundings and reminded her of Drew's. And right now they were warm with empathy.

"They scare you to death so you're angry, but you want to smother them with love at the same time because you're so glad they're all right."

Alyssa smiled at the apt description. "You have kids?"

"Not yet," she said, and flicked a glance at the man beside her. "But I remember my mother wearing the same expression."

Alyssa stole a look at the man herself; he'd be enough to have any woman thinking about forever. She'd noticed the engagement ring on the woman's left hand, and suppressed a little sigh. It must be wonderful to have done it the normal way, fallen in love, planning a life from the beginning. She looked upon her own plain, gold wedding band as a symbol of everything she'd done wrong as a stupid, naive girl.

"I'm Hayley Cole," the woman said. "This is my fiancé, Quinn Foxworth."

"I'm Alyssa Kiley," she said, not willing to release Luke enough to shake hands. Neither one of the people before her seemed to take offense. "Thank you for bringing him home."

"And this," Hayley added with a gesture toward the dog, "is Cutter. It's him you really have to thank, he found Luke and brought us here."

Alyssa was loath to let go of Luke, but the boy was starting to squirm, his gaze fastened on the dog. Reluctantly she let him wiggle down. To her surprise when the dog moved, instead of going straight to Luke he came to her, and sat at her feet. She looked down at him, a little startled by the intense, steady gaze. She felt drawn, and leaned over to put a hand on the dog's silky head.

"Well, thank you, Cutter," she said, not sure what else to do.

The dog lowered his head in what for all the world looked like a nod of acknowledgment. As she stroked his fur, she felt oddly soothed, calmed, as if she'd finally accepted that Luke was truly all right.

"What an…interesting dog," she murmured.

"You don't know the half of it," Quinn Foxworth said, his tone wry. Alyssa looked up at him, and saw nothing but bemusement and appreciation there. Except when he looked at Hayley, and she saw a loving warmth she'd never seen in a man's eyes before.

Certainly never in her husband's. At least, not directed at her.

As if her thought had conjured him, a vehicle turned the corner, fast enough to make the tires squeal a little in protest. Hayley and Quinn looked, but Alyssa didn't, she knew who it was. And his mood probably wouldn't be any better now than it had been this morning. Worse, in fact, now that she'd called him home from work for what turned out to be nothing.

She glanced at Luke, who was on his knees beside the dog, hugging him fiercely. She thought about sending him inside, but before she could decide, the dark blue pickup stopped in the driveway with a final bark from the tires and it was too late.

"I'm thinking you should handle this one," Hayley said quietly to Quinn. "He doesn't look happy."

"Drew never looks happy," Alyssa said. Only when she heard the words spoken did she realize how sad they really were.

She tried to imagine how the man who erupted from the vehicle must look to them. Certainly a million times more intimidating than her annoyingly fragile looks. Drew was tall, lean, and after years of hard work looked as powerful as he was. There wasn't a touch of softness about him, except perhaps in the unexpectedly vivid green eyes. Where Doug had had a refined face, a soft, sweet smile and a ready, carefree laugh, his brother's jaw was strong, his face uncompromisingly masculine, his smile rare and his laugh almost nonexistent. She thought she remembered, years ago, that he had smiled, even laughed, as readily as anyone. But it had been so long she wasn't sure anymore.

He quickly gave the newcomers—including Cutter—a suspicious once-over. But the moment his gaze came to rest on Luke, some of the tension visibly drained out of him. He truly did love her son, Alyssa thought. She couldn't deny that. She'd always known it. It was, after all, why she was here.

Drew crouched beside the boy. "You're all right?" he said. Luke looked up at him, his mouth tight as he nodded.

Drew let out a breath as if he'd been holding it. They were a contrast, Drew's dark hair glistened with rain, while Luke's even damper hair was a darker shade of his father's dirty blonde.

Luke looked up then. "Am I in trouble? For running away?"

Something pained flashed in Drew's eyes. "If you're in trouble for anything, it's for how you scared your mother. And me."

Luke's eyes widened. "You? You're never scared."

"I love you, buddy. That gives you the power to scare me."

"Oh."

Drew straightened up, gave Luke a moment to think about that before he went on. "Something you want to say to your mother?"

It was more suggestion than question, and Luke didn't miss it. With a heavy sigh the child released his hold on Cutter's fur and straightened. He turned and looked up at her. "I'm sorry, Mom."

She didn't know whether to hug him again or order him to his room and lock him up until he was twenty-one. Or thirty.

"How did you sneak out so quietly?" she asked instead. Luke usually made enough noise to cover for a battle invasion.

"I waited until you were in the bathroom. You had your purse and makeup and stuff, so…"

Alyssa felt color creep up her cheeks and barely managed not to look at Hayley and Quinn. That made it sound like she was a woman who cared more for her appearance than taking care of her child, when in fact she'd gone in there because she knew she was going to start crying again, and she didn't want Luke to see that. His witnessing the latest argument was bad enough.

"I didn't mean to make you mad," Luke said.

"You didn't. You scared me, too."

"I'm sorry."

"Promise me you'll never do that again."

The boy studied the well-muddied sneakers that had been nearly new when he'd put them on this morning. "I promise." He looked up. "Could I play with the dog a little?"

Alyssa glanced at Hayley. "He's welcome to for a few minutes," the woman said. "But we won't take up residence, I assure you."

Alyssa smiled. She could like this woman.

Luke looked at Drew. For an instant Alyssa wondered if he'd withhold the threat to punish the boy. But even as she thought it she discarded it as unfair. Drew was stern, perhaps, stricter than she, but he wasn't mean.

"For a few minutes," he said.

Luke darted off with Cutter at his heels. As they went the dog looked back over his shoulder at his people, and Alyssa had the oddest feeling the glance was making them uncomfortable. Even the impressive Quinn, who was reminding her more of Drew with every silent moment.

"He certainly messed up those new shoes," Alyssa said, her adrenaline-fueled relief finally ebbing and leaving her a bit shaky.

"He's a boy," Drew said. "It'll happen."

Drew had never worried much about that, either, at least, not like she did. He didn't like waste, but he didn't consider normal boy wear and tear on things waste. She'd been afraid of the cost of things when they'd first settled in here, he could be so intimidating, but it had been clear from the beginning that Luke was his soft spot.

"I'm a little confused," Quinn said, looking at Drew. It was the first time he'd spoken in some time, and as Drew turned to look at the man Alyssa could see the assessing going on. It always happened with Drew, that quiet appraisal. She would have put it down to some primal male thing, except that he did it with women too, in a non-sexual way. It was one of the many, many ways he differed from Doug, who had taken pride in never judging anyone.

Of course, in the end he'd paid the ultimate price for that lack of judgment.

"Luke said his mom is his mom, and called you his dad, but said you're really his uncle," Quinn said.

"None of our business, honey," Hayley said softly.

"If it's true, no. But if Luke ran away because something more than a family spat is going on, then—"

"Oh, no," Alyssa exclaimed. "No, you mustn't think that! Drew would never, ever hurt Luke."

"It's all right, Lyss."

Drew had apparently drawn his conclusion about Quinn Foxworth because he nodded in approval. And he met Quinn's gaze head on.

"I appreciate your concern. Alyssa and I are married, but Luke is my nephew, technically."

"And you're raising him."

"Yes. I'm the only father he's ever known. My brother sure as hell wasn't up to the task."

And there it was again. Alyssa felt the old, familiar jab of pain at the cold, dismissive tone in his voice as he spoke of his brother. It was always there, it seemed, just sometimes closer to the surface, as it had been this morning, sparking the argument that had sent Luke running.

"Drew, please, not now," she said softly, looking over to where Luke was romping with the dog, who now seemed nothing more than the perfect child's companion.

His jaw tightened, but with a glance in the same direction, he nodded. His tone was neutral when he turned back to the pair before him. "Thank you for bringing him home."

"Thank Cutter," Hayley said. "He found him." She looked at Alyssa. "He was very cautious, your Luke. Said you told him people sometimes use animals to lure kids."

"For all the good it apparently did," she answered wryly.

"Oh, it did," Quinn assured her. She appreciated that. "He wasn't about to let either of us near him. That's why we had Cutter backtrack him here. That interested him enough to get him to come home."

Drew glanced once more at the boy and dog, who were rolling around on wet grass as if it were a warm, sunny day. "That must be some dog."

Hayley laughed. "We could tell you stories. But now, I think we should leave you to...resolve this."

Drew nodded. "We need to talk to him some more."

"Don't you need to get back to work?" Alyssa asked.

"This is more important," Drew said, and started across the yard to collect Luke.

"Nice that he puts that first," Hayley said, sounding as if she were making an effort to be noncommittal.

"He always puts Luke first," Alyssa said.

That was our deal, after all, she thought. And Drew kept it. Of course he did, he was Drew.

She'd made the best bargain she could, at the time. Her choices had brought them to the brink of disaster, and Drew had saved them. He'd promised them safety, a home, and to love and care for Luke as if he were his own. And he'd delivered on every one of those promises. Unlike his brother, Drew Kiley's word was his bond, and he lived up to it.

And if things had changed, if she had changed since then, it wasn't Drew's fault. It was hers.

As usual.

Chapter 3

"That has got to be an interesting household," Quinn said as they walked back to the park, taking the same shortcut through the trees, since Drew had told them it was a good mile if they went by road. Plus it offered some protection from the suddenly increased rain.

"Indeed," Hayley said, looking back to be sure the reluctant Cutter was actually with them. The dog had been very hesitant about leaving his new playmate. "But Luke wasn't scared. Of either of them."

That had been her first fear, that the boy had run away to escape some kind of abuse. But the way he'd been with his mother, and his…uncle, had clearly negated that idea.

"No. Nervous about being in trouble, but not scared." Quinn grimaced. "No love lost between those brothers, though."

"No. Even with one of them dead. Sad."

"He's doing the right thing."

"Drew? Yes, he is." She dodged a low-hanging branch.

"But I have the feeling things are going to be very interesting around there this afternoon."

Cutter woofed, low and with emphasis.

"I know, dog," Quinn said. "But we don't mess in people's private lives, buddy. Not what Foxworth does."

The dog made another sound, one Hayley thought sounded rather disgusted.

"But if Luke had been afraid…" She was still fairly new to all the ins and outs of the Foxworth Foundation, and wasn't sure exactly where the line was in some situations. And this situation was certainly unique. She couldn't imagine they'd come across a family like this one, consisting of a boy and his mother, who was married to his dead father's brother.

"We don't do domestics," Quinn said. "But if there was reason to suspect he was being abused, we would at least look into it and then turn it over to the right people," Quinn said. "We'd never walk away from something like that."

Hayley looked back once more. The trail through the trees had turned westward, and Luke's home was now out of sight.

"I wonder what kind of argument's going to break out next," she said.

"Let's just hope it's out of that kid's earshot," Quinn answered.

With a sigh Hayley nodded. Then they cleared the trees and stepped back into the open space of the park. Rain was pelting them now, hard and steady.

"We're going to get soaked," Quinn said.

"I think that ship already sailed," Hayley retorted.

"Guess we'll have to go home and change clothes."

She flicked him a glance, saw nothing but obvious innocence in his expression. For a guy who had a poker face that wouldn't quit, she knew exactly what this meant.

"You just want my clothes off," she accused, but laughter broke through in the middle.

"Damn straight," he said.

"You go first," she teased.

"My pleasure," Quinn said, and there was so much heat and outright need in his voice she was surprised she wasn't already steaming.

She spared another thought for Drew and Alyssa Kiley, wondering if they ever shared moments like this in their odd relationship. If she had to guess, she'd sadly say no. They didn't have the air of a couple that was intimate at every possible moment. She wondered if they were at all, given the nature and circumstances of their being together.

And then they were in the car, Cutter loaded in the back where he promptly sprayed the interior with a hearty shake, and all she could think about was getting her man home and licking every raindrop off the body she knew so well.

Drew was thankful Alyssa didn't seem inclined to fight with him. Maybe she was just so thankful Luke was home safe, thankful that they'd dodged a large bullet, that her relief made her more forgiving. Or maybe, as he had, she'd just learned the futility of it. All they did was go round and round in the same old rut, digging it deeper and deeper with each circuit.

More likely she just felt like he did, now that the adrenaline that had spiked when she'd called to tell him Luke was missing had begun to ebb. The thought of Luke out there, alone, lost and maybe scared, had knifed at him. That it was probably his fault had only driven that knife deeper.

He paced the living room, seeing nothing of the familiar surroundings. He'd built this house for them, done much of the labor himself, but it all meant nothing. None of his success, his work at building the business his grandfather had begun, of hanging on to it through the toughest times, and now building it again, meant anything next to the biggest job he'd ever taken on.

He worked hard at being a father. Harder than at anything in his life. It wasn't in his nature the way it seemed to be in Alyssa's. She was automatically loving and understanding and generous—too generous in some cases—by nature. And it was that generosity that got them into trouble. Or more accurately, his reaction to it. Because that generosity made her excuse Doug even after what he'd done. And that clawed at something buried deep inside him. Made him, to his shame, lash out every once in a while.

And if he sometimes wished for a little more of that generous understanding for himself, well, that was his problem. She'd agreed to this arrangement for Luke's sake, because at the time she'd had little choice. She wasn't the one who was now chafing under the terms.

She hadn't asked him to fall in love with her.

She still loves Doug, he reminded himself. For all his sins, she still loves him, and probably always will. It didn't matter that he didn't understand it, didn't understand what she'd seen in his brother that had made her willing to throw her life away for him.

He'd long ago admitted he knew what Doug had seen in her, although he had his doubts whether his feckless little brother had seen the real woman behind the sweet face and the big, innocent blue eyes. In his more sour moments he suspected it was that innocence that had drawn Doug; it took a certain amount of innocence to be taken in by his act.

And there he was again, striking out even in his mind. Doug was dead—and hating him for what he'd done was pointless.

"We did this."

Her voice was soft, almost a whisper from behind him. He spun around. She'd gone up with Luke to get him warm and dry, and set him up with his current favorite book. He was already reading well for his age, on to third-grade level readers, and Drew knew that was thanks to Alyssa. Not only had she read to him regularly, she'd made up a game where she'd written simple words on cards and hidden them around the room in reachable places for a child. Then she'd sent Luke off on a treasure hunt, making him tell her what words he'd found. At first Drew had thought it kind of silly, but when he'd seen the results—and heard Luke's proud crowing when he got one right—he'd quickly changed his mind.

"Yes," he said, his voice nearly as quiet as hers. "We did."

"It has to stop, Drew."

"Yes."

"What can I do to make that easier?"

God, he hated this. She was being so reasonable, so understanding. And he felt like a fool because the only answer he had was "Stop loving my brother."

"I'm not Luke," he said, not quite snapping. "Don't treat me like a six-year-old."

"Luke," she said sweetly, "is leaving temper tantrums behind."

He drew back sharply. Opened his mouth, ready to truly snap this time. And stopped.

"Okay," he said after a moment, "I had that one coming."

"Yes."

In an odd way, her dig pleased him. Not because it was accurate, he sheepishly admitted, but because she felt confident enough to do it. She'd been so weak, sick and scared when he'd found her four years ago, going toe to toe with him like this would have been impossible. But she was strong now, poised and self-assured. And he took a tiny bit of credit for that. She'd done the hard work. Once she'd gotten well she'd pulled herself up and found her way, but he'd given her the means, and the protection she'd needed to get it done.

"You've come a long way," he said quietly.

"Because I don't cower anymore?"

He frowned. "I never made you cower."

For an instant she looked startled. "I never said you did."

She crossed her arms and began to move, pacing almost the same track he had taken around the living room.

"You saved us, Drew, don't think I don't know that, or will ever forget it. I have come a long way, and it's in large part because you made it possible."

It was a pretty little speech, a sentiment she'd expressed more than once. And not so long ago it had been enough. More than enough. It had told him he'd done exactly what he'd intended. That he'd accomplished his goal. That she was stable now, strong, and he'd had a hand in that.

And it wasn't her fault that wasn't enough for him anymore.

"That's what we dull, boring rocks do," he said, using his brother's terminology. Doug had always insisted it was a joke, but Drew had always known there was a certain amount of venom behind it. His insisting it was a joke just made Drew look touchy if he took offense. Doug had that little game down to a science.

Alyssa turned then. "There's a lot to be said for being the rock of the family."

Yes, she had come a long way. There was a time when she'd meant it just as Doug had, but no more. He had to give her that.

"Is there?" he asked.

"Yes. We've been safe, thanks to you. Back then I didn't appreciate how important feeling safe and steady was. Now I do."

He supposed that was something.

For a moment she just looked at him. One hand stole up to push her hair behind her right ear. She'd gotten it cut recently. He'd thought he would miss the long waves of golden blonde, but he liked this smooth shape, how it swept forward onto her cheeks, making her eyes look even bigger and bluer. He'd wondered what was behind the radical change, but had been wary to ask. Their relationship was such a minefield sometimes. She too often took a simple question as a criticism, when he never meant it that way.

But when you practically force somebody to marry you, you took what you got, he supposed.

"Thank you," he finally said. That had to be safe enough, didn't it?

"Thank you," she said, "for not blaming me."

His brows lowered in puzzlement. "Blaming you for what?"

"Luke slipping away."

He drew back slightly. "It wasn't your fault. He's a smart kid, he knew when to sneak out."

"Which brings us back to why he did it."

Drew let out a compressed breath. "Okay. I get it. It was my fault."

"I'm not saying that."

"Then what are you saying?"

"I'm saying I appreciate that you don't hold your feelings about your brother against Luke."

"Appreciate?" What an insipid, bloodless word that suddenly seemed. "I love him like he was my own."

"I know that," Alyssa said in that patient way of hers that worked wonders with Luke but tended to spark his temper. "I know you love him completely. But Luke needs to know his father loved him, too."

"His father didn't even stick around to know him."

"That wasn't by his choice, Drew. You know that."

"His choices led to everything that happened. Can't you see—"

He cut himself off when he realized he was just repeating the exact words that had started this whole thing this morning. Just like that they were back in that circular rut. *He* determined to make her see, and *she* determined to hang on to her rose-tinted memories.

And the way things were going, they could well spend the rest of their lives there, endlessly circling.

He was going to lose her. He could feel it. What they had was a facade, a construct that had served a purpose that was now accomplished, and should be demolished before it collapsed under its own weight.

They weren't just circling each other, they were circling the drain.

Chapter 4

"Please, Mom?"

Luke's voice had taken on the wheedling tone that made Alyssa laugh but drove Drew nuts. But he didn't react. He knew it was because it reminded him of Doug, who had had that perfected at Luke's age. He hated to think there was anything of Doug in this boy he thought of as his son, although he knew there likely was. It was bad enough that he looked so much like him, but any hint that he'd inherited other things worried him.

But now he made himself chalk it up to typical six-year-old behavior and not a sign of hereditary, blatant self-absorption. And he told himself the actions of a six-year-old were not a predictor of the man Luke would become.

But he had less luck telling himself that the very thing that irritated him about that tone was what made Alyssa laugh; it reminded her of the man she'd loved. Still loved. Didn't the fact that she still wore that damned necklace that Doug had given her prove that?

"Dad? Can I?"

"Not by yourself, if that's what you mean," he said.

"I should say not, young man," Alyssa said, her tone so heartfelt in its agreement that Drew felt his irritation ebb away. Luke was just a six-year-old boy who wanted something, not a fledgling narcissist.

"Well, you could come," Luke said. "We can even walk on the sidewalk if you want," he added generously.

"Well, now, there's a selling point," Drew said drily.

Alyssa laughed. She did so easily now, and Drew caught himself again remembering the days when she had been too ill, and too frightened for herself and her son to laugh at all.

Seems like we switched places, he thought. She'd blossomed, while he'd…retreated. He supposed he should be thankful she wasn't the nudging, prying sort, or he'd lash out even more; a public display of his private pain wasn't in his nature. Or hadn't been, until lately.

Of course, maybe she wasn't the nudging, prying sort because she didn't care. She might *appreciate* him—yeah, he hated the word all right—but that didn't mean she felt anything more.

"Please? He might be there already."

Drew snapped himself out of his useless reverie. "Or he might not be at all," he warned.

"He will be. I just know it."

It wasn't what he'd planned on doing this Saturday morning, but Drew found himself assenting anyway. He didn't want to take any chances. Things had been peaceful, relatively, even pleasant for the last week, but they'd been kind of walking on eggshells, too.

"All right. I'll go with you."

He felt rather than saw Alyssa's startled glance. Usually she was the one to give in first.

Luke crowed. "Yahoo!"

"But you're still restricted," Drew warned. "You stay in sight at all times, no running off on your own."

Usually Alyssa thought his penalties a bit too strict, but she had no quibble with this one. Which told him how scared she'd been last week. She'd already been on edge, thinking somebody had been watching her. And Luke taking off had been the tipping point.

"Go get your duck boots on, a sweater, and your blue jacket," she instructed.

The boy grimaced, but was wise enough even at six not to push his luck. He darted up the stairs.

"I can go with him," she said when he was out of earshot.

"I think we both should," he said.

Her brow furrowed. He frowned; was just the idea of a walk with him so bad?

"I'm sure you have other things to do," she said.

Was there annoyance in her voice, or was he imagining it? There had been a time when he'd been able to read her better. But she wasn't the same foolish girl she'd been when she'd run off with Doug at seventeen, believing they were eloping, only to find he had no intention of marrying her. Not even—or rather especially—when she'd gotten pregnant.

Nor was she the same shattered woman he'd found two years after Doug's death, alone, in a hospital and seriously ill, and unable to care for herself or her toddler son. Alyssa had been a broken woman. And the nephew he'd never even met was in the custody of Child Protective Services.

No, she'd healed, gradually, gotten stronger. And she'd grown up. Rather quickly, once she saw the chance to get her son back. Then she'd sacrificed everything to keep Luke safe and happy.

She'd even married him.

She was staring at him now. "Two sets of eyes to keep on him," he said.

"You don't think he'll run away again?" Anxiety spiked in her voice.

He hadn't meant to do that. "No. But it can't hurt, can it?"

He wanted to ask if the idea of a walk with him was that horrible, but he didn't want to hear the answer so he kept quiet.

"No. It's a good idea. If he sees us going together, maybe he'll think—"

She broke off suddenly, as if she'd realized what her next words would have sounded like.

Drew didn't need to hear them to know what she'd been going to say. Maybe Luke will think we're okay, that we're a real family, that the only parents he'd really known were really together.

When in reality they were anything but.

Without a word, he walked over to the coatrack by the door and grabbed his rain jacket. He took Alyssa's down as well and held it for her as she slid her arms in. A nice, husbandly gesture.

Right.

He knew too well he would never be able to make Alyssa happy, not in the way Doug had. No amount of telling himself it had only been teenage infatuation could change that.

They walked, slowly since the rain had for the moment lightened to more of a heavy mist. He wished he could kid himself that they were a normal, ordinary, happy family out for a Saturday morning walk. But his own actions, calling out to Luke to remind him to stay in sight, were a reminder they were not. As was his wife's nervous edginess, the way she keep looking around, over her shoulder, as if she expected something or someone to jump out at her.

She must still be having that feeling of being watched. He didn't sense anything, but he wasn't sure he would. He was just a guy who went to work every day and tried to keep things together. Alyssa had the imagination in the family. Maybe that's what had drawn her to Doug, who had always been full of wild, impossible plans.

But he didn't discount her feeling. Because he knew something she didn't yet, because he'd only found out the week before Luke vanished. He hadn't been sure how to tell her, had been working up to it, and then the whole thing with Luke had happened, and even though that had turned out fine, she was still shaken. So he'd held off telling her what he'd learned. But he'd renewed the vow he'd made on the day she'd agreed to his plan. He would keep both her and Luke safe. And he would. No matter what.

"He *is* here!"

"Yes, it seems he is," Alyssa said to her delighted son. "How did you know?"

Luke slid her a sideways look. "He told me."

"Who told you?"

"Cutter."

She had no idea what to say to that piece of fancy, so she merely laughed. In her heart, she was happy the boy could even manage such fanciful thoughts still. Because of his rocky start in life, he was ahead of many kids his same age in leaving childhood behind. But he was clearly able to still indulge in wild imaginings, and somehow that comforted her.

"Can I go now?" Luke asked, trying to tug his hand free from hers.

"No," she said. "We need to talk to his people first."

But it seemed the decision was out of her hands, the dog was already racing across the park toward them. She saw Hayley and Quinn spot them, and Hayley gave a friendly wave as they started their way as well.

The approach of the happy dog was too much for Luke, and he broke loose to run toward him. The dog yipped in greeting, and immediately dropped into what was clearly play mode, front end down, tail up and wagging.

"Hello," Hayley said cheerfully as they joined them. Quinn merely nodded at them both. "I should have known there was a reason Cutter wanted to come here this morning."

Drew blinked. "What?"

"He was determined," Quinn said drily.

Alyssa laughed. "You say that like it was his idea."

"Oh, it was," Hayley said. "He made it quite clear."

"He's a dog," Drew said, rather pointedly.

"Maybe," Quinn said in the same tone.

Hayley laughed, probably at their expressions. Alyssa guessed she looked as skeptical as Drew did right now.

"It's kind of hard to explain," Hayley said. "*He's* kind of hard to explain. But trust me, he brought us here, not the other way around."

Drew was looking at them in that assessing, considering way of his. "He brought you," he said slowly.

"He's got his ways," Quinn said. "He usually just makes your life impossible until you do what he wants."

"But he's helpful, too," Hayley said, still chuckling. "He brings us our outdoor shoes. That's usually our first clue we're going somewhere. Then we wait to see if we're walking or going in the car. Today was the car."

"I suppose he gives you directions, too?" Drew sounded more amused than sarcastic, Alyssa thought. Thankfully, since he could carve a turkey with that sharpness sometimes.

"Actually, he does," Quinn said. There was something, Alyssa thought, about this big, strong and clearly tough man accepting the eccentricities of a dog that warmed her. "It sort of consists of blessed silence when we're going the right way and booming barks if we dare make a wrong turn. If we're lucky, we figure it out before we go deaf."

"We figured this one out fairly quickly," Hayley said.

"Which is why we can still hear well enough to have this conversation," Quinn said, his mouth quirking.

Something about this made Drew grin suddenly. Alyssa's breath stopped in her throat. She tried to remember the last time she'd seen it, and couldn't. Doug's smile had been easy, his grins frequent.

And worth less because of it?

Alyssa blinked. What an odd thought to have.

"Can we go now?" Luke said, on the edge of a whine.

"Is it all right if they play for a while?" Alyssa asked.

"I think that's why we're here," Hayley said.

Taking that as assent, Luke dashed off, Cutter at his heels.

"In sight!" Drew called out the reminder.

"A little fallout from last week?" Hayley asked.

Drew nodded. "He scared his mother half to death. I don't want him forgetting that any time soon."

It was such a simple statement, Alyssa didn't know why it made her throat tighten up. She had appreciated the edict Drew had lain down, even appreciated the way he'd done it, approaching Luke for a man-to-man talk in a way that had the boy listening carefully, wide-eyed and intent. And for a six-year-old, Luke had followed the rule pretty well.

"At that age, boys need rules," Drew had said after he'd sent Luke to bed that first night, telling him to think about it until he went to sleep. "They need to know where the boundaries are."

"What about girls?" she'd asked, grateful enough at his reaction to this entire episode to merely tease.

Drew had given her a sideways look. "No idea," he said. "I never was one."

No, Alyssa thought now, *you certainly never were.*

"—in construction?" Quinn was asking Drew. "Mind if I pick your brain a little? Thinking about some remodeling of our building."

"Sure," Drew said.

"We'll keep the rascals in sight," Quinn promised Alyssa as they walked toward where boy and dog were romping in some self-invented game of tag that had no rules Alyssa could discern.

"It's silly, I suppose," she said to Hayley as the men walked away, talking. "But I'm still nervous."

"Not silly at all."

"I think Drew thinks I'm too jumpy, or imagining things. But I'd been feeling like somebody had been watching me, and then Luke vanished…."

"Someone was watching you?"

"No, probably not really. It was just a creepy feeling."

"Quinn taught me that those feelings are often just your brain interpreting signals so fast that what's really a logical process seems like a leap of intuition."

Alyssa blinked. "Really?" She wasn't sure if she was referring to the idea, or Quinn saying it.

"I've learned he's right. If you go back over the details of what made you feel that way, you sometimes find there were a lot of little things that, added together, made your brain make that jump."

It made sense to her, and she promised herself when she had a quiet moment she'd try to do that. In the meantime, she was grateful to Hayley for not simply brushing it off.

"Drew obviously cares a great deal about you and Luke."

Alyssa said the one thing she was certain was true. "He feels responsible for us."

"You have an…interesting family relationship."

"Ya' think?" Alyssa responded with a laugh. "I know, it seems weird to those on the outside, me being married to the brother of my son's father. But I don't want to think about where we'd be, where Luke would be, if he hadn't found us when he did. I can honestly say he saved us."

"Quinn kidnapped me." Hayley said it as casually as if she'd said they'd met at a community picnic.

Alyssa blinked. "He what?"

Hayley explained about the night the proverbial black helicopter had dropped into her life and changed it forever.

"What," Alyssa said, her eyes wide, "exactly does your fiancé do?"

"He fights," Hayley said proudly.

So he was military? Alyssa had thought he might be—something about the way he carried himself. "Navy?" she asked, since this was Navy territory around the Sound. She thought he might even be a SEAL, he was just that impressive.

"Former Army. He used to be a Ranger. But he's still a fighter. Only now he fights for people in the right who can no longer fight for themselves."

Chapter 5

Alyssa blinked. She glanced across the park to where Drew and Quinn Foxworth were watching Luke and the dog play. It sounded so…noble, that sentiment. No wonder Hayley sounded proud.

"Why?" she finally asked.

"Because once he was helpless in the face of tragedy. He lost hope. He made it his mission to help others who were feeling that way. And I'm proud to be part of that now."

Helpless. Oh, how well she knew that feeling. She would never forget, never wanted to forget, and was determined she would never be in that position again. It made her even more curious about these people.

She looked across the green expanse toward the swings, where Luke was weaving around the uprights with Cutter hot on his heels. Drew and Quinn were right there, deep in conversation but clearly with an eye on the boy.

"Is that why he joined the service?"

Hayley nodded. "But things changed. He was butting

heads more than he was seeing eye-to-eye. So he left, and that was the beginning of the Foxworth Foundation."

"He has a foundation?"

"Started by him and the only other Foxworth left, his sister. Now it covers most of the country, from five regional locations." Hayley glanced over to where Luke and Cutter were now wrestling happily. "But we're the only ones with a dog as a team member," she added with a grin.

Alyssa, still nervous about Luke, had been doing the same regularly, checking on the pair. "He's…quite something, your dog. Where did you find him?"

"I didn't. He found me. Turned up on my doorstep when I needed him most, after my mother died."

Alyssa's gaze shifted back to Hayley. "Like he found Luke when he needed him most?"

"Exactly. It's what he does. He finds people who need his—or Foxworth's—particular kind of help."

Alyssa sighed. "I'll be forever grateful to him for bringing Luke home." Hayley met her gaze, and there was something warm and understanding in her eyes, something that made Alyssa add rather pitifully, "I wish he could help us."

"Don't be so sure he can't," Hayley said.

"Can he help Drew stop hating his brother?" Her tone was bitter, but she couldn't help it any more than she'd been able to stop the words from slipping out.

"Does he? Really?"

"Close enough."

"Seems rather pointless to hate someone who's dead," Hayley said, her tone so neutral Alyssa knew it was intentional.

"It is, but he can't let go. It's the only pointless thing he does in his life."

"Why?"

"It's a long story."

"We have all morning," Hayley said, gesturing toward

the romping dog and child. "I think they're having so much fun it would be sad to interrupt them."

Alyssa smiled. Luke was having fun, and it warmed her heart. Plus, there was something about this woman that made this feel more like sharing with a trusted friend than airing dirty laundry. So Alyssa answered her.

"Doug was very different from Drew. He was sunny, happy, carefree. Drew's always been so serious, responsible."

"Some would say," Hayley said in that same, neutral tone, "the latter makes the former possible."

"That people like Doug can only be carefree if people like Drew do the serious stuff? Yeah, I've heard that. Repeatedly." At Hayley's look, she added quickly, "Oh, not from Drew. He doesn't say stuff like that, at least. I've heard it from other people. Even from guys who were supposedly Doug's friends."

"What does he say?"

Alyssa supposed she wanted to know what their fight had been about. Her instinct was always to keep quiet, if only because she didn't want to whine. She'd been that way for too long, and she was determined not to revert.

"That Doug was lazy, always looking for the easy way. That he'd slid through life on looks and charm. That he wanted to be rich without putting in the work. That he was irresponsible."

"Any of that true?"

Alyssa shrugged. Contrary to what Drew believed, she'd come to terms with many of the realities of Luke's father a while ago. "Probably most of it."

Hayley's brows rose. "If you agree, then what is there to fight about?"

"Because Drew also thinks Doug never loved me, not really. That he abandoned me when I got pregnant. Because I got pregnant. It's not true."

Alyssa stopped herself when she heard her voice rising.

"It's okay," Hayley said gently. "An understandable hot button."

Odd how her voice was so comforting, Alyssa thought. She felt like she could tell Hayley the whole story and she would understand. Maybe because she'd suffered the loss of someone she loved, too. Whatever it was, she found herself pouring out the whole story.

"I fell in love with Doug Kiley when I was fifteen. The way only a teenager can. A year later, he finally noticed me. My parents hated the idea because he was four years older. His parents weren't too happy either. So they tried to break us up."

Hayley rolled her eyes. "Oh, and that always works so well."

Alyssa smiled, surprising herself. She rarely spoke of that time anymore, and it never made her smile, but somehow with Hayley it was different.

"We ran off together when I was seventeen. For a while it was fun, we had adventures, he called them, up and down the west coast. And then I got pregnant."

"Where were you then?"

"California. It was the end of summer, and we were broke. Doug said you could practically live off what people left on the beaches."

"And not get cold at night," Hayley said.

Alyssa liked that she got that, and didn't judge. "Yes. Anyway, I had to go to a free clinic to be sure, but I was pregnant."

"That must have been a little scary."

"It was. But I was…happy, too. I loved Doug, and I was young enough to feel like having his baby was a sign of that." Her mouth quirked ruefully. "Shows you how stupid I was."

"How did Doug react?"

Alyssa sighed. "I didn't tell him, for a while. He was worried about just getting us enough to eat."

"And when you did?"

Alyssa looked over at Luke, the single consistent light in her life since that awful day. "He got scared. He said we were broke, we couldn't have a kid. He wanted me to get rid of it, so we could go on just like before."

"Ah."

The sound Hayley made was noncommittal, nonjudgmental. It enabled Alyssa to go on. "If it had been sooner, I might have done it. Probably would have. But I waited too long. I'd felt the baby move. And I couldn't."

"A tough decision."

She didn't tell Hayley Doug had become angry about it. He'd spent days trying to talk her out of going through with it. Then he'd turned on the charm full bore, sweet-talking her with stories about the future she was risking. She wasn't sure where she'd found the strength to resist, but she had. And then Doug had lost it. She'd never seen him so furious, didn't even realize he was capable of such anger.

And then he'd walked out. Just to cool off, she was sure.

And she'd never seen him alive again.

"Doug was killed a few days later. He'd gone out looking for a way to get money, to take care of us. He hooked up with this really creepy, shady guy we'd met on the bus to L.A.—Baird Oliver. It was all his idea. I know he was only able to talk Doug into it because he was so scared."

"They did something stupid?" Hayley asked softly.

Alyssa nodded. "They robbed a convenience store. Baird got away, but he was caught later. Doug crashed running from the police. He was killed."

"And you were pregnant and alone."

She nodded. "I know it was wrong, the robbery. But he was desperate. And Baird was persuasive, in a slimy kind of way. Doug just wanted to take care of us."

"You think he changed his mind about leaving?"

"I know he did. He didn't have the money, so he couldn't

have been running away like Drew says he was. And he was headed back, not away. He was coming back to get me."

"You must have been terrified."

"I was. The next couple of years were hell. I knew I couldn't come home, my parents hadn't spoken to me since we ran off. Getting pregnant, having Luke, would only make it worse."

"That's sad."

"Yes."

"So what did you do?"

Alyssa laughed, only this time it was full of scorn, directed only at herself. "I brilliantly got so run-down trying to work three jobs and still take care of Luke that I got sick, which became pneumonia, and I ended up in the hospital." She looked at Luke once more. "They took him away from me, Hayley. He was the only thing I had left of the man I'd been so crazy in love with, and they took him away."

Hayley took in an audible breath. Alyssa liked her even more for her expression of genuine sympathy. "What happened?"

"Drew," she said simply. "He found us. Saved us. Both of us. He took care of me when I could barely lift a finger to help myself for weeks. And he got Luke back, out of foster care. And I will always, always owe him for that."

She meant it. Even though occasionally, after incidents like last week's, she had to remind herself just how much she owed him.

And how impossible it would be to ever really pay him back.

Chapter 6

"Careless, foolish, and impossibly self-centered his entire life."

Drew kept his voice low even though Luke was so raptly involved with his new playmate he doubted he would have heard anything short of a bomb going off. He didn't care anymore how the boy had known the dog would be here in the park, he was just savoring the expression of delight on Luke's face.

"And you're obviously not," Quinn said. It was so matter-of-fact Drew felt oddly pleased. "How'd that happen?"

Drew shrugged one shoulder. "Doug was kind of sickly when he was a baby. So everybody fussed over him. Then later he was so damn cute and clever, everybody spoiled him. He was smart enough to figure out early that he could charm people into just about anything."

"And it's a lot easier than working."

Drew studied Quinn Foxworth for a long moment. He

instinctively liked the man, for his brisk, businesslike manner, and the innate steadiness he sensed in him. And the obvious fact that he was crazy in love with his Hayley, and wasn't afraid to show it.

He envied the man that.

"Yes," he said finally. "And Doug was all about the easy way. But Lyss still insists he was trying to get money to take care of them both when he was killed."

"But you don't believe that."

"More likely he was trying to get enough money to run from the responsibility. He didn't have it on him when he died, so I've always thought he didn't want to get caught with it and it was stashed somewhere for him and his scumbag partner to retrieve later."

"The partner that went to prison?"

Drew nodded. "Baird Oliver. That robbery wasn't his first foray into crime."

"And they never found the cash?"

Drew shook his head. "Wasn't in the car when Doug crashed and Oliver didn't have it on him, either."

"So your brother's motives are what you were fighting about?"

Drew sighed, looking again at Luke, glad simply to see the boy so happy. "More who he was. Or wasn't."

"And you each have your own version."

"Yes," Drew admitted. "But mine's based in fact, hers is based in…fantasy. Some sort of dream image she's always had of him."

"Incompatible visions."

"Exactly." He let out a compressed breath. "We agreed early on to not discuss it, because it just degenerated into scenes like last week. Our marriage may be…just a business arrangement, but the fighting isn't good for Luke. And he's old enough now, he's starting to ask difficult questions."

Quinn studied him for a moment. "About his father?"

"Yes. I wanted to settle that as soon as he was old enough to understand, to tell him the truth, but Lyss kept putting it off."

"Because she didn't agree that what you wanted to tell him was the truth?" Quinn suggested.

"Probably," Drew said with a glum expression. "I didn't mind that she wanted him to know about Doug, he is his biological father. But she didn't want him to hear anything negative, anything at all."

"Which makes a dead man the perfect father. He can do no wrong."

Drew's breath stopped in his throat. He stared at Quinn. How many times had he thought just that, and then hated himself for it?

Quinn shrugged. "I tended to idealize my own father, after he died. And it took a while before my sister could get me to remember he hadn't always been perfect."

"She's older?"

"A little." Quinn grinned then. "Or a lot, sometimes. Our parents always said they had a wise, brilliant kid and a smart but stubborn one. I'll let you guess which was which."

Drew smiled, an odd enough occurrence while talking of his family situation that he was acutely aware of it.

"So what do you do about it?" Quinn asked.

"What can I do?" Drew answered wearily. "I kept hoping she'd eventually realize that what she thinks she knows isn't the truth, but she's determined to hang on to that idealized image." He shook his head sharply. "But it's not all her doing. I let her most of the time, because I just don't want to fight that fight. I don't want to fight with her at all."

Quinn's steady gaze sharpened, and Drew wondered if he'd let too much show. He wasn't sure why he was talking so much to this guy he'd just met a week ago anyway. He never talked about all this to anyone.

"So, this is just a business arrangement," Quinn said, not even making it a question.

"It took me two years to find them, after Doug was killed. When I did, Lyss was really sick. Exhaustion, pneumonia. They'd already taken Luke, put him in a foster home. She couldn't take care of herself, let alone him. Getting married was the fastest way to get through it all."

"You would have had claim on Luke by blood, wouldn't you?"

"Yes. But he needed his mother, too. And she needed help. And—"

He cut himself off. This was insane. He wasn't going to explain to this near-stranger why he'd done what he'd done. Let him think whatever he was going to think. He was regretting already that Foxworth knew as much as he did.

When did you start running off at the mouth? he asked himself sourly.

He should get Luke and Alyssa, and they should just go home. The fight was over, and Luke had scared them enough that he thought they might be able to avoid the heated exchanges in the future. It would be hard to pry the boy away from the dog he was having so much fun with, but—

Almost on the thought, the dog stopped mid-romp. He spun around on his hindquarters and stared at Drew. And then he bolted, straight toward them.

Cutter sat, not as Drew would have expected, at Quinn's feet, but at his own. The animal stared up at him intently. No, more than intently. That gaze was intense, and seemingly impossible to look away from. Drew thought of tales he'd read as a boy, of sheepdogs who controlled their flock with just the power of their eyes, and cattle dogs who did the same. He'd always thought it a bit fanciful. Now he wasn't so sure.

"Uh-oh." Quinn's voice was wry, almost wary sounding.

Drew lifted a brow at him. "Your dog trying to tell me something?"

"He's expressing an opinion, yes." Quinn crouched down beside the animal, who only flicked a glance at him. "We can't, boy. We don't do domestic. It's not our place."

Drew shifted his gaze from the dog back to the man, who had seemed perfectly sane moments ago. Yet now here he was, talking to a dog as if the animal could comprehend every word. *We don't do domestic*... What the hell did that mean?

Cutter let out a low sound, not a growl but a sort of whuffing bark. It sounded oddly insistent.

"No, Cutter," Quinn said.

The insistent bark came again just as Luke, clearly curious at the departure of his delightful companion, came up to them.

"Do you have to leave?" the boy asked, looking crestfallen.

"We should," Quinn said, "but I'm not sure he's going to let us."

"Okay, this is crazy. He's a dog," Drew said.

"Sometimes," Quinn said. "Sometimes I'm not sure what he is."

"Quinn?"

Hayley's voice came from behind him, and Drew turned to see the woman and Alyssa approaching. Lyss was smiling, and he was thankful to Hayley for that if nothing else.

"Do we have a…situation?" Hayley asked as they came to a halt. She was looking at the dog.

"It seems we do."

Hayley frowned. "Did you tell him this was personal, not really our business?"

"I did. He's not listening."

"I think," Drew muttered, "I've lost my mind. We need to get out of here."

"And away from the crazy people who talk to a dog like he's a person who can understand?" Hayley said.

Drew blinked. "I…."

"It's okay," Hayley said with a smile that was impossible to ignore. "We understand, believe me. It took us a long time to accept that…he really does understand. Not the words, perhaps, but he knows what's going on."

"Well, I don't," Alyssa said, watching this all with much more amusement on her face than anything else.

"He knows there's a problem," Hayley explained. "And it's in his nature to want to fix it."

"You mean to want us to fix it," Quinn amended drily.

"Well, yes," Hayley agreed with a laugh. "It is our function to figure out what he wants and try to do it."

This time Drew and Alyssa were united. They both looked from the dog to his people in wary disbelief.

"You're saying he wants to fix *our* problem?" Alyssa asked.

"He wants it fixed, yes," Hayley said. "He likes people. He loves some. And he doesn't tolerate fixable problems well."

Drew looked back at the dog, who was still staring at him in that way that made him faintly uncomfortable. "Fixable?"

"Yes. But he thinks everything's fixable. At least, he has so far."

"I don't think so," Alyssa said. "Not this time. I've been trying for years."

Drew's gaze snapped to his wife. "What are you talking—"

"Let him try, Dad!" Luke said, sounding anxious, as if he thought a fight was about to start. "Please? Mom? Maybe he can help. He's really smart."

"This," Drew muttered, "is ridiculous. We're down the rabbit hole."

"Luke, honey, why don't you and Cutter go play a little

more, because we will have to leave soon," Alyssa said. "Let us talk to Quinn and Hayley."

Luke hesitated as Cutter didn't move. Hayley stroked the dog's head. "Go ahead, boy. We'll talk."

The woof that came this time was much more pleased sounding. And Drew shook his head sharply at how willing even he seemed to be to assign human emotion to the dog. But the pair raced off to continue whatever boy-dog game they'd made up.

Alyssa watched her son go, then looked at Quinn. "Hayley told me what you do. What Foxworth does, I mean. And it sounds good, and noble, and all that. But there's nothing you can do to fix us."

Drew winced inwardly. She sounded so certain. Not that he thought this Foxworth outfit could fix them, but Lyss sounded so sure they couldn't be fixed at all.

And she was probably right.

"Drew told me about his brother," Quinn began.

"Oh, I'm sure he did," Alyssa said, her voice fairly dripping with resentment.

"I only told him the truth," Drew said.

Hayley stepped in before things escalated, saying calmly, "And Alyssa told me her side of things. Which I'm sure is very different."

Drew stayed silent this time, reminding himself of his determination to never fight over this again.

"You each have your opinions, your interpretations of what happened, then," Hayley said.

"I know what happened," Drew said.

"You weren't there—I was," Alyssa pointed out.

"You weren't with him when they robbed the place. Or when he crashed, thank God. And you never accepted the truth, even when the cops told you." So much for his determination, Drew thought.

"The police didn't know, either. They didn't know Doug, not like I did. They assumed."

"So," Quinn said, "neither of you knows for sure what was in his head, you just have what you believe but can't prove. And the two versions are not compatible. That about it?"

"I know," Alyssa said stubbornly.

"And you can't fix willful blindness," Drew snapped.

And there they were, back to square one.

Quinn sighed. He looked at Hayley. "I'm not sure even Foxworth can fix this one. How do we prove what was in a dead man's heart?"

"But Cutter…" she said.

"I know. He's as determined as I've ever seen him."

"We could look into it, couldn't we?"

"Wait. You're saying you'd go against your own policies because of a dog?" Drew asked, sounding as incredulous as he felt.

"Not just *a* dog. This dog," Quinn said. At Drew's look he chuckled. "Believe me, not so long ago I sounded just like you. But it's hard to argue with the kind of stats this guy has piled up."

"So, he's never wrong, is that what you're saying?"

"No. He just hasn't been yet."

Hayley cut in. "Maybe somebody, somebody not emotionally involved, might know something. If anybody can find somebody like that, Foxworth can."

"Somebody without a dog in this fight, you mean?" Drew joked, unable to quite believe he was taking this discussion even semi-seriously. "This is crazy."

"On that, I agree," Alyssa said. "Dog aside, I don't want anybody digging around in this. Luke's been through enough. I'm not going to risk destroying his image of his father."

Drew's stomach knotted. Had she really said that? Did she even realize she had acknowledged the possibility that there even was a risk of that image—that illusion—being destroyed?

That quickly, Drew changed his mind. From what Quinn had said, Foxworth was big, had great resources, better people, and tremendous results. They also had time, time the police never had, and as Quinn had explained, once they took a case, they never gave up unless their client told them to.

It was almost dizzying how quickly he'd flipped, but Drew couldn't deny the allure of this being settled once and for all. But he knew Alyssa would never voluntarily seek out truth that might contradict her image of Doug.

But if Foxworth could do it…

"—I appreciate the thought, but no," Alyssa was saying.

"It's going to be interesting," Quinn said. "We've never really tried to pull Cutter back once he's gotten his teeth into something, so to speak."

"Maybe he's right," Drew said.

"What?" Alyssa's head snapped around and she stared at him.

Careful, he cautioned himself. *There's only one way to get her to see reason.* And in this case, it had the advantage of being true, and being the one thing that had made him sickest about this whole thing.

"Luke," he said quietly.

"I told you, I won't have him thinking his father was some common criminal who didn't love him!"

"That's not the reason to do it," Drew said, keeping his voice low, even with an effort.

"Then what is?" she demanded.

"He doesn't even have to know. I swear to you, even if I'm proved right, we don't have to tell him."

"Then what is it you're after, Drew?"

"I'm after a way to clear the air between the parents he has now. Because a six-year-old talking about going away because he thinks it will make us happy is nothing to ignore."

Alyssa opened her mouth. Shut it. And as if he could see

it, he sensed the fight drain away. As always with her, Luke came first. And the truth of what he'd said was undeniable.

She looked over to the boy and the dog. Then back at him.

"How do I know you mean it, that you won't tell him anything bad they might find?"

Again the admission. Drew's hopes rose. He tried to quash them. It was too early, he couldn't let himself think that way. "Have I ever broken my word to you?"

She looked unhappy about it, but she said, "No."

"Then let them look. Maybe they won't find anything, but maybe they will and we can put this behind us once and for all."

"What if they find you're wrong?"

He didn't think that was going to happen. But if by some chance Foxworth found something that proved Doug was who she thought he was, at least with her, then he deserved better than he'd gotten from his big brother.

"Then I'll join your chorus to Luke," he said.

Something flashed in her eyes then, and he knew he'd won.

"Done," she said.

And Drew wondered what on earth he'd gotten them into. All because of a dog.

Chapter 7

"I hope you know what you're doing," Quinn muttered to the dog at his feet. Cutter looked up at him steadily.

"I believe that's his 'Of course I do. It's you humans who are slow on the uptake,' expression," Hayley said cheerfully.

"We humans," Quinn said, "are reluctant to handle familial dynamite."

Hayley glanced over to where Drew and Alyssa were standing at the third-floor window, Drew holding Luke up so he could see the bald eagle sitting on the branch of a large maple amid the evergreens. The boy was babbling excitedly; he'd never seen one so close before.

"Maybe we should have Kayla and Dane talk to them about misguided brotherly love," Quinn said, and Hayley looked at him to see that he'd followed the direction of her gaze. Hayley had no doubts that Kayla and Dane Burdette would be willing. They felt, as did most of Foxworth's former clients, that they owed them whatever they might ask for.

"I get your point, but I'm not sure this situation is the same. Brother and brother, not brother and sister. It's different, the relationship between brothers, isn't it?"

"Probably. More competitive, maybe," Quinn said. "So, you believe her version?"

"Let's just say I don't disbelieve anybody at this point."

"But they can't both be right."

"I didn't say right. I think they both see what they see, through their own filters. And the truth is probably somewhere in between."

The eagle lifted off, having spotted something worth investigating. Luke shouted "Look, look!" as the majestic bird dove, then soared before disappearing to the west.

"Beautiful, isn't she?" Hayley said, walking up to join the trio at the window.

"It's a girl? How do you know?" Luke asked.

"The females are bigger," she answered. "Her mate's noticeably smaller."

Luke glanced from her to Drew. Drew nodded. "They are."

"That's weird."

"We'll go to the library and find a book about them," Alyssa said.

"Can't we just go on the computer?"

"The pictures are better in a book, and you can look at it by yourself after we read it together. When you're done with your schoolwork."

Luke frowned. "We're not learning about birds yet."

"Then you'll be ahead of everybody, won't you?" Drew said.

Luke's frown vanished. "Yeah!"

Hayley glanced at Quinn. *Competitive* was definitely the word with boys, she thought. He was grinning at her as if he knew exactly what she was thinking. And he probably did. The closer their wedding got, the more excited she was; the thought of sharing the rest of her life with this man was more than she'd ever dared hope for.

And all thanks to that furry rascal Cutter, who chose this moment to rise and come to her, as if he'd sensed her rising emotions. Unable to hold it all in for a moment, Hayley crouched beside the dog and hugged him fiercely.

"Thank you, my friend," she whispered.

Cutter nuzzled her, whuffing softly. She felt the quick swipe of his tongue over her chin.

"Why are you thanking him?" Luke asked. Hayley looked up to see the boy looking at them curiously.

"Because he found Quinn for me," she said.

"Oh." Luke looked doubtfully up at the man beside her. "He did?"

"That he did," Quinn confirmed.

"I thought you said he found people in trouble."

"He does."

Luke's eyes widened as he looked at Quinn. "Were you in trouble?"

Even a six-year-old can see Quinn isn't a man to find himself in trouble often, Hayley thought with an inward laugh.

"No," Quinn said, "but I was definitely lost."

Hayley felt her eyes sting at his heartfelt declaration. But Luke just nodded. "Oh," the boy said, as if it all made sense now. As perhaps it did. "Can we go outside and play?" he asked, petting Cutter.

"Not while *we're* inside," Alyssa said quickly. "Maybe later."

Luke looked crestfallen. "I wanted to look at the eagle tree."

"If you'd be comfortable with it," Quinn said, "I can have somebody out there with him, while we go over what we've found so far."

Alyssa blinked. "What you've found? But we only agreed to this a couple of hours ago."

"Foxworth works fast," Hayley said. Quinn had called ahead to Tyler Hewitt, their tech genius, and gotten him started. By the time they'd arrived here at the Foxworth building, he'd already sent the basics. And one possibly very pertinent fact.

"So can we, please?" Luke asked.

"Liam will take good care of him," Quinn said. "Heck, they'll have fun. He's an outdoor guy, a dog guy, a tech guy and our best tracker."

Drew reacted to that with a small chuckle. "That's quite a résumé."

"A tracker?" Luke asked.

"Yep. He could follow a trail through the trees for miles, if pressed," Quinn said. "He's the one who found where our eagle's nest is."

Luke's eyes widened. "Really? Could he show me?"

"That might be a bit too far for today. Why don't you meet him, see how it goes?" Quinn leaned over to the boy. "I hear he also carries those little candy bars all the time," he said in a loud whisper. Luke grinned.

Alyssa looked at Drew, who nodded. So however unusual their relationship was, she did accept his input when it came to Luke, Hayley thought.

Quinn took out his cell and buzzed the comlink. "Need you to watch out for our young friend and a certain dog outside for a bit." There was a pause before Quinn laughed. "Yeah, I'm sure Cutter does need watching more than Luke."

He ended the call and slipped the phone back into his pocket.

"Cutter, take him down to Liam," Quinn said, gesturing at Luke.

The dog was on his feet instantly. He walked a few steps forward, then stopped to look back at the boy. Luke looked at his mother.

"It's all right," she said, although Hayley thought she heard a bit of doubt yet.

"We'll sit at the table by the window," she said. "You'll be able to see them."

Alyssa let out a breath and nodded. "Thank you."

With a whoop, Luke took off after the dog and they heard the clatter as the pair went down the stairs.

And now, Hayley thought as they went to the table she'd mentioned, to open that package of familial dynamite, as Quinn had put it.

"The first thing you need to know, if you don't already," Quinn said, "is that Baird Oliver is out."

Alyssa's breath caught audibly. Her gaze shot to Drew. He wasn't sure what to say or how to say it. And in that moment of indecision, she got there.

"You knew!"

"Lyss—"

"You knew he was out?"

He sighed. "I've been tracking it, yes. I knew it was nearly time, so I started making calls. And found he'd already been let out, three months early." His mouth twisted. "Nice, for a guy with a record pages long, everything from petty theft to assault with a deadly weapon."

"And you didn't tell me?"

"I only found out for sure a little while ago. Just before this whole thing with Luke, and I didn't want to upset you even more."

"So you decided to keep me in the dark? When the career criminal who got Luke's father killed is out?"

"I was going to tell you, just not then."

"And the week since?"

Drew flicked a glance at the couple opposite them. It was awkward, but he didn't see any way out of it. There was only one reason he hadn't told her Doug's partner in crime had been released and was now a free man.

"It's been so…nice, I didn't want to ruin it."

Her eyes widened slightly. And to his surprise, she smiled. A warm, acknowledging smile.

It had been nice. They had both been so relieved that Luke was all right, so focused on the boy and his welfare, that things had been quite pleasant. Something he should remember, Drew told himself. All it really took to keep her happy was that Luke was happy. He had the feeling she'd be content living in a tiny apartment somewhere, on a tight budget, doing without, as long as her son was happy.

And the biggest thing she could probably do without was him.

But that smile…

"We're trying to track him down," Quinn said briskly, as if he was used to emotional moments like this occurring in his workplace. As, given the work Foxworth did, perhaps they did. "But since he served his entire sentence and isn't on parole, that's going to take a little time."

"Because he doesn't have to check in with anyone?" Alyssa asked.

Quinn nodded. "He's free and clear."

"Except for that matter of a felony record," Drew said.

"Yes. But all I meant was that no one has any leverage."

"I'm hoping," Drew said, "that since it's been three months, he either can't find us or isn't looking."

Quinn's gaze sharpened. Then he gave Drew a short nod of approval. "Glad to see I don't need to explain that."

"Wait," Alyssa said. "You think he'll come looking for us? Baird? Why?"

"I just think it's better to be cautious," Drew said.

"Always wise when dealing with a man with his kind of rap sheet," Quinn said.

Alyssa watched Drew for a moment. "That's why you had that alarm system put in this summer, isn't it?"

"Partly," he admitted.

She'd teased him then, about being paranoid. An alarm

system seemed completely unnecessary on their quiet little street in their quiet little neighborhood in a quiet little town. But he'd simply said he wanted them safe when he was working long hours on a job, and he was having one installed at the office anyway for insurance reasons. Which was at least partially true. He didn't see any point in reminding her that Doug's co-felon would be released soon. And she'd looked over at Luke, busily drawing a picture of their hike the day before, and thanked him.

She'd even reached out to him that night. It had been a long time, and he was hungry enough to take what she offered, even knowing it was out of gratitude rather than love. It didn't happen often, but considering they'd started out with her insisting she would never, ever sleep with him he supposed it was something. He'd found it amazing how you could almost get used to not having sex if you went long enough. Like you went numb or something. Except for those times when the need became overwhelming and he'd resorted to the oldest method in the world, with stupid fantasies about his wife running through his head.

He saw her cheeks turn pink, knew she was remembering that night as well. It had been good, even she couldn't deny that. But she'd been so glum afterwards, as if she felt guilty, he knew it would be a long time before he got that offer again. And he'd spent a long time after that cursing his dead brother for having such a hold on her. He just didn't understand it. She was a bright, clever woman, why couldn't she see who Doug really was?

Alyssa turned away, looking out the window where Luke and Cutter were playing under the watchful eye of the guardian Quinn had promised. Liam Burnett looked young from here, but Quinn had assured them he was more than competent.

"He's been trained by the best," Hayley had added with a loving glance at her fiancé. "And young enough he'll probably end up playing right there with them before long."

Drew wondered what it would be like, to have your woman look at you like that. He knew Alyssa respected him, was grateful to him, and—God help him—*appreciated* him. But love him, the way Hayley clearly loved Quinn? No. And he had no right to expect it. Ever.

"We'll find Oliver, wherever he went," Quinn promised now. "And no matter how long it takes. We're dealing with a different sort of situation now."

"More what you usually do?" Alyssa asked.

"Yes," Quinn agreed, "but we won't stop on the other. We'll just add finding Oliver to it. And if necessary, once we do we'll keep an eye on him from then on."

Alyssa turned back. "That could get expensive," she said with a frown.

Drew hadn't even asked. Her safety and Luke's was something he didn't put a price tag on.

"Foxworth doesn't charge," Quinn said.

Drew blinked. "What?"

"Once we decide to take on a case, we fund it."

Suspicion bit, deep and hard. "And just how do you manage that?"

"We're funded by a trust, set up with my parents' life insurance."

"They're both gone?" Alyssa asked softly.

Quinn nodded. "Years ago."

"I'm sorry."

There was no doubting the genuineness of her tone. Alyssa had that down to her bones, that capacity of empathy. Perhaps because of what she herself had been through, she had a knack for making people realize she truly did know how they felt. He used to wish she'd use some of that on him, but soon decided it was just as well she didn't know how he felt. Especially after he'd made the stupid mistake of falling in love with her.

"It was the Lockerbie bombing," Hayley said.

Drew sucked in a breath. He'd been a kid at the time,

but he remembered his parents' horror. Alyssa had only been a baby, so while she knew of it, it likely didn't have the impact it had for him.

"That was the terrorist attack, the passenger jet?" she asked.

Quinn nodded. "They were both on board."

"My God," Alyssa breathed. "How awful. I'm so sorry. You must have been very young."

Again the empathy fairly glowed from her, as if it were a tangible thing between her and the person she was feeling it for. He wasn't used to that kind of introspection, he just went along day by day doing what had to be done. Alyssa sometimes unnerved him with her observations, leaving him wondering how she knew such things about people, things they never said.

And wondering whether to be hurt or thankful she didn't seem to ever turn that capacity on him.

"I was ten," Quinn answered.

"And alone?"

"I had my sister. She was four years older and practically raised me from then on. Our uncle really tried, but he wasn't cut out for kids."

"Is that why you joined the military?" Alyssa asked.

"Mostly," Quinn said.

"And then the bomber got released in a backroom deal," Hayley said. "That's why Foxworth does what it does. Quinn didn't ever want anyone to feel as helpless and wronged as they did when that happened."

"So you used your parents' insurance money to set up Foxworth?" Drew asked. "Must have been a nice inheritance."

"It helps that my sister turned out to be a financial genius," Quinn said with a grin. "Thanks to her we have facilities in all four corners of the country, plus headquarters in St. Louis."

"Does each one have its own helipad?" Drew asked;

he'd noticed the windsock next to the square of concrete outside the warehouse beside the green, three story building they were in now.

"Not all, not yet," Quinn said. "We're working on that."

"And is every Foxworth building unmarked?"

Quinn's gaze sharpened once more. He leaned back in his chair, and again gave Drew a nod of approval. "You noticed that."

"Hard to miss."

"Not for some," Quinn said. "Let's just say some of the people we help have enemies who aren't too happy about it."

"Why do I get the feeling your help isn't limited to just avoiding domestic situations and tracking down released ex-cons?"

"Because you're a smart guy?" Quinn suggested. He studied Drew for a moment. "You ex-military? Law enforcement?"

"No," Drew said, then added with a crooked grin, "I was a Boy Scout once."

"You still are," Alyssa said.

Drew's head snapped around. There hadn't been a hint of a dig in her tone, although he knew there was a time when there would have been. Back when Doug had used it as an insult. My brother the Boy Scout, he'd said constantly.

I've got no chance of matching you in the good little boy department, so maybe I'll just have to go for the bad instead.

The laughing statement that had haunted him for years now echoed in his head. Nothing else Doug had said or done had hit him quite the way that had. For a long time he'd felt almost responsible for his little brother's twisted mindset. As if he'd set an impossible standard to live up to. He'd never felt he was anything special, he'd just tried to do his best, make their parents proud, but apparently in the process he'd somehow made Doug feel inferior.

But Alyssa was smiling at him.

He felt the strongest urge to call this all off. To go back, to try and hang on to the mood of the last week. It had been, on the surface, the life he'd dreamed of with her. And if they could hold on to that, maybe he could work on the rest, maybe someday she might actually look at him the way she'd once looked at Doug.

He tried to scoff himself out of that silly idea, but it clung stubbornly to the edges of his consciousness. But now he knew he had to decide, and decide now. For so long he'd wanted her to see the truth, wanted her to see the real man—or rather, boy—his brother had been. And on that day he'd realized he loved her, he knew he'd wanted her to see Doug differently in the hope that she would then be free to see him differently.

But now he wondered if it would be worth it. How would she react if he destroyed that rose-colored image she had?

If he let this go on, and Foxworth somehow found the answers and proved him right, what would he be left with?

Chapter 8

Drew was glad things had slowed down as winter approached. Usually he fretted about the downturn as construction slowed, especially since he kept paying his crew to stay on, but this time he was glad of it. And if having him around more irritated Alyssa she didn't show it. She simply said the more time he spent with Luke, assuring him he was loved and needed, the better.

Personally, he thought the best thing they could do for Luke now was present a united—not loving, that was too much to ask—and calm front. Like the home front he'd had, his parents love for each other had never been in doubt, and he'd turned out okay.

Then again, they'd raised Doug in the same atmosphere.

But they'd also spoiled him more, after his rocky start. And once he'd learned to use his innate charm to manipulate adults, it was all over.

The call from Foxworth came in just after they'd dropped Luke off at school. Part of that united front, they'd both hugged him and waited until he was inside the long, low, northwest-style building. Alyssa had sighed as she wondered aloud how long before being hugged by his mother in public would be unacceptable. Then the call had come, and they quickly scuttled the plans they'd had to go shopping to replace Alyssa's computer, which had been acting up lately, and headed for the unmarked, green building.

It had only been three days since they'd been here. He hadn't expected anything new so quickly, despite Hayley's assurances. They were the best at what they did, she'd said, and apparently she was right. Even if he still wasn't exactly sure what all it was they did. He was sure of why, though, after the story they'd heard, and that kind of motivation was hard to disagree with.

When they arrived, Cutter was outside and raced up to meet them. He greeted them both with a bump of wet nose, then looked toward the car.

"Sorry, buddy, Luke's at school," Drew said with a laugh at the dog.

Cutter whuffed softly, sounding dejected, as if he'd understood perfectly his new playmate wasn't coming. Alyssa smiled and patted his head.

"Maybe next time," she said.

Cutter then turned and trotted toward the building. They followed. At the door he rose up on his hind legs and batted at a metal square on the wall. A handicapped door activator, Drew realized as the door swung open, and couldn't help grinning at the clever dog.

The moment the door was open Cutter trumpeted out a bark that sounded for all the world like an announcement.

"Not quite a doorbell, but effective," Drew said.

Alyssa laughed, which pleased him a lot more than it probably should have. But then, she usually did. It was only that one sore spot that was ever a problem, as far as he was concerned.

Of course, Alyssa could have an entirely different viewpoint. He'd always expected that one day she'd want out of their arrangement. They'd talked about that, before they'd gone through with it. They'd left open the option that if either of them found someone else, they'd be free to go. He'd made her promise she wouldn't sneak, but would tell him honestly. She'd cringed at that one, but said nothing. Probably felt she had no right to, after sneaking off with Doug.

But she'd changed, grown so much in the last three years, sooner or later she was going to get tired of being tied to a man she didn't love, a man who reminded her in the worst possible way of the man she had loved. It was why he kept his feelings buried, as deep as he could. Because telling her how he felt would more than likely hasten that day.

Buried might not be enough, he thought as they walked through the door Cutter had opened for them. He might just need to pour cement over them, too.

They came into the downstairs living area that had so surprised them the first time they were here. It had been like walking into a warm, welcoming living room, a leather couch, a couple of chairs arranged around a coffee table on a thick, cushy-looking area rug. They were all facing a gas fireplace that was turned on, warming the room visually as well as temperature-wise. He'd admired the efficient arrangement of the small kitchen along the back wall, and the way the island separated it from the rest of the space.

Hayley was already there, with a laptop open before her on the heavy coffee table. Cutter trotted over to her, sat, and leaned into her. "Ah, there you are."

"Is he your official greeter?" Alyssa asked with a smile.

Hayley laughed as she stood up. "One of the many tasks he's taken on, yes."

"Pretty smart trick, with the door," Drew said.

"Quinn put it in mostly for him. He's a clever boy," Hayley said, scratching a spot just behind the dog's right ear.

The sigh of pleasure was almost human, and Drew found himself grinning again.

"Good morning." Quinn's voice came from the back as he came down the stairs, a plain manila folder in his hand. "Cutter rounded you up, I see."

"That he did," Alyssa said.

"Maybe we should get Luke a dog," Drew mused aloud.

"Yes," Alyssa agreed instantly. "I didn't realize until I saw them together how much he'd love one."

"I know just who you should talk to," Hayley said. "Laney Adams. She's the girlfriend of one of our guys, and she runs the grooming shop here in town. She knows all the dog folks around."

"I think we should adopt one, though," Drew said. "Help a homeless one."

Alyssa glanced at him, her expression unreadable. At least, to him. But oddly, he saw something change in Hayley's expression, as if she somehow knew exactly what Alyssa was thinking.

Women.

"Perfect," Hayley said. "Laney donates groomings to the local Humane Society, prettying up the shelter dogs so they have a better chance. She knows a lot of folks there. And the dogs. She'd know which ones might be really good for Luke."

"I like her already," Alyssa said.

"Of course, Cutter found Laney her own dog," Quinn put in.

"What?"

"She'd been thinking about a dog for the shop, as a greeter, as you called it. And she made the mistake—or the right call—of discussing it in front of Cutter. A week later he brought Teague a tired, scared, skinny and very dirty pup who'd obviously been lost for a long time."

"Teague is…?"

"Teague Johnson. Works for us."

"Her boyfriend?"

Hayley nodded. "So now Murphy has a good home and a job."

"Wait," Drew said. "Back up here a minute. You're saying Cutter understood that discussion?"

Quinn smiled, his expression one of a man who'd been down this road, and remembered how ridiculous it seemed. "You have a better explanation?"

"You're assuming cause and effect, here," Drew said.

"Post hoc, ergo propter hoc?" Quinn said.

"Exactly."

Hayley looked at Alyssa and winked. "I love it when he talks Latin."

Alyssa sighed. "I have no idea what that even means."

"After this, therefore because of this, literally," Drew said. "It's a logical fallacy. The assumption that because something happens after something else, it happened because of that something else."

"Glad you got something out of that college education," Alyssa said, her tone so sour it was almost bitter. Drew winced.

"I've told you more than once you could go back to school if you wanted to. We'd manage." He knew one of the regrets she had about running off with Doug was tossing away the scholarship she'd earned.

"I know you have. But I made my choices, I have to live with them."

"But you don't have to keep on punishing yourself for them," Drew said gently. "Life's done that enough already."

"I'm sorry." The look she gave him then washed away the sting he'd felt at her jab. One thing about Alyssa, if she apologized, she meant it. She glanced at Hayley and Quinn. "And sorry we always seem to air our private problems in front of you."

Hayley waved off her words. "Part of our charm, people feel comfortable."

Quinn, who seemed a bit more uncomfortable about it all, cleared his throat in a wordless reminder of why they were here. Hayley picked up on it instantly.

"I thought we'd sit down here by the fire, since it's a cold, damp morning," she said.

"It's nice," Alyssa said. She'd taken a seat on the couch. Drew hesitated, then sat beside her, but not too close. She didn't react, so he guessed it was all right. And acknowledged briefly how tired he was of guessing with her.

"It's a lot nicer than when I was living here," Quinn said with a grin.

"You were living here?" Alyssa looked around.

"Before I met Hayley, yes."

"Met?" Hayley said with an arched brow.

"Okay, kidnapped."

Drew gave her a startled look. Hayley laughed. "It's a long story. Alyssa can tell you, if you want, I gave her the short version. But now let's get onto your situation."

Alyssa, Drew realized suddenly, was very calm about this. Given that Foxworth had agreed to dig into the truth about Doug, he would have expected her to be a little more nervous. Maybe he'd been wrong thinking she might have accepted the possibility that he was right about his brother. It surely wouldn't be the first time he'd misinterpreted her. The last three years had been a major learning curve.

Quinn set the folder down on the table.

"Drew, I assume you know about your brother's juvenile record."

"Yes. You were able to get that?"

Quinn nodded. "Rules change after a death. Assault, arson, car theft…quite a résumé before he even hit sixteen."

"But that's not right," Alyssa exclaimed. "He never assaulted anyone, that was just a misunderstanding. He might have bullied that kid a little, but that was all. And it wasn't arson, that was just a silly prank that went wrong. And the car thing, that was just joyriding."

Drew stared at her. "What?"

"He told me all about those things. How it all got blown out of proportion."

"Lyss, he went to juvie. For six months. If it had just been joyriding, and if not for the arson, he would have gotten probation or something."

She shook her head. "He told me the truth about it all. It was just the judge didn't believe him."

"It was that the facts proved otherwise," Drew snapped.

He felt a sinking sensation somewhere low and gut-deep. He got up almost convulsively, and walked over toward the fireplace, staring down into the flames. He had an odd sensation of muscles twitching, demanding he move more.

He wanted to run. He realized it with a little shock, he who faced up to life and difficulties. He didn't run. At least he never had. But he wanted to now, and he hated the feeling. He rested an arm on the wood mantelpiece, as if that would anchor him in place. And after a moment his muscles gave up the demand. As if fighting the urge had weakened him, he let his head drop to rest on his forearm. He did feel weak. Tired. Disheartened.

He felt something brush his leg, looked down to see Cutter, who had been quietly snoozing on the rug. The dog nuzzled his other hand, rubbed his head against his knee as if he'd somehow sensed Drew's inner turmoil.

Maybe they were right, he thought rather numbly, and the dog really did read minds.

Now if you could just change minds, he silently told the animal staring up at him. Instinctively he reached to pet the dog's head. And felt oddly better for it. It seemed to ease the roiling in his stomach, at least, even if it did nothing to solve the problem.

Except for moments of weakness, they'd stuck to the agreement not to discuss Doug. But one of the results was that he'd never realized until this moment just how little she knew of the real man his brother was. He'd thought she just refused to admit it, but now he saw that she honestly believed the falsified version of his life Doug had given her.

He heard Quinn talking quietly to Alyssa. He couldn't quite hear the words, didn't care. Hayley rose and came to stand beside him.

"Let's take Cutter for a little walk," she suggested, her voice low enough not to interrupt whatever Quinn was telling Alyssa.

He shook his head. He'd beaten the urge to run, he wasn't going to do it now.

"Please." She was already pulling the hood of her sweater up over her hair. "Quinn's very, very good at laying out facts for people. Give him a chance to get through to her."

The implication that they saw the facts themselves, saw the truth about his brother, made him feel a little less hopeless. Still he hesitated to leave, even for a few minutes, in the midst of this. A second later he felt a nudge behind his knees. Cutter, he realized, had gone behind him and added his own urging to Hayley's persuasive power.

He gave in then, grabbed up his own jacket. The moment they stepped outside into the clearing Luke had been playing in he felt better, despite the light rain that was falling.

"I'm sorry, Drew," Hayley said. "You just have to remember how young she was."

"I know how young she was. I met her for the first time after I came home from college. She was sixteen then. And I knew by the way she acted that Doug had her snowed. A year later she ran off with him."

"At seventeen, the romantic image of a bad boy with a heart of gold is almost irresistible to some girls." She glanced back toward the building. "And very hard to let go of." And then she looked at him, her green eyes warm, sympathetic. "Even if they have a real heart of gold right in front of them."

Her words drained even more of the tension out of him.

He closed his eyes for a moment, then opened them to look at her.

"Quinn is a lucky man," he said.

"Yes," she said with a quick smile. "But then, I'm a lucky woman."

Drew smiled back, feeling somehow better. He rubbed at the back of his neck. Tension always seemed to settle there, and now that it had eased slightly, the muscles were tired.

"I've been trying to figure her out for three years now. She's far from stupid, so I never got why she was so loyal to Doug, after he got her into so much trouble and then abandoned her when she needed him most."

"She never saw the real Doug," Hayley said.

"I should have known. I'd seen him do it with our folks, and others, put up this facade, this carefully constructed image that was all they ever saw."

"And that's all she ever knew of the man who fathered her son."

"So it seems. I guess I just never thought he'd do it with the girl he supposedly loved."

"Which says as much about you as it does about him," Hayley said with a warm smile that made him think yet again that Quinn Foxworth was a very lucky man.

Chapter 9

Alyssa stared at the records spread out before her. The papers alone she could dismiss, they were, after all, just one person's interpretation of what happened. And cops, Doug had often told her, wrote things that proved their case, not always the truth. She'd wondered why they picked him to harass, but it had only been a brief thought, quickly forgotten when Doug launched into her favorite subject—the wonderful life they were going to have once they were free of all this and away from his parents and hers.

They had to wait until he was twenty-one, he'd said, because then he'd come into a small inheritance left by his grandmother. His stick-in-the-mud brother had used his to help fund college, but he wasn't about to throw his away like that. He was going to get out there and *live,* not spend hours in some musty hall reading about other people's lives.

She'd only found out later that Drew hadn't wanted to go to college at all, he'd wanted to stay here and work in the business. But his grandfather had pushed for college, and Drew respected the man. So he'd made a deal with his grandfather, that he'd go to college, as long as he could come straight back when he was done. And true to his intent, he did just that. He'd graduated with honors, but was on his way home the very next day.

While she and Doug were still playing out their teen romance back here. She would have left with him before that, willingly. Sixteen was the age of consent in Washington, she told him, he wouldn't get in trouble, even if he was four years older than she. She loved him, madly, she told him.

Madly.

She'd come to accept that she hadn't seen things as clearly as her seventeen-year-old self had thought. It had been a long process of ruefully admitting she'd been more than a little foolish.

But she'd never thought herself blind. Until now.

It was the video that had chilled her.

She wasn't sure how they'd gotten them, but supposed since Doug was dead, it didn't matter, and Quinn had said Foxworth had friends in a lot of places, and very good ones in law enforcement. It helped that they never wanted credit for what they did, even if it helped solve something the police hadn't been able to.

It was undeniably Doug. In small interview rooms, in apparently three different places, one after the arson arrest, and two following the stolen car incident. Quinn had set the laptop in front of her and played them, one after the other. She watched as he admitted to it all, the police versions, not the sad tales he'd spun for her.

She'd never seen that Doug before. Had never heard such things spoken by him. Foulmouthed and arrogant, disdainful and smug, she was hard-pressed to simply chalk it up to him reacting to being in police custody. She tried, told herself he was just acting that way because he was scared. It even worked.

Until Quinn had called up a fourth video.

This one wasn't Doug. It was Baird. An interview done after his conviction for the robbery, when he had nothing to gain by lying or to lose by telling the truth. And in the part Quinn made her watch, he was talking about her.

"Doug's bitch? Yeah, I know her."

An unseen questioner asked, "Did she know about your plan?"

"Nah. Doug'd never tell her. Didn't want the grief."

"Grief?"

"He said she's the whiny, good-girl type. Good for sex, but not much else." Baird grinned at the camera, waved with his left hand in an obscene gesture. He was left-handed, she remembered. Inanely. "He said I could do her, if I wanted. But I knew she was knocked up, and it kind of took the fun out of it, you know?"

For a moment Alyssa just stared at the frozen image in the video clip Quinn had stopped.

She'd known the police suspected she'd been involved. It had been only to be expected, given her connection to Doug. But they'd been surprisingly gentle with her, more than she'd ever hoped. So she owed Baird Oliver for not getting sucked further into that investigation? Ironic, she supposed. Perhaps she should thank him someday.

Maybe you should thank him for not taking Doug up on his generous offer to use you like a whore. After you were pregnant with his son.

She told herself Baird was lying. But Baird had never hidden who he was or what he did, it was out there for anyone to see if they really looked. She'd seen it enough after Doug had taken up with him, to her dismay.

In the beginning he'd promised her it was only temporary, that Baird had plans that would get them back in the money again, after they'd blown through what was left of the inheritance. And then she'd found out she was pregnant, and Doug went a little crazy. He'd screamed at her for being careless, as if she'd been the only one involved. As if it were all her fault. Worried about how he would provide for them, she'd told herself. But now she was having more trouble than usual hanging on to the old excuses.

Because Drew never blames you for anything, and you've gotten used to it?

It was a thought she'd never had in quite that way before. It was true, though. Doug had often blamed her for anything that went wrong, so often she'd come to accept it. But Drew never did. If anything he took the blame on himself. And then fixed whatever had gone wrong, as best it could be fixed. She hadn't realized until this moment how much she'd come to rely on that steady support, to count on it always being there.

She'd been so sure that if Foxworth found anything, they would find proof that Drew was wrong.

Now she wasn't sure of anything.

"So, how did you get through three years without hashing this out?"

Drew sighed. He had never talked about this with anyone. But somehow he knew that he could tell this woman. Or Quinn. And it would never go beyond them. He'd done a little homework on Foxworth before their call had come today, and had been both surprised and a little awed by what he'd found. They'd helped a lot of people around the country, people up against odds that seemed impossible, people who had no other recourse in their battle against anything from rank injustice to the proverbial fighting city hall.

People who felt as helpless as Quinn had when the person responsible for the deaths of his own parents had been released under false pretenses, with little or no thought for his hundreds of victims.

"We made…a deal. Not talking about Doug was part of it. But sometimes, like the day we all met, we blow it." He grimaced. "Most times it's me. I never mean to, but…"

"A deal?"

He let out a compressed breath. "A sort of business arrangement. When I found them, Alyssa was so sick she couldn't take care of herself or Luke. In fact, I probably only found her because she was in the hospital. But I wanted Luke to be with family, taken care of, provided for."

"So, you married her?"

"I know, I could have made legal arrangements to become his guardian, I had a blood claim, but he'd already been taken away from his mother. Setting it up would take a lawyer, and it would have been long, complicated and expensive. And Luke would have to stay in foster care while it was being done. I thought the time and money could be better spent taking care of them."

"And she agreed?"

He let out another breath. He didn't like talking about it, didn't like the way it all sounded, but now that he'd started he didn't quite see how to stop.

"She was so weak, and grief-stricken over Doug's death. And she was scared for the future. Scared she'd never get Luke back. She was really on the edge. Getting married seemed to offer the fastest solution."

"And you got Luke back."

"It still took a while, had to go to family court, but it was a lot faster. We got him in time for his third birthday." His mouth quirked. "Sometimes I guess being a boring straight arrow pays off."

"I happen to be very fond of straight arrows," Hayley said. "I'm surrounded by them here. And I don't find them boring at all. And obviously Alyssa must find something appealing about them as well."

Drew blinked. "What makes you think that?"

Hayley shrugged. "She's still with you. She's healthy, back on her feet—she could make her own way." She lifted a brow at him. "Unless you're holding her prisoner, of course."

Drew pulled back in shock. "What? No! Of course not."

"So she could leave any time, right?"

He looked away. He didn't want to think about that. "Yeah," he muttered.

For a moment he stared at the tree, the maple among the firs, thinking that the eagle had it right. Just watch the world, hunt and fly. Sounded like a pretty good life to him just now.

"So when did you actually fall in love with her?"

He froze. After a few seconds of uncomfortable silence he opened his mouth to deny it. He'd never said it out loud to anyone, as if he could continue to deny it as long as he never said the words.

He glanced at Hayley. She was looking at him, an expression of warmth and understanding on her expressive face. "I don't meddle," she said softly. Then, with a smile, she added, "I leave that to Cutter. He's better at it anyway."

He nearly laughed, and the pressure eased.

"I'm not sure when it happened. I realized it on her birthday last year," he finally answered. "She'd changed so much. Grown. She wasn't that sick, scared girl anymore. She was a woman, smart, kind, strong and the most loving mother I'd ever seen."

"And lovely."

"Yes." It would be foolish to deny that when the proof was sitting right inside that door. Alyssa was lovely. The big blue eyes, the wispy blonde sweep of hair, that ever so kissable mouth…

"I gather she doesn't know?"

He shook his head, sharply. "And she can't. That wasn't part of the deal."

"At her request or yours?"

His brows lowered. "Hers. She was clear about it. That's one of the reasons she said yes. She'd never love anybody again anyway, so she might as well marry me so Luke could have a stable home with family."

"So, she's changed in every way…except that one?"

He frowned, puzzled. "What?"

"You said she's grown, gotten strong, changed so much since you found her in that hospital. But that single thing hasn't changed? She's still cut herself off from love with all the dramatic flair of that seventeen-year-old who ran off with your brother?"

He stared at her. "I…never thought of it that way."

Cutter, who had been investigating an apparently fascinating bit of greenery off to their right, suddenly lifted his head and looked toward the building. He abandoned his inspection and trotted over to them. When he had their attention he started toward the back door they'd come out through. At about ten feet away, he stopped and looked back.

"I guess it's safe to go back," Hayley said.

Drew blinked. But he couldn't deny he was glad of the interruption at this particular moment.

He looked from her to Cutter and back. "You mean he's psychic, too?" he asked drily.

"Sometimes," she said, "I would find it hard to deny that."

Her tone was such a combination of love, ruefulness and acceptance that he couldn't help smiling. And he felt much better as they headed back inside. Nothing had really changed, after all. He'd known he could never take Doug's place with Alyssa. Had never wanted to. He wanted his own place.

And getting that was up to him.

Something had definitely changed. Drew sensed it the moment they got back inside and he saw Alyssa's face. She looked shaken, unsettled, rattled…something. And she wouldn't look at him. He wanted to ask her what was wrong, but the presence of Quinn and Hayley stopped him.

Quinn. What had he done? What had he told her, shown

her? His gaze flicked to the other man's face. To his surprise, Quinn gave him a barely perceptible nod.

What the hell did that mean? Was he admitting he'd put that look on her face? Telling him it would be all right? What?

"I was just telling Alyssa that we're waiting on some further details from L.A. About the robbery. A friend of ours with the local sheriff's office, Detective Dunbar, used to work there. He's making some calls."

"You think they'll tell him more than they told me back then?" Drew asked.

"Frankly, yes," Quinn said. "Cop to cop, and all. There are things the police don't always tell family, if they don't think it's necessary." He flicked a glance at Alyssa. "Contrary to what some think, they have hearts. They don't want to hurt anyone who's already grieving, with things they might not need to know. At the time, anyway."

"Or send someone who's already hurting so badly over the edge." Hayley said it to Drew, but she was looking at Alyssa, who was still staring at her hands, folded and still in her lap.

He wanted to go to her, to steady her, tell her everything would be all right. But he didn't know what had happened, what Quinn had told or shown her, so how could he promise that? He wasn't Doug, who made wild promises assuming he'd never be held to them. If he made a promise, if he gave his word, he would damn well keep it. He—

The familiar sound of Alyssa's cell phone broke off his thoughts. She jumped slightly, as if she'd been a million miles away and had been yanked back to the present and this place.

Or maybe just back with Doug, before her life had fallen apart.

"Sorry," she said, aimed at Quinn and Hayley. "I have to get this, it could be school, about Luke. There's a lot of flu going around right now."

Her insistence, Drew knew, wasn't lingering concern after the boy's stunt, she'd always been that way. To her, it was simply being a mother.

She dug into a side pocket on her purse, the big leather bag he had teased her about so often. Once she had dumped it out on the floor, gone through item by item and explained why it was in there, how often she used or needed it, pointed out that most of the things that were in there were for Luke, like the mini first-aid kit for scrapes and cuts, two of his small metal cars to keep him occupied during unexpected waiting time, extras of the vitamins he always forgot to take before rushing out the door in the mornings, sanitary wipes for grubby hands, and a half-dozen other things he never would have thought of.

He'd thrown up his hands, admitting defeat. She'd smiled at him then, and they'd both ended up laughing when he had offered to carry the bag for her with all the officiousness of a trained valet. It had been a sweet moment, a memory he treasured. A memory that had given him hope.

Until the next time he slipped up and they'd fought about Doug.

She had the phone out, frowned at the screen before tapping it and putting it up to her ear.

"Hello?" A pause, then, "Yes? Who is this?"

Three things happened simultaneously.

Alyssa went pale.

Her eyes widened in shock.

And Cutter launched to his feet, seeming suddenly twice as big as he was as he zeroed in on Alyssa. Drew gaped at the dog for an instant, but quickly dismissed the oddity and went into action himself.

"Lyss?" Drew cross the distance between them in one long stride. "Luke?" he asked, his heart hammering in his chest. "Is it Luke?"

She shook her head. Shook it again, sharply.

She hit the mute command, then looked up at him. Her eyes were still wide, her expression stunned.

"It's Baird," she said.

Chapter 10

Quinn moved so quickly it startled Alyssa almost as much as the unexpected, unwanted call. He signaled everyone to be quiet as he grabbed for the laptop. Alyssa was thankful for that; the computer's screen had still been frozen on the image of Baird's snigger, and seeing that while hearing that never-forgotten voice in her ear had taken the breath out of her.

"What is it, Alyssa?" that voice said. "So glad to hear my voice you can't even talk?"

"Try and keep him talking," Quinn said. "Hayley, call Ty. See if he can at least start a trace."

For a moment Alyssa couldn't seem to move. But then Drew was there, sitting beside her, putting a strong, warm arm around her. She unmuted the phone.

"I'm just surprised, that's all."

"You shouldn't be."

Although he didn't say it in the menacing tone she knew he was quite capable of, it sounded ominous just the same.

She knew Drew had heard by the way his arm pulled her closer. She leaned into him, grateful for his solid strength.

"Where are you?"

"Oh, I'm close. Very close."

Her hand tightened around the phone. She heard a low sound, realized it was Cutter, growling. The distraction of wondering, even if only for a split second, how the dog had known instantly this caller was a threat, enabled her to get a grip on her nerves.

"When did you get out?" she asked, although she already knew. Quinn had said to try and keep him talking, but she had no idea what to say to this man who had destroyed her world and ended up almost costing her her life, almost landed Luke forever in the grinding machinery of the system.

No. Drew would have found him. Even if you had died, Drew never would have stopped until he'd found him.

She supposed that the thought that hit her now, when she was talking to the man who had so led Doug astray, wasn't really surprising. The certainty with which it struck didn't even surprise her, not anymore. She'd spent three years with Drew Kiley, and she knew now that behind that cool, businesslike exterior was a very strong, very determined man.

A man who loved Luke and took care of him as if he were his own.

"—time off for good behavior," Baird was saying in her ear. She gave herself an inward shake; she should be paying attention, he might say something she should know.

"Good behavior? You?" She managed a laugh.

To her surprise, Baird laughed, too. "Nah. It was money. It always is, innit? They let a bunch of us out, because the government needs to study butterflies more than it needs to keep harmless folks like me locked up."

That jab got her full attention. "Harmless? Tell that to Doug. Oh, wait…"

She heard a long, low whistle. "You grow some teeth while I was inside, honey?"

"Don't call me honey!"

"Why not? I was thinking now that Doug's out of the way, we could hook up. You know you always wanted to."

Alyssa's stomach churned. She'd only occasionally thought about this man in the last three years, she'd been too busy getting well, then taking care of Luke, trying to make up for the chaos of the first couple of years of his life. But it had only taken a minute for it all to come roaring back, how much she hated him. Just the idea of being with Baird Oliver was enough to turn her stomach.

In the midst of that flood of emotion, she realized Drew's arm had tightened, that his entire body had gone rigid. Somehow that enabled her to keep back the flood of invective she wanted to unleash on this man. Drew was worth a hundred, a thousand of this piece of slime.

A sudden, vivid memory shot through her mind, of that summer day just a few months ago, when her gratitude to Drew and for all he'd done for them had welled up inside her and she'd reached out to him. He'd kept his promise, he'd never pushed her for more intimacy than she wanted to give, but that day it was she who wanted it.

And had found an entirely different kind of connection, a kind she'd never known before. He'd been gentle, then urgent, then surprisingly fierce, but through it all she felt treasured in a way she'd never felt with Doug.

It had been a stunning realization for her, and she'd been wrestling with it ever since. And somehow hearing this sleaze make lewd suggestions to her crystallized things so clearly she couldn't believe she hadn't realized it before.

"—too bad you kept the kid. I figured you'd be smart enough to get rid of it, one way or another. But then, I always thought you were smarter than Doug said you were. I mean, coming back here, getting his rich, big-shot, old-school brother to take care of you and the brat? That's genius."

How did he know where she was, that she and Luke were with Doug's brother? She shivered, her mind racing through possibilities. With Drew's arm steadying her, she somehow found the cool to come back at him again. "Genius? No, genius is not even being able to pull off a convenience store robbery without getting caught. And getting your partner killed in the process."

"Hey, bitch, I didn't get him killed. He's the one who drove into that pole on the way to our meet-up. And I only got caught because I trusted him to show up."

Trusting Doug had seemed to get a lot of people in trouble, she thought. And realized with a little jolt that her thought was something Drew would say. In fact, was very like what he'd said that had begun the argument that had convinced Luke he should run away. And now here she was thinking the same thing. Had these few minutes on the phone with Doug's old partner caused that? Had it been what Quinn had shown her? Or had it simply been the years since with Drew, the years of safety, security and tender care that had changed the way she looked at things?

All of it, she thought. She'd changed, and Baird's trash talk had sparked the realization.

She glanced at Quinn, who was still working on the laptop. Hayley, with the phone still at her ear, was leaning over him, occasionally whispering something to him. She tried to keep going.

"How did you find me, Baird?"

"Aw, that's easy enough. They teach us computer skills inside, you know, so we'll be able to find jobs when we get out. God bless all that social media crap."

She frowned. "I don't do any of that."

There had been no reason. Even her parents wouldn't speak to her, and she surely didn't want to try and contact any old friends, not after the mess she'd made of her life.

"But ol' big brother's company does. Lots of helpful information there."

Drew stiffened again. She knew there was nothing specific about her, and especially not Luke, on the Kiley Construction website, or any of the accompanying social pages. Drew had been very careful. The most personal thing mentioned at all was in the "about us" section, in the story telling how the company had been started by Drew's grandfather, expanded by his father, and was now being run by a third generation Kiley, Drew, who had grown up in the county, gone away to college at his grandfather's insistence, but come back home.

She sucked in a little breath as something struck her. Had Drew done that, kept the personal information skimpy, for just this reason? She'd always thought that since their marriage was just an arrangement, like any other business dealing he had, that he hadn't bothered to acknowledge them in his professional literature. But now, suddenly and belatedly, she was wondering if this had been why. Had he feared that someday something like this might happen?

"You're lying, Baird. There's nothing about me on any of that."

"But lots about big brother. Fine, upstanding businessman that he is, all about customer service, he even gives his cell phone out to his customers so they can reach him any time. All I had to do was ask."

There was a sudden tension radiating from Quinn and Hayley. Were they getting close to tracing the call? *Keep him talking,* she told herself. *You know he loves to brag, keep him talking.*

"But that's still not me. How did you get to me, to my cell phone?"

"Easy. Once I had Doug's brother's, I figured yours would be with the same company, given he's taking care of you and Doug's brat. After that it was easy. You know they're not the most secure databases these days."

"How did you even know I was with Drew?"

"Hell, that was even easier. After I got out, I just played up how worried I was, how guilty I felt about what had happened to you and the baby after Doug died."

"Please. You never gave a damn about me. You were the one always after him to leave me behind."

"You did cramp his style a bit." Oh, that was Baird all right. Let nothing get in the way of what he wanted. "I'm not as good an actor as Doug was, but I'm okay. Some sob sister of a social worker looked it up for me. All she'd tell me was that Doug's brother had stepped in, but that was enough. It's not like you were in witness protection or something. Easy-peasy. So here I am."

Just how close was he, really? "Here?"

"Of course. You're really out in the country, aren't you? I mean you can go for miles without even a stoplight, nothing but damn trees. I can't imagine you being stuck there all this time. You were all about the bright lights, big city."

Her breath caught. Was he really here? She shivered. Drew grabbed her free hand, squeezed it. She steadied herself. Cutter began to pace, clearly unhappy. *So am I, dog,* she thought.

"What is it you want, Baird? I know you don't really give a damn about me, or my son."

"Hey, just trying to be polite. I'm rehabilitated, you know."

Alyssa believed in redemption. She herself was living proof, was she not, that it was possible? It might take her the rest of her life, but she would make it up to Luke for the rocky start. But Baird Oliver? No. If anything, he sounded more slimy, more conniving than ever.

"Give it a rest, Baird."

"Don't be that way, honey—"

"I told you—"

"All right, all right. Let's get to business then."

Here it came, she thought. "We don't have any business."

"Oh, come on now. You know what I want."

"No, I don't."

"Of course you do. I want my share."

"Your share of what?"

"Of the money."

"What mon—"

She broke off midword. He couldn't mean what it sounded like.

"Don't lie to me. I know you have it."

"Are you talking about the robbery money?" Her voice rose slightly, she was so incredulous.

"Don't play stupid, either. I've waited a long time for this."

"I never even saw that money."

"That's bull. I know you have it. They never found it, so Doug must have given it to you. He was probably trying to rip me off, keep it all. If he hadn't died in that crash, I would have probably killed him myself."

"I don't have it. I never did."

There was a moment of silence. Alyssa felt Drew's tension even as he held her. He was probably the only reason she was still upright. She glanced at Quinn, who nodded and held up a note pad where he'd written "Pinging off a tower north of Seattle."

So he wasn't literally right here. But he was still too close. Across the Sound, yes, but still, too close.

"Doug owed me seven grand," he said, "plus interest over all this time. I figure that's about a nice even ten. That's how much I want."

"I told you, I never even saw that money."

"I don't believe you. If you don't have it, it's because you spent it."

"I didn't. I never saw it. I never saw Doug alive again after you left that night."

There was a long pause before he spoke again.

"You'd better get it, then. In fact, this'll be better. They won't be tracing money you just give to an old friend."

"How do you expect me to get that kind of money?"

"Borrow it from the rich brother, Mr. Straight Arrow."

"I can't do that."

"Why not? He can't be that smart. You conned him into taking care of you."

If you only knew, she thought, her hand tightening on the phone. *Drew Kiley is the smartest person I've ever known.* She didn't, couldn't acknowledge just now how his accusation that she'd conned him stung.

"I can't take more from him."

"I'm being generous, I only want my half, what I've got coming to me." He talked as if Doug had stolen hard-earned wages from him, she realized. She truly did not understand how this man thought. She knew how hard Drew worked, the long hours he put in, and yet Baird had felt he could steal from the store owner who had probably worked just as hard, and claim it was his due. "Besides, you owe me."

"Owe you? You got Doug killed!"

"He did that all by himself, honey. But I'm the one who kept them from dragging you into it. I told them you didn't know about it, or you'd have been in jail right beside me."

"But I didn't know about it. I never would have gone along if I had."

"Cops didn't think so."

The memory of the video went through her mind. Of him telling them she hadn't known about the plan.

"Why did you do that?"

"Maybe I thought you'd be grateful. Show me a little gratitude. On your knees, maybe." He laughed. "But mainly because I knew Doug would have left the money with you."

"He didn't."

"It doesn't matter. I don't care if it's *that* money, as long as the amount is right. And I don't care how you get it. But you will."

"I—"

"Listen to me, you little bitch. That money is mine, and I will collect it. I don't give a damn where you get it, but get it."

"And if I do, then what?"

"Well, if you're going to turn down my offer to show you what it's like to be with a real man, then I'll just be on my way."

A real man. Scorn bubbled up in her, but she held back the biting words she wanted to say. She didn't want him to get mad and hang up. But would he, when he was trying to get something out of her?

"That's better. You just be a good, quiet little girl. I'll give you three days to come up with the cash."

"No way I can do that."

"You will. Or you'll be very sorry. And you know I can make good on that promise."

"What if I just call the police?"

Baird laughed. It was a nasty, unpleasant sound. "You so much as breathe in the direction of the cops, you'll be even sorrier. After all, I'm just an old friend, coming to get something you were keeping for me."

"You think they'll buy that?"

"Why not? There won't be anyone left alive to contradict me."

Her breath jammed in her throat. She felt Drew move as if to grab the phone. She twisted away, she had to keep him out of this. This was her fault, not his, and it was hers to deal with.

"I'll be in touch, Aly-girl," Baird said cheerfully, as if he hadn't just threatened her. The use of Doug's old nickname for her sent a shiver through her. She sat there listening to empty air for a long moment, feeling as if she'd somehow slipped back in time.

Don't have too much fun, Aly-girl.

The last words Doug had ever spoken to her echoed in

her mind. She'd always thought the words frighteningly prophetic. But after what Quinn had shown her today, she wondered if they'd been goodbye.

But it didn't matter now. What mattered was that her past had crashed in on her, on them.

And she hadn't realized just how much she treasured this life she had now, until the threat of losing it had loomed up before her.

Chapter 11

"You think he's been over here?" Drew felt an overpowering urge to get up, to walk, to pace as Cutter had been doing. After recounting the phone call—with admirable accuracy, Drew thought—Alyssa was clearly shaken, and he didn't want to leave her side until she was steadier.

"No way to know," Quinn answered. "We weren't expecting a call, or we might have been ready for it and better able to pin him down."

"I should have been expecting it," Drew said flatly. "Especially after Lyss said she felt like she was being watched."

He heard her gasp, realized she hadn't connected the feeling she'd had with this yet.

"You think it was him?" she asked, her eyes wide.

"We don't know, but it's not an unreasonable assumption." Quinn's voice was brisk, unrattled, and seemed to help Alyssa calm a little.

"Even Seattle is too close," Alyssa said. "But if he's been over here? Watching me, following me?" She shuddered, stopping it with an effort Drew could see. He supposed it could be worse. She could have been glad to hear from Doug's old friend. That would have been the icing on his cake.

Hayley had been busy on the laptop, but now she stood up.

"Everybody has his picture," she said.

"Good. Teague's on the other side with Laney today, he can keep an eye out."

"North of Seattle's a pretty big cornfield," Drew said.

Quinn nodded. "I don't expect Teague to find him. But he can come back that way, and you never know."

"Shall I call Brett?" Hayley asked.

"Brett?" Drew asked.

"Detective Dunbar." Quinn nodded. "Yes, since he's already partly read in. See if we can send him a picture. Maybe he can get the ferry people to keep an eye open. One of the advantages of living someplace that's a little hard to get to."

"Will he do that?" Drew asked. "I mean, technically Oliver hasn't done anything yet, except show up in the vicinity and make a threatening phone call."

"True enough. And 'You'll be sorry' is a pretty vague threat. But Brett's a different sort of cop. The fact that Oliver has shown up here at all will make him take notice."

"But what if he doesn't look like that mug shot anymore?" Alyssa asked.

Good, Drew thought. She was thinking now.

"I had Ty do a modified one, too, without the buzzed hair," Hayley answered. "And he may have jail tattoos now." Is there anything else we could add to the description?"

"Only if you can figure out how to make it slimy. He was very creepy."

"He still is," Drew said, getting up at last now that she seemed steadier. "He threatened you, Lyss."

"I think he was just trying to scare me into getting that money for him. He wouldn't really hurt me."

Drew opened his mouth to tell her she was being naive, but Quinn beat him to it in a much more productive way.

"Don't count on that," he said. "He was arrested for attempted murder of his girlfriend when he was nineteen. They couldn't prove it, and she was uncooperative, so he skated."

At Quinn's words Drew spun around to look at Alyssa. Her eyes were wide, her lips parted. She hadn't known that, he could see that clearly.

"Now do you get it? This isn't one of Doug's silly capers, this is serious. Deadly serious."

She leapt to her feet. "Of course, I do. My son's father is dead because of this man. There's nothing silly about that."

And just like that they were at loggerheads again.

On the edge of his vision Drew saw Hayley and Quinn exchange a look. No doubt regretting they'd gotten involved in this. This was a far cry from simply digging up past history. Drew guessed he should be thankful they'd involved their detective friend, since obviously this was now out of their bailiwick.

"Let's go, Lyss. We need to go get Luke. Then you're going someplace safe."

She blinked. "What?"

"You and Luke. We'll get you someplace safe, then I'll deal with Oliver."

"Deal with him? Deal with him how? Weren't you just telling me how dangerous he is?"

"That's why I want you and Luke someplace safe."

"You want to pull him out of school and for us to go hide somewhere? He'll be terrified! He's had enough of that in his life."

"Lyss—"

"He'll be fine at school, and at home it's safe enough, with the alarm system."

"I'm not taking any chances."

"Except with yourself?"

For a moment he just stared at her. A few minutes ago she was so angry at him she was shouting, now she was worried about him taking chances? Just when he thought he had her figured out, she threw him another curve.

"What are you going to do?" she asked.

"Pay him off, if that's what I have to do."

She drew back slightly, her brows raised. "You? Pay off an…extortionist? Doesn't that go against the Boy Scout code?"

He didn't even react to the dig. "I'll do a lot more to keep my family safe."

"But ten thousand dollars—"

"That's really rather…small, for an extortion," Quinn said neutrally. "I wonder why."

"Maybe he's got himself convinced he's really owed it," Hayley said. "That it's really his money."

"That sounds like him," Alyssa said, and Drew cringed inwardly at the bitter, broken tone that had crept into her voice. He could only imagine how she must feel, the past she thought she'd fought her way out of hovering again. "He would feel that way, as if robbing that store was as much work as running it." She glanced at Drew. "Ten thousand might not be much for an extortion, but it's still a lot—"

Drew cut her off with a wave. "I'll manage."

He turned to Hayley and Quinn. He wondered how often they'd listened to people argue about their personal problems in front of them. He felt a little embarrassed that they were doing it so often. But that was over now.

"Thank you for your help," he said.

"You say that like we're done," Quinn said.

Drew looked at the other man. "Aren't you? This is a lot more than just digging into the past now."

"We don't quit until you tell us to," Quinn said.

"But Oliver could be dangerous."

Hayley laughed, startling him. "Maybe you need to dig into the Foxworth past a little," she said. "They've handled much bigger, and more dangerous fish than Baird Oliver."

Drew glanced at Alyssa. She looked as surprised as he felt. "What exactly does Foxworth do?" she asked.

"A little bit of this, little bit of that," Quinn said.

"Do you remember the headlines a few years ago," Hayley asked, "about the American woman and her daughter who got kidnapped and held by a drug lord down in Mexico?"

Alyssa shook her head, which didn't surprise Drew. At that time, she'd been struggling to survive, already sick and afraid. But he remembered.

"They were rescued, right? Snuck out right under the cartel's noses? The husband hired some private security team to—"

He stopped abruptly. Stared at Hayley, then Quinn.

"You? Foxworth did that?"

Quinn gave a half shrug, as if it had been nothing more than a day's work. And Drew found himself believing it. There was more, much more to Foxworth—both man and organization—than he'd understood.

"You realize," Quinn said in that same calm, unruffled tone, "that if you pay Oliver off, there's no guarantee he'll go away."

"Or not come back for more," Hayley added.

He knew in his gut they were right. And for the first time in his adult life, he couldn't decide what to do. He would do anything to protect Alyssa and Luke, but knowing what to do was something else. He knew how to design and build a house from the dirt up, he could handle a computer or a bulldozer, he could work twelve hours a day six days a week and still play with Luke on the seventh day, he could even throw a football pretty damned well, but this, this was out of his league. And he knew it.

"We can help you keep them safe," Quinn said quietly.

Drew's gaze shot to the other man's face. His eyes were clear, an icy sort of blue that spoke of cool determination. Drew was used to assessing people, it was how he'd acquired the solid, steady work crews he had today. But this was about more than who would show up for work on time, who was a skilled carpenter, stoneworker or painter. Much, much more.

"That's my job."

"Yes," Quinn agreed easily. "I would feel the same way. But let us help."

"How?"

Cutter barked, sudden, sharp and startling them all.

"Well, there's one quarter heard from," Quinn said.

Cutter walked over and sat in front of Alyssa. He looked back at Hayley, his gaze intent in that way Drew had noticed before.

"I think he's volunteering," Hayley said.

Drew blinked. "What?"

"Consider him an addition to your alarm system," she said. "He's very good at it."

"And there's a lot to be said for an alarm system that can bite," Quinn added.

"Wait. You're giving us your dog?"

"Loaning," Hayley said. "And frankly, when he does that—" she gestured at the animal "—we're not really involved in the decision. He's already made it."

Alyssa was staring at the dog. Then, slowly she reached out to stroke his head, then scratch the spot the others had scratched, just below his right ear. Cutter leaned against her.

"Luke would love it," she said. There was less stress in her voice, and that touch of panic was gone. What was it about that dog?

"And he will guard Luke with his life," Quinn said.

Drew grimaced at the thought that might even be necessary. "He really barely knows Luke."

"But he picked Luke," Hayley said.

"You're doing this because a dog wanted to play with a kid in a park?"

"Welcome to our world," Quinn said with a grin. "We'll send you some human help, too. Liam will be by later, and starting tomorrow he and Teague can trade off standing watch. Then when Rafe gets back from D.C. we'll add him in."

They must have looked startled, Drew thought. And frankly, he was. The dog was one thing, but guards?

"It'll only be until we find Oliver," Hayley said. "And that won't be long."

"You sound awfully confident."

"I am," she said simply. "Because I know Foxworth."

Drew gave a doubtful shake of his head. "I'm still not sure Lyss and Luke shouldn't go somewhere else, where he can't find them."

"That's an option," Quinn said. "We have a couple of safe houses available."

His perception of Foxworth shifted yet again. A couple of safe houses? Just how big was this operation?

"I don't want to scare Luke," Alyssa insisted. "And I don't want him to miss school. He's getting so good at reading, I don't want that to stop."

"I want him—and you—safe," Drew countered.

"Then keep us safe. Let them help."

Drew turned back to Quinn. "Just who are you guys?"

"The best at what we do."

"Not that I track stuff like this, but I've never heard of you before now."

"Good," Quinn said. "We work on referral only. Or lately," he added with a wry quirk of his mouth, "upon Cutter's insistence."

"I looked at your website. It's kind of vague."

"Intentionally," Quinn said. "You want references?"

Drew wondered if that was a gibe, but after a moment studying Quinn's steady gaze, decided not.

"You have them?" he asked.

"From around the country," Hayley said proudly. "In fact…" She looked thoughtful as she pulled the laptop back toward her, quickly typing something into the location bar of the browser already open. "I thought I saw…"

Drew's brows furrowed as the Kiley Construction website came up. She clicked through to the video he'd had done a couple of years ago on the arts center project. The finished building, with its soaring front facade and glass-fronted lobby that looked out over an inlet had become a landmark in the county, and it was their best advertising. As he often did, he took video of the entire process, and it had turned out so well he'd handed that off to a local company that did high-quality promotional videos, and they'd turned out an impressive bit of marketing.

"I thought so," Hayley said as the credits rolled by at the end of the piece. "Sound Digital Video."

Drew had no idea what that had to do with anything, but nodded. "Yeah. Sergei and Dane, the guys behind SDV, are great. And they're local. I try and stay local whenever I can."

"Dane Burdette is one of those references you wanted."

Drew blinked. "What?"

"In fact, it was his now wife's brother we went looking for," Quinn said. "Same sort of situation. Differing views, as it were."

"How'd that one turn out?" Drew asked drily.

"Why don't you call and ask him? That's how we work."

"You let other people blow your horn?"

"Pretty much," Quinn said with a shrug.

"Word of mouth," Drew said.

"The best advertising. Not that we need it." Quinn grimaced in turn. "There is, sadly, no shortage of people getting screwed over in the world."

Drew made the call. All he had to do was mention Foxworth, and Dane was on the phone instantly. His praise was effusive and clearly heartfelt. And he told Drew of all the others he'd talked to before he'd agreed to let Foxworth get involved. Told how they'd helped everyone from a man up against a crooked zoning official to a grieving family dealing with a suicide, to a stolen locket that was the only memento a girl had from her deceased mother. And Foxworth had put their full force into righting the battered worlds of many varied people.

When the man got to the part about Foxworth having trackers and a sniper Drew turned to stare at Quinn. When Dane told him about Cutter being installed in their motel room as a living burglar alarm, his gaze shifted to the dog, and he found himself shaking his head.

But most of all, they had kept Kayla safe, Dane told him.

And that, Drew thought, was the bottom line.

"They were really Cutter's first case," Hayley said when he hung up, smiling at what was probably a boggled expression on his face. "Well, after Quinn and I, anyway."

"How'd he find them?" Alyssa asked.

"At the post office," Hayley said. "It's a long story."

"Like you being kidnapped?"

Hayley grinned. "That story's ongoing."

"Not for long," Quinn said rather fervently.

Hayley lifted a brow at him. "Counting down the remaining days of your bachelorhood?"

"Counting down the days till my real life starts," Quinn said.

The air between them was suddenly charged, electric. Drew wondered what it must be like to have that kind of connection.

He stifled the urge to look at Alyssa. It was pointless. They would never have what Quinn and Hayley had.

Doug had seen to that.

Chapter 12

"Really? He's going to stay with us?"

"Just for a while," Alyssa reminded her son, who was hugging Cutter with obvious delight. They sat in one of her favorite spots, the front porch swing Drew had built for her by hand. She'd never asked for it, but he'd noticed how often she sat out there, watching Luke play, and without a word he'd set about making it more pleasant. It's something Doug would never have thought of, and even if he had he could never have done it. He'd had to ask her for help putting together a cardboard box once.

"You'll have to help take care of him," Drew said to the boy. "Are you big enough to do that?"

Luke drew himself up to his full three foot eleven and stuck out his chest. "I'm big now, Dad. I can do it."

"I'll bet you can," Drew said, tousling the boy's hair with a gentle hand.

Alyssa turned slightly, not wanting either of them to see her eyes glistening with tears. Luke was getting so big.

She needed to measure him again, he was probably even taller than three-eleven now. And Drew was so good with him. There was just something about that big, strong man being so gentle with a little boy that tugged at something deep and primal in her. It really was boiling things down to their essence. And for all their disputes, she had never once doubted Drew was a good man. He was the best thing that could have happened for Luke, and she'd long ago decided she'd gotten the best of the deal.

"Are you all right?"

Alyssa sighed. Drew put an arm around her, and she leaned into his steady warmth as Luke and the dog began their unique game of tag once more. She didn't know how long they'd been sitting there when it occurred to her that it was a weekday, and for Drew a workday. Not that he didn't work more than his share of weekends, too, during the high season. Which this was not, but still, she knew there was paperwork to do, designs to work on, permit forms to handle, it never seemed to end for him. He'd taken the rest of the day off after Luke had run away, but except for the visits to Foxworth, he'd been back to working normal—for him—hours since.

Until now. After Baird had called.

"You're not going back to work?" she asked.

He shook his head. "No."

"Drew—"

He held up a hand. "Brilliant though that dog may be, I'm not putting my family's safety entirely in his…paws."

She smiled in spite of herself. "But won't you get behind?"

"I can do a lot of the paperwork from here. Kevin is taking over at the Harkness site."

"And you're okay with that?"

While she wouldn't call Drew a control freak, he did like to stay on top of everything they did. It was his name on the company, he always said, and he was responsible.

And she could hardly complain about that, or the long hours it required, when in essence the same applied to her and Luke. His name was on them, therefore he was responsible.

"Kevin is due to step up. I think he's ready. Now we'll find out."

"It's a good thing you did, taking him on like that. A lot of people wouldn't."

Drew shrugged. "I knew he was a good kid. He just got way off track there for a while, after his father died."

Alyssa opened her mouth to say that she wished he'd given his own brother that much consideration. But she didn't. He would just say Kevin had an excuse, Doug had none. And no amount of her telling him he'd changed, that he'd grown up in the years after they'd run off would get through to him. He had those last images of Doug etched so deeply into his memory they were probably unassailable.

Just as she had the memories of those videos now, videos of the man she'd adored seeming like someone completely different.

Or had it been when he was with her that he was different? Which one had been the real Doug, and which the act?

She didn't know. She knew what she wanted to believe. And that alone scared her. She wasn't a teenager anymore, and that she wanted to believe so badly made her wonder just how well she'd left that foolishness behind.

"At least he'll be so tired he'll sleep like a rock tonight," Drew said, watching as Luke shrieked delightedly as Cutter wrestled with him, then pulled back to run around him in swift circles, and barked happily.

Alyssa smiled. She'd been smiling quite a while now, taking as much delight in seeing her son so happy as Luke himself was in the play with his new-found best friend.

"That alone might be reason enough for a dog," Alyssa said.

Drew chuckled. It wasn't quite a real laugh, but it was as close as he'd come for a while, so she'd take it. "Maybe we should talk to… What was her name? The lady from the groomer's?"

"Laney, I think Hayley said. Yes, maybe we should. She might know a good dog from the shelter, one who would be good with Luke. He—"

She broke off midsentence. Cutter, one instant crouched down in the front-down, tail-up universal dog play signal, in the next was upright and rigid, a fierce, terrifying snarl ripping from his throat. Alyssa cried out, for a split second fearing the dog had turned on Luke, but it was clear the animal's attention was elsewhere. He was staring toward the trees, where Luke's path to the park was.

Drew had leapt up instantly, vaulting over the porch railing and hitting the ground running. In that moment, as if he'd only been waiting to be sure the human protector had realized the danger, Cutter took off. Head down, tail out, barking in fierce warning, he headed toward those trees at a dead run.

"Get Luke inside!" Drew yelled, and headed after the dog. Alyssa ran to the boy, who seemed bewildered.

"What happened, Mom? Why did Cutter get mad?"

"I think he smelled something that could be dangerous," she said.

Luke's eyes widened. "You mean like a bear or something?"

"Or something," she said grimly.

"Dad will scare it away," Luke said confidently.

She picked him up and started backing toward the house, her gaze fastened on where her husband and the dog had vanished into the trees. She felt like she should do something, anything. Call the police? Call Foxworth?

Idiot, she told herself. Get Luke inside and lock the door. Doors. Windows. Everything.

Luke protested as she headed up the porch steps, having to tug him every step of the way.

"No, we need to help!" the boy said, squirming mightily in his effort to escape. He was getting so big it was all she could do to hold on to him.

"Luke—"

"Mom, we have to go, Cutter and Dad might need our help!"

She heard a car in the distance, the bark of tires on asphalt as somebody took a turn too fast.

"Trust them," she told Luke as she pulled him inside.

They waited, her anxiously, Luke rebelliously. He clambered up on the chair that sat by the front window and looked out in the direction his father and new companion had gone. Alyssa kept her gaze on her son, half-afraid he'd bolt out the door if she turned her back. If it was just her she would go after Drew, but it wasn't, she had Luke and it was her job to keep him safe.

Minutes ticked by, and she was on the verge of calling for help when the pair emerged from the same spot they'd gone in.

"There they are!" Luke yelled and ran for the door. Alyssa let him go, and followed.

Cutter was trotting beside Drew, looking up at him intently. Drew reached down and rubbed that spot that seemed to be the dog's favorite. Her gaze sharpened as she realized he was holding his other arm, the left, rather oddly. And the shirtsleeve was rolled up, on that side only. Was he hurt?

Luke burst through the door, running toward Drew and the dog. Cutter spotted him and erupted into an equally fast run. They collided and went down, Luke on top of the dog, who seemed to have twisted so the boy would fall on him and not the rocky ground. The dog inspected the boy as if to be certain he was all right, then proceeded to make him giggle by licking every bit of skin he could reach. And for that, she owed that dog a hug herself. But first…

"Was it…him?" she asked as Drew arrived on the scene of the happy reunion.

"I don't know. Only person I saw was over by the park, not even near the house. I didn't get a good look at him." He glanced at Cutter. "That guy's got one heck of a nose. Or set of ears. That's nearly a mile away."

"What happened?"

"He went over the fence at the park."

"Over the fence? That's…suspicious, isn't it?"

"The way he ran, yes. Had a car on the other side, so I couldn't catch him before he was in it and gone. It may not have been Oliver, but he—" he nodded at Cutter "—didn't like him, that's for sure."

"Did he— Drew, you're bleeding!"

He looked at the arm he'd been holding oddly. "Was. It's stopped now."

Luke had heard her exclamation and came running over. The thought of Drew hurt surpassed even Cutter, she was glad to see.

"What happened, Dad?"

"Got caught on the top of the chain-link fence."

"Do you need to go to the E.R.? Stitches?" she asked.

"No," he said quickly. "It's fine. In fact, it came in handy."

She blinked. "What?"

He held the arm so she could see. And there, on the inside above the wrist, were three numbers and a letter.

Written in blood.

She stared at him. "License plate?"

He nodded. "What I could see of it."

"Dad, that is so cool!" Luke said with little boy fascination.

She supposed she should be thankful for the childlike resiliency. Now that his furry friend was back, and his father was relatively okay—and had assumed major cool status by writing in his own blood—Luke was merely excited, not scared.

"Let's go inside, clean that up," she said. "Luke, would you go in and get the first aid kit from the bathroom?"

"Sure. Come on, Cutter!"

"I want to call Foxworth," he said as the boy raced inside. "It's probably nothing, but I don't like it anyway."

She nodded. "They should know, I guess."

"And I want to thank them for the loan of Mr. Good Ears," he said.

"It is reassuring," she said with a laugh, relief finally pushing back all the horrible thoughts that had been racing through her mind in the last few minutes. She opened the door and held it for him. Ignoring the fact that he was the one bleeding, he gestured her inside first. Ever the gentleman, she thought, then was distracted by the unfamiliar but welcome sound of a dog's toenails on the wood floor.

"He certainly went from playmate to protector in a fraction of a second, didn't he?"

"He did. And I don't want to think about how close that guy could have gotten if Cutter hadn't been here to hear him. Or smell him. Whatever he did."

"What about calling the police?" she asked.

"That, too. Although since I can't say it was him, or even give a good description, and he wasn't even close to our property, I'm not sure what they could or would do."

He walked over to the kitchen island, where they kept a notepad and pen. He transferred the information from his arm to the pad just as Luke and Cutter arrived with the white plastic box with the red cross on the lid.

"You call, I'll clean," Alyssa said. "And Luke, you be my assistant and hold that steady for me, okay?"

The boy straightened proudly. "I can do it."

And in the midst of it all, knowing someone, even if it hadn't been Baird, was snooping around, knowing he'd been within even a mile of Luke, knowing Drew had been hurt, however minor, in chasing after him, somehow amid all that chaos Alyssa felt an odd sense of warmth and comfort as the three of them huddled together. A sense of family, sticking together no matter what. That she could even feel like that in the midst of all this amazed her.

Drew had given her that.

And of all the many things he had done for them, that was the most important. And yet he had done it without thought, without hesitation. And continued to do it, every day.

Yes, there was a lot to be said for being the rock of the family.

Chapter 13

"Brett!"

Hayley's smile and pleased greeting brought a matching smile to the face of the tall, rangy man she'd opened the door for.

"Hayley," he acknowledged.

"Well, Detective Dunbar," Quinn said as he finished the phone call he'd been on and walked over to shake hands, "didn't expect to see you in person."

"I was in the neighborhood, literally," Dunbar said. "Just wrapping up a burglary case. I heard your ex-con may have shown up near your client's house?"

They'd gotten used to the fact that very little happened that Dunbar didn't know about. Once it was on his radar, he had an amazing ability to track it all. Hayley had a feeling it was because there was nothing else in his life. They didn't know that much about him, personally. But they knew what mattered; he was dedicated, honest and caring, and had left the big city. More than once Quinn had said

Brett Dunbar was the kind of man Foxworth wanted, and that he'd hire him in an instant if he ever left law enforcement. But being a cop was in Dunbar's blood, and Quinn didn't think he'd ever leave it behind.

Which was, in the end, a benefit to Foxworth anyway. He liked what they did, and had helped them many times since they'd first encountered him last year.

"Not too close, thankfully, but in the vicinity," Quinn answered. "Drew took off after him, got a partial plate off the car. Looks like a rental car, probably from Sea-Tac."

"That's what I heard."

Quinn knew it was Dunbar who had cleared them for routine checks on such public records, which had sped things up considerably on their end. Not that Tyler Hewitt, their tech genius, or even Liam couldn't find the information in their own way, but Quinn preferred to go through the front door when it came to the police.

"We can't prove it was him, Drew didn't get a good enough look, but it only makes sense. First the call, then he shows up at the park with a kid's play area closest to the one location he knows, Drew's office."

Dunbar nodded in agreement. "Typical predator behavior. I'd keep an eye on all the places kids congregate."

Quinn nodded in turn. "Luke's the most vulnerable target in all this."

"I talked to my buddy down in L.A.," Dunbar said. "He talked to the guy who popped Oliver for the two-eleven. And the traffic investigator who worked the crash that killed Kiley."

Quinn lifted a brow. "Didn't expect that so quickly. Thank you."

Dunbar shrugged. "Always like to know what there is to know on a non-rehabbed felon on my turf. Especially one trying out extortion."

"Did they have anything?"

"Oliver's tough. Not smart, but at least shrewd. He

turned down the chance at parole, served his entire sentence by choice. Didn't want to be on a leash when he got out."

Hayley shook her head. "That's quite a price to pay."

"Tells you a lot about him," Dunbar said. "He's a big-picture kind of guy."

"And I get the impression Doug Kiley was the opposite," Quinn said.

"Don't know," Dunbar said. "He was already dead, so all they had to go on was what Oliver said. At first he tried to pin it all on him, but his ego got the better of him and he couldn't quite stick to the role of follower. And he was pissed, because the car Kiley crashed was his."

Dunbar reached into his jacket pocket and pulled out a folded piece of paper. "Buddy sent me this. Given the circs of your case, thought you might want it."

Quinn took the page and unfolded it. There was a sticky note at the top in Dunbar's writing. Quinn scanned it all and quickly realized what it was. "Thanks, Brett. This may help."

"Good. I'd better get back and close out this case. Got three more on my desk."

"You work too hard," Hayley said.

"Taxpayers deserve their money's worth."

"Would that everyone felt that way," Quinn said with a grin.

"You're coming to the wedding, right?" Hayley asked.

"I don't do weddings," Dunbar said.

Quinn winced, hoping Hayley's feelings hadn't been hurt by the flat response. She had told him once that their friend was hurting way down deep over someone, but he'd thought she was just being a romantic. But maybe she was right. As she so very often was.

"But for you two," Dunbar went on, now with a smile, "I'll make an exception."

Hayley hugged the man, and Quinn wished he'd had a camera at the ready to capture the startled look on his face.

"I'm holding you to that," Hayley said.

"Don't cross her," Quinn said to the clearly bemused detective.

"Wouldn't dream of it."

"Someday," Hayley said after he'd gone, "he's going to find someone who can lift that cloud he lives under."

"Figure that's the answer to everything, do you?" Quinn teased.

"It worked for me," she said simply.

His heart took that little leap it always did when she said things like that. She told him so often, in words and a million other little ways, how much she loved him, but it never, ever lost its impact.

"What was it he gave you?"

Quinn had to shake himself out of thoughts of luring her back to the small bedroom in the back corner, where he'd once spent his nights. "It's a property inventory. Of the things Doug had on him and in the car when he crashed."

He peeled off the sticky and handed it to her, curious to see what might jump out at her on the list.

"Twenty-three dollars," she murmured as she read. "Not much for a guy who just knocked off a convenience store for nearly fifteen thousand." Then, a moment later, "No photos in the wallet. Not even of Alyssa."

"And phony ID."

"Under a phony name," she said, still reading. "I wonder if Alyssa even knew he was using another name."

"Don't know. Brett's note here says they checked that name for addresses, bank accounts and any potential hiding places for the cash, but came up dry."

Hayley nodded, but kept reading. He saw the moment when she stopped, when her brow furrowed and her gaze narrowed. She looked up at him.

"A receipt from a bus company?"

Quinn smiled. He'd known she'd catch it. "Yes."

"Tickets?"

"Doesn't say, but what else would you buy from a bus company?"

"Some of them carry packages, don't they? He could even have sent the money somewhere that way."

Quinn's smile widened. "Have I ever told you how brilliant you are?"

She smiled back. "I believe you have, on a fairly regular basis."

"Good."

She gestured at the note. "We have to find out."

"We know he was getting ready to run, one way or another, judging by this. It was almost seven years ago, though, so I don't know if they'll be able to track where he was going."

"We have to find out what that receipt is for. For the Kileys, it could all hinge on that."

He'd been focused on the logistics, the where and when, and had for a moment missed the human significance. But Hayley hadn't.

"Yes," he said slowly. "It could."

"Eagle feather."

Luke laughed. "You got it right!" he exclaimed as he opened the door for Liam Burnett.

The man stepped into the kitchen and smiled at Alyssa as if to let her know all was well outside the house. Then he grinned at Luke.

"I'm good with passwords, but you should still look through the peephole. Make sure it's me." They'd tried to make it a game for Luke, and thus far it seemed to have worked. He didn't seem worried, just having fun.

"But the peephole's too tall," he explained to Liam. "And you sounded like you."

"Use the chair. And are you saying I talk funny?" The mock outrage was so over the top even Alyssa smiled.

Alyssa watched as the boy and the man bantered. Liam

Burnett had arrived as promised, and already he and Luke had settled into a sibling-style relationship. At times, the two decades between them seemed not to matter at all. Luke had no trouble accepting what they'd told him, that Liam was a friend who'd be visiting for a while. Of course, it probably helped that Liam looked much younger. He had to be almost her age, but he looked not much older than a teenager.

And with Luke, he acted much younger. Quinn had assured her he and the boy would get along, and he'd been right. Quinn seemed to be right about most things. And if he ever veered wrong, he had Hayley to straighten him out. He freely admitted it, saying it in a tone of love and admiration that made Alyssa more than a little envious.

"Dinner's almost ready. Liam, you will join us, won't you? Luke, you need to go wash up."

Luke's expression changed, but before he could make his usual protest, Liam stepped in. "Smells great! I'll wash up for a chance at that. Bet I can beat you," he added to Luke.

That quickly the boy shifted, and raced off to the bathroom without another word.

"Well, that was easy," Alyssa muttered.

"Little competition always spices things up with us guys," Liam said with a grin that fit well with the faint Texas drawl. And she noticed he did as promised, and headed for the kitchen sink to wash his hands.

She thought again of the moment when Liam had faced her so openly, admitting that he had a police record. That he'd been on a very wrong path when, a few years later, Quinn had found him and given him a chance to get straight.

He'd asked if she was comfortable trusting him with Luke, in view of all that.

"I've got no high ground to stand on when it comes to teenage mistakes," she'd told him, appreciating his honesty and trying to answer it in kind. "So, I'm all about second chances."

That had sealed the deal, and she hadn't had a second thought about it.

Drew, who had been outside preparing the steaks for the grill, came in then, and looked at Liam. "You find anything?" he asked.

Liam shook his head. "All clear. I went down to the park. Found the sign where the guy was yesterday, more where you chased him, but nothing more recent. And it doesn't look like he was headed this way at all. Doubt he knows you live this close. I think he was just scoping out the park because it's obviously where kids hang out."

Alyssa's stomach knotted at the thought of Baird even thinking about kids at all. She tried not to let it show as she handed him a towel to dry his hands.

"Wrist okay?" Liam asked with a nod at Drew's left arm.

Drew glanced at the neat bandage Alyssa had applied. "It's good."

Liam nodded.

"How could you tell the difference?" Alyssa asked. "Where Drew was chasing him, I mean?"

Liam shrugged. "Clear as can be, when you know what to look for. The guy was careful walking around the park, so there was only a footprint or two, and a couple of ferns he stepped on still buried in mud. Going out, he was running, broke a lot of branches in that direction, and the footprints were deeper."

"Some of that was me," Drew said.

"Yes," Liam agreed. "But he had on city shoes, slick soles."

"I should have caught him, then," Drew said drily.

"He was too close to the fence, so he got over. Otherwise Cutter would have caught him."

A soft whuffing sound came from the corner of the

kitchen, where Cutter was curled on the blanket Alyssa had put down for him.

"Yeah, you," Liam said with a grin. "You may be a better tracker than I—slightly—but only because you're lower to the ground and have that nose. You don't read signs worth a darn."

The whuff came again, and this time it sounded oddly dismissive. Liam laughed.

Luke skidded into the kitchen on Liam's last words. "You're a tracker?"

"I am. I could track an armadillo across the entire state of Texas."

"An arma-what?"

"Armadillo," Liam said. "They're sort of the armored tank of the animal world."

Luke's eyes widened. He looked at Drew for verification. The simple gesture set up an odd sort of ache inside her. Luke trusted Drew implicitly, without question. Which was proof she had made the right choice.

For Luke, anyway.

"Sounds about right," Drew said. "They have a shell that's really hard, and in plates, like old suits of armor that knights wore."

"Knights? Like the King Arthur story Mom read me?"

"Just like."

"I've never seen one," Luke said.

"And you won't, up here," Liam said. "They get cold too easy, so they stay where it's warm for the most part."

This inspired Luke to ask a string of questions that had Liam working to keep up. Drew smiled at the exchange as he gathered up the meat to head out to the grill. One of the first things he'd done at this house was to build a cover over a section of the deck; if you liked to barbecue, and lived in the Northwest, it was almost a necessity.

"You don't really have to feed me," Liam said to Alyssa. "I could—"

Alyssa waved him off with a smile. "I think Luke would be upset if you didn't eat with us."

"I would," the boy chimed in.

"And the more he trusts you the better, at the moment," Alyssa said.

"Thank you," Liam said. "I just wanted you to know it wasn't expected."

"So, exactly how," Drew asked later, when they were well into the meal, each steak done as each person liked them, a knack Drew had that Alyssa hadn't ever quite mastered, "did a Texas boy end up working for Foxworth?"

"Simple. I tried to hack them."

Both Alyssa and Drew set down their forks at that one. "You what?"

"On a dare. See, there was this buddy of mine, who didn't believe they were who they said they were. All that fighting for the little guy against impossible odds stuff was bull, he said."

Eating resumed. "How did he even know about them?" Alyssa asked. "I thought they went on referrals only."

"They do. Some relative of his got in trouble over some stupid law. He actually saved a kid's life, but he trespassed on government property to do it, and they arrested him. Foxworth stepped in, and made it go away. My buddy didn't believe that's what they did, and for free."

"And you set out to prove that?" Drew asked.

"No, he did. I set out to find out the truth." He glanced over at Luke, whose interest had faded a bit since they'd left the fascinating subject of armadillos, which Alyssa had promised him they would look up after dinner.

When he saw Luke seemed more interested in his dinner, Liam went on. "I had…a history of poking around where I shouldn't, computerwise. Got in trouble a couple of times. I wasn't on a good path, as my momma used to say."

"How much trouble?" Drew asked, not in an accusatory way, but more curious.

"Enough. Detective Dunbar is a lot nicer."

That easily, he'd admitted to Drew, who hadn't heard his confession to her, that he'd been in trouble with the police, but in a way that Luke wouldn't figure out. Alyssa appreciated that, although she wasn't sure it might not be a good thing for Luke to know being in trouble once didn't mean you had to stay there.

"Then I met Quinn," Liam said. "Well, he sent Rafe after me first, to bring me in to talk, and believe me, that was enough to scare me straighter than any arrow."

"Rafe?"

"Rafer Crawford. You haven't met him. He's back in D.C. on a private thing for Quinn." Liam took a sip of water before adding casually, "He's our sniper."

The forks went down again. Drew and Alyssa stared at him.

"What's a sniper?" Luke asked.

"Let's work on the armadillo, first," Alyssa said, recovering quickly.

Her distraction succeeded.

"So you met Quinn," Drew said, skipping over the comment that had made his brows shoot upwards.

"He gave me a chance, a bigger chance than I ever expected. First just at the tech end, but I wanted more. Once I'd proved myself, he saw that I got trained, and put me on his own team."

"So you're not ex-military."

"Nope. A lot of Foxworth personnel are, but not all. But they trained us, so we're good. We—"

He stopped as his phone chimed. He excused himself and went out to the deck to answer.

"Did you know his mom and dad have a bunch of dogs?" Luke asked. "Not like Cutter, he said, there's only one of him, but they have a bunch of hunting dogs. I'd like to go to Texas and see them."

"I think you just want to see the armadillos," Drew teased.

"Them, too!" Luke exclaimed just as Liam came back into the room.

"Quinn," he said, gesturing with the phone. "He and Hayley want to see you. Apparently, they've figured out the phone call."

Alyssa looked at Drew, then at Luke, uncertain. She trusted Liam, because she trusted Hayley and Quinn and they trusted him, but also because he was so good with Luke. But her common sense told her not everyone who was good with kids had good intentions.

"Can't they come here?" Alyssa asked.

"They could," Liam said, "but if our guy's anywhere around and sees them, he might get suspicious. Think you called the—" He stopped, glancing at Luke.

The cops, Alyssa realized he'd been about to say. "But you're here."

Liam laughed. "Quinn's the one who looks like a cop. Or Teague. Rafe looks like he just came off a battlefield. Me, I'm just the kid next door."

"But—"

"I'll keep him safe, Alyssa," Liam said, and as he met and held her gaze, there was suddenly none of the kid about him. "I'm trained and prepared to do whatever it takes."

She believed him. And a glance at Drew told her he did, too.

"Take Cutter with you," Liam said.

"Aww," Luke said.

"I think Hayley misses him and would like a visit," Liam explained to him. "You get that, right?"

"Okay," Luke said reluctantly.

"C'mon, bud. We'll find something to do."

"Can we look up armadillos?" Luke asked.

"We sure can, buddy. There are different kinds, you know. And the giant armadillo is bigger than you are."

Luke's eyes widened anew, and he leapt to his feet. "Can we go now?"

"No," Liam said. "We're going to clean up the kitchen first, like my momma taught me."

Luke groaned. Alyssa laughed. "Okay, I'm sold. He can stay."

But as she and Drew went to the garage and got into his truck, letting Cutter hop into the small backseat, she wondered just what Foxworth had discovered.

And if Baird was even closer—and more dangerous—than she feared.

Chapter 14

"Thanks for coming," Hayley said as they sat around the fireplace once more. Cutter, after his effusive greeting to her, had plopped happily at her feet. Alyssa marveled anew at the dog, who was clearly devoted to her, yet had insisted, in his clever way, on being with them. "I know it's hard to leave Luke just now, but Liam will take very good care of him."

"They get along very well," Alyssa said.

"Sometimes Liam's just a big kid himself," Hayley said. "But he's very good, and that innocent face is a good disguise."

"I get the feeling he's a lot tougher than he looks," Drew said.

"He is," Quinn said as he sat down in the chair opposite Hayley, "as tough as he needs to be."

"It's not that I don't trust him," Alyssa said, "it's just that I've never left Luke with anyone else." She grimaced. "There *is* no one else."

"I'm sorry about the rift between you and your parents," Hayley said gently. "I wish they would have listened."

Alyssa pulled back slightly. "Listened?"

"To Drew. It's their loss, not even getting to know their grandson."

Alyssa looked at her husband. There was something about the set of his jaw that told her he hadn't expected this, would have been happier if it had never been said. And wasn't about to say anything more himself.

She shifted her gaze back to Hayley.

"Drew…talked to them?"

"You didn't know?"

"No. I didn't."

Hayley glanced at Drew. "You didn't tell her? That you tried several times to patch things up?"

"I didn't see the point. They said no. Why hurt her more?"

Alyssa turned now to face the man seated a couple of feet away from her on the couch. "You talked to them? About me?"

He sighed. He hadn't thought about the other things Foxworth might uncover, he'd been so focused on them proving the truth about Doug.

"I told them how you'd changed, you'd grown up, what a great mother you were." His jaw tightened. "I wanted you to have somebody besides me, just in case."

"In case what?"

"Things happen."

It took her a moment to realize what he meant. When she did, an icy chill swept through her, a chill no fireplace could beat back. Something happen to Drew? Impossible. The man truly was a rock.

"Besides, I wanted Luke to know his grandparents, the only ones he has left since my folks died."

She stared at him. She didn't know how much time passed, silently, as no one said anything else. She understood, she couldn't think of a thing to say herself. Finally she managed to speak, her voice tight.

"I could have told you it was pointless. My parents, especially my narrow-minded, cold-hearted mother, will never change."

"I realize that, now." He rubbed at the back of his neck, as if he were trying to ease a tension nothing could really ease. "I should have realized it sooner. They didn't listen when I talked to them back then, either."

Alyssa froze. He'd talked to her parents back then? "What do you mean?"

"When I told them that by trying to break you and Doug up, they were only driving you closer together. But they slammed the door in my face then, too."

She felt more than a little stunned. She'd had no idea. "I...I'm sorry," she said rather lamely.

He shrugged. "My folks weren't happy, either. They didn't like the fact that you were only sixteen and Doug was twenty. It was the only time I ever saw them actually criticize him, the only time they ever stood up to him." He sighed. "And they blamed themselves—and me—from the moment you two ran off."

A hollow ache rose to replace the chill inside her. It was a physical thing, an empty feeling that had become familiar now, she'd felt it so often in the last year or so. It was an odd sort of ache. Not pity, not even really sympathy. All she was sure of was that he was a good man, the best kind of man, something she'd never appreciated when she'd been young and foolish. Something she had in fact disdained, preferring Doug's carefree, laid-back attitude to his older brother's overblown sense of responsibility.

That sense of responsibility that had saved her life, and saved Luke from foster care, and given them a kind of security and comfort she never could have provided on her own, not then. And now she knew he'd tried to help even back then, even when he should have been wrapped up in his own life at what, twenty-three or -four?

And here he is, she thought, trapped, shackled to a woman he doesn't love, for the sake of a child he does.

Cutter moved then, got up from his bed by the fire and walked to the couch. He sat between them, looking from Alyssa to Drew with that intent expression she found both amusing and unsettling. Instinctively she reached out to stroke his dark head. To her surprise, as soon as her fingers touched the soft fur he twisted his head, and with exquisite care caught her wrist with his teeth. He tugged her hand, gently, until it was on the cushion between them. Then he went to Drew and nosed at the hand that was resting on his knee, nudging it in Alyssa's direction.

Cutter persistently pushed at Drew's hand. They realized at the same instant what the dog was doing. Alyssa's gaze shot to Drew's face, just as he glanced at her. He looked back at the dog, then, tentatively, reached out and touched her hand.

"Is that what you wanted?" he asked.

But the question wasn't necessary. The moment their fingers connected, the dog stopped. He sat once more, watching, and Alyssa wondered if they separated if the dog would begin again. She had a feeling he just might. Apparently so did Drew, because he curled his hand around hers and left it there. Because of the dog, she told herself. Certainly not because he felt the same little jolt she felt.

"Well, I see Cutter agrees with me," Hayley said.

Alyssa turned to look at the woman who already felt like a friend. "Agrees with you?"

"That you two need to take a long look at exactly how you feel."

Alyssa flushed. Instinctively she started to pull her hand free. But Drew held on. She flicked him a sideways glance.

"Dog," he said, as if it were explanation. And while perhaps it was, there was something else in his expression, some suddenly unbanked heat in his eyes, that made her wonder if there was more to the way he kept her hand in his warm clasp.

"In the meantime," Quinn said brusquely, "Two things. Taylor, our tech guru, figured out exactly how Oliver found your cell, Alyssa."

She felt a sudden tension in Drew's fingers as he shifted his focus to Quinn. "How?"

"He's not as smart as I feared," Quinn said. "Or as good at hacking. Tyler, on the other hand…"

"Are you saying Liam isn't the only former hacker you've hired?" Drew's tone was dry as his mouth quirked upward at one corner.

Quinn smiled. "It's a fact of life these days, you need people who know their way around. And having people who know what the bad guys can do and how is even better."

"Especially," Hayley added, "when they're good guys at heart, and love the challenge of taking down the bad ones."

Quinn smiled at her before going on. "Tyler found that a series of numbers issued by your provider were called in rapid succession over the course of seventy-nine minutes. All from the same burner phone. And all numbers in close proximity to your number, Drew."

Drew's fingers tightened around hers. "You mean he took my number, the one from the website, and just started…calling?"

"He clearly assumed that both your phones would be from the same provider," Hayley said, "and chanced that the numbers would be close."

"They were," Drew said grimly. "They're on the same plan. And only two numbers apart."

Quinn nodded. "Since the prefix was the same for all numbers issued in this area, he started with varying the last number in the sequence. Then the third. And so on, until eventually he got it right."

"Damn," Drew muttered, and sank back into the couch

cushions. And finally he let go of her, lifting his hands to rub at his eyes as if they'd suddenly become impossibly gritty.

"Like I said, not as smart as he thinks he is, but apparently he's dogged. Pardon the term, Cutter," Quinn added when the dog, who had settled near Drew and Alyssa's feet, lifted his head to look at him.

Alyssa suppressed a shiver. How could she have been so stupid? "So if I hadn't admitted who I was when he called, he would have just kept calling other numbers?"

"Likely," Quinn said.

A different kind of chill swept her. "Oh, God. This is all my fault."

Drew bolted upright. "Like hell. If anything it's my fault for putting my number out there like that."

"That's just good business," Quinn said. "And one of the reasons your reputation is what it is in this county."

"He's right," Alyssa said, trying not to shiver. "I'm the one who blithely said yes when he asked if I was Alyssa Kiley. I should have known."

"You couldn't have," Drew said.

She lost the fight and the shiver seized her. Drew moved then, pulling her against him. She let him, in fact went willingly, needing his steady strength, his warmth at this moment more than she needed her next breath. And refusing to admit even to herself that maybe, just maybe, she wanted more. That was a complication that might just lose her even this much comfort.

"But I should have realized, once I found he'd gotten out," Drew said.

"You didn't know him," Alyssa said. "I did."

"It's no one's fault," Hayley said quietly. "No one living a normal life expects it to explode like that with a simple phone call."

"And assigning blame doesn't solve the problem," Quinn said briskly. "Here's where we are. Oliver wants money. He knows roughly where you are now, and it's a small town. He knows you two are together. And he knows you have Luke."

Alyssa shivered anew, more fiercely. Drew tightened his arm around her.

"The sheriff's office knows about him now," Quinn continued, "and Dunbar at least is taking it seriously. But there are only so many of them, and as you said, he hasn't done anything yet but make an unspecifically threatening phone call. Borderline extortion at worst."

"What about the guy near the park, and the car I saw?" Drew asked.

"Rental, found abandoned near the ferry landing on the island. Out of gas."

Drew frowned. "Headed which way?"

"Away," Quinn said.

"So he may be gone?"

"Or want us to think he is."

"So what do we do now?" Alyssa asked, hating how her voice trembled but unable to help it. She knew Liam was with Luke now, but she couldn't beat back the feeling she should never have left him. Once she had him back within reach, she never would again.

"Option one is we take you all to a safe house, where you stay under guard until we or law enforcement find this guy. Downside to that is that Seattle's a big city, and easy to get lost in, and over here there are a ton of places to hide and not be seen by anyone, let alone the police. It could be a very long haul."

"And he may really be gone," Alyssa said, realizing even as she said it how naive that probably sounded. And she of all people, she who knew how slimy and downright evil Baird Oliver was, should know better.

"Maybe," Quinn said, and she was thankful there was no criticism or judgment in his tone. But she knew he didn't believe it.

Neither, apparently, did Drew. "If he was stubborn

enough to keep calling number after number like that, I doubt he's going to give up so easily. Even if that was him, and Cutter scared the heck out of him."

The dog woofed softly at the mention of his name, but didn't move from his appointed spot at their feet. He really was something, Alyssa thought.

"If he thinks Cutter is ours, he might think twice about trying to find us at home after he chased him," she said.

Quinn nodded.

"But that doesn't help us catch him," Drew said. "And even if we did, what could we do? He hasn't really done anything yet. The sheriff—"

"—has less leeway than we do," Quinn said. "Trust me, when we catch him, he will be convinced of the wisdom of leaving you alone."

Something in the way he said it made Alyssa almost pity Baird.

Almost.

She reached down to scratch Cutter's ear, thankful that he'd found them and brought them to Foxworth.

"What do we do now?" she asked Quinn.

"Take Luke to school every day, personally. Hand him off to someone you know, pick him up the same way. Let them know there's reason to be sure he's not released to either you or Drew or one of us. Keep him with you every moment he's not in school."

Alyssa nodded. Quinn continued.

"One of us will always be with you until this is over. The rest of us will keep hunting for Oliver."

Drew grimaced. "So I just stay out of the way, huh?"

Quinn smiled in understanding. "I know it goes against the grain. But we're trained for this. Let us do it."

"I'd rather be out there hunting for him," Drew said.

"Perhaps," Hayley said quietly, "you should ask Alyssa which she would prefer."

Drew looked at her then, and she answered instantly.

"Stay safe, with us." Something flashed in his eyes and she quickly added, "For Luke."

Drew gave a wry look at Hayley. "You knew I couldn't say no to that, didn't you?"

"Think of yourself as another line of defense," Quinn said.

"At least you didn't say 'last' line of defense," Drew said with a grimace.

"Best, maybe," Quinn said. "You'd lay down your life for them, wouldn't you?"

"Yes," Drew said, without a second's hesitation.

Alyssa's breath caught in her throat. There could be no doubting the sincerity of his answer. And the very thought rattled her to the core.

It was Luke he really meant, she told herself. Luke he really loved enough to die for. Not her. And she would do well to remember that.

Chapter 15

Hayley woke up quickly when Quinn's phone rang just before dawn. The days of waking up slowly were behind her for good, it seemed. Quinn always seemed to be instantly alert; for her it was a longer process.

As usual, Quinn sounded as if he'd been awake all along when he answered. He listened for a moment before saying. "No. That's enough. Come on home." Then, after an even briefer moment, "Yes, I still want his ass. In fact, I want it personally. And now that you've found this out, we'll get it. Head on back. A month is more than enough in that cesspool."

He ended the call and set the phone back down on the nightstand.

"Rafe?" she asked.

Quinn turned to look at her in the shadowy room. "How'd you guess?"

"Shortest phone call ever with someone you haven't seen in a month."

She saw him smile, even in the darkness. "That's Rafe, all right."

"Besides," she added, "he's the only one who's gone, therefore the only one who can head back."

"Ah, my brilliant soon-to-be-wife," Quinn said, lying back and pulling her down beside him.

"He found something, didn't he."

It wasn't a question. Again, it was Rafe. He might not be as comfortable in the big city anymore as he'd once been, but he was just as efficient. And she'd learned early that he had a reputation that got things done in certain quarters, in ways no one else could match, not even Quinn.

"Yes," Quinn said.

"Do we have a name? Is he still alive?" She wasn't sure joking about it was wise, but Quinn wasn't reacting as she'd thought he would once they got a lead on the mole who had almost gotten them killed on the mission where they'd first met.

"No name yet, just an agency. Lucky for him. Rafe doesn't have much tolerance for traitors."

"Was the leak where you suspected?"

Quinn's expression darkened. "Yes."

Hayley drew in a deep breath. That meant they were dealing with a federal agency. A very powerful one. "What will you do?"

"Keep going until we have that name. And then I'll take him down," Quinn said matter-of-factly.

"But if he covered his tracks so well that it took this long to just find out where he works, will you be able to prove it?"

"There will be a way. And if not, we'll make one. Or we'll prove something else. This wasn't his first rodeo."

"What if now he knows we're looking for him and runs before we can get him?"

Quinn gave her a sideways look. She realized her mistake and laughed. "Sorry. Rafe. I should have realized. No way he knows."

He laughed with her, a sound she never tired of hearing. A warmth she'd never known before him welled up and she reached for him, still amazed at how quickly it came over her, this unrelenting need for this one man.

It was much later, with the gray light of a winter morning lightening, if not brightening, the room, that Hayley brought up the current situation.

"Those two," she said in a lazily sated voice, need to take off the masks."

"Meaning?"

"It's obvious Drew loves her. And I think she loves him. But they're so locked into their 'arrangement' that neither one of them is willing to let down and risk saying so."

"You sure about that? Seems like it's the kid who's holding them together."

"I think that's what they tell themselves. She thinks he's only with her for Luke's sake, and he thinks she's only staying married to him for Luke's sake. He feels guilty because what seemed like the best solution at the time, when she was so sick and weak, is unacceptable now. Because now he loves her. And she feels she owes him everything for saving him, but indebtedness isn't love. And she can't see past that to how she really feels. But she won't leave, because of that debt, as well as for Luke. He's the only father Luke has really known. Which is another sore spot, because of how Drew feels about Doug. Alyssa wants Luke to know and love his father, but that's hard to do when the guy who's stepped into that job feels that way. And neither of them really knows who's right, they only know what they think is right."

Quinn was staring at her. "I think my head's going to explode. How do you do that? We've known them for a little over a week, and you've got every facet of their situation figured out."

"But it's obvious, once you talk to them."

"I think," Quinn said wryly, "that Cutter chose to show up on your doorstep because you're kindred spirits. Mind readers. Something."

"I miss him. House seems so quiet without him."

"He'll be back."

"I know." She smiled. "He is a working dog, after all."

"He gives the phrase a whole new meaning," Quinn said with a chuckle. He pulled her close. "I miss him, too."

Hayley sighed contentedly. "I love you, Quinn Foxworth. And I love how you've changed my life."

And I hope, she added to herself, *that we can help Drew and Alyssa find this for themselves.*

"If the place is still standing when this is over, it will be amazing," Drew said, watching Luke and Cutter, trapped inside by heavy rain today, tear through the house in some crazed kind of race that changed direction at whim. They'd been at it for at least ten minutes now, ever since Teague Johnson, who had arrived to relieve Liam, had gone outside to have a look around his new assignment. He'd arrived after dark, which came early this time of year, and come in through the back, by stealth.

Drew understood why once he'd seen the man; Liam could be anybody's kid brother or visiting cousin, but the first thing you thought when you saw Teague was military or law enforcement. And if Baird Oliver ever managed to find them here, if he was watching, he would assume they'd called for help, against his instructions.

Luke and Cutter made another circuit, this time careening off the living room couch. Drew winced.

"I just look at it as a very tired boy in the making," Alyssa answered. "And that's a good thing come bedtime."

"You're an optimist," he said. What he didn't say was how he admired that quality in her. Along with many others.

That he'd slipped from admiration into much deeper waters was something he tried not to dwell on. Things were tense enough between them now, even without her knowing he'd committed the unforgivably stupid act of falling in love with her.

"If I'm an optimist, I learned it from Doug."

And there it was. Digging at him again. "Doug wasn't an optimist. He just never accepted reality."

"And you can't accept that he ever did anything good." She let out an audible sigh. "You just can't help yourself, can you? You have to diss him at every opportunity."

"No more than you can help throwing out the bait," Drew retorted.

She went still. Thoughtful. Then, with a small nod, she said, "I suppose I had that coming. I do have the need to test the water, see if anything's changed."

Drew studied her for a moment. "Did you expect it to?"

"Not really."

"What Foxworth has found so far only confirms what I always thought. You know now how much he lied to you."

She flushed slightly, and it bit deep that he took that tiny reaction as a sign of progress. Pitiful.

"That's mine to deal with. But I also know your mind is made up, and always has been. And if you won't change it for Luke, you surely won't change it for me."

He only wished he could. But he'd grown up with Doug, he knew how he manipulated, how he put up a front, showed people what they wanted to see. And if you resisted, he became the walking definition of "charm offensive." And people fell for it. They always had.

Except for him.

"The truth is," he stated flatly.

"Which is your version, of course."

"I—"

He broke off as Cutter peeled away from the chase and skidded to a halt in front of them. He looked at them, from one to the other, and let out what for all the world sounded like a disgusted sigh.

Luke quickly noticed the loss of his racing partner, and trotted over.

"Are we in trouble?" he asked warily.

"No, of course you're not."

The boy looked at them doubtfully. "You look mad. Are you fighting?"

Drew heard the note of fear in Alyssa's voice as she answered quickly, "No!" He knew she was thinking that the last time Luke had heard them talking like that, he'd run away.

He put his arm around her, pulling her close. He had to take a deep breath to steady himself against the electric charge that ran through him before he spoke. This was impossible, he thought. He couldn't keep doing this. He wanted her too much.

But for Luke, he did it.

"We were just disagreeing," Drew said, earning him a panicked glance from Alyssa, who had avoided looking at him from the moment he'd touched her. "About what kind of dog we should get," he finished.

Alyssa's expression shifted instantly to one of relief and thanks as Luke lit up. "Really? I mean, I'd rather have Cutter, but he already belongs to someone."

"Yes, he does." *And I think I'm thankful for that,* Drew thought.

Cutter's head came up sharply, and for an instant Drew thought the dog had somehow read his thought. But then his head snapped around toward the back of the house. Drew tensed, but Cutter's tail came up and wagged slightly as he woofed a welcome and trotted that way. Drew followed him, reassured by the dog's reaction but still cautious.

And he felt a jab of anger, that they were reduced to this, living with armed guards—he'd noticed the weapons both Liam and Teague discreetly carried—all because of Doug.

But then, if it wasn't for Doug there would be no Luke, and that didn't bear thinking about.

As for Lyss, he thought, and the idiocy he'd committed by falling for her when he never, ever intended to…sometimes he couldn't bear thinking about that, either.

Chapter 16

Cutter sat expectantly at the door that went from the mudroom into the backyard. A moment later the door clicked, opened.

"Eagle feather." Teague called out the password they—or rather Luke—had picked out. Not that Cutter's reaction hadn't been enough. The man stepped into the mudroom, water streaming off him as Cutter greeted him with a welcoming sniff.

Drew studied the man for a moment. He was about his own height, and looked lean and fit. His sandy-brown hair was clipped military short, and the quiet confidence in the clear blue eyes was reassuring. Although it was Drew's job to keep Luke safe, it was good to have backup you had faith in. He was starting to feel that way about all of Foxworth.

"Hey, buddy," Teague said, ruffling the dog's fur. "What's up?"

"I think he was chewing us out," Drew said wryly as Teague carefully shed his dripping jacket and hung it on the rack beside the door.

"Oh, he's good at that," Teague said with a grin.

Now that he'd properly greeted his colleague, Cutter went back to Luke. The boy wasn't quite as comfortable with Teague yet, as he had become with Liam, but he still smiled at him.

"As you were," Teague said to the boy.

"What does that mean?" Luke asked as Alyssa joined them, grabbing a towel from the shelf next to the kitchen door and tossing it to Teague.

"It means go back to what you were doing," Drew said while Teague dried himself off. "Then again," he added, looking at the tossed throw rugs and one askew chair, "maybe not."

"We'll go watch TV, then," Luke said. "Come on, Cutter."

For a moment the dog hesitated, looking at Teague. The man nodded and made a gesture with his hand, then Cutter trotted off after Luke.

"What was that, he was waiting for the okay?" Alyssa asked with a laugh.

"He takes his job very seriously," Teague said, and Drew wasn't sure how much of it was a joke. "Normally, I'd take him with me to check the perimeter, but I thought I'd save you wet dog."

Drew laughed at that. "Something to remember," he said.

"So what was he chewing you out about?" Teague asked.

Alyssa gave Drew a sideways glance. "I think he thought we were fighting."

"Oh." Teague looked suddenly uncomfortable.

"It was more of a difference of opinion," Drew said wearily. "A very old one."

"Okay, he was chewing you out, then. He's big on people getting along," Teague said. "Just ask Laney."

"Your girlfriend?" Alyssa asked.

Teague nodded. "Thanks to Cutter."

Drew lifted a brow. "She's your girlfriend because of a dog?"

Teague laughed. "Sounds crazy, doesn't it? But it's true. We were having…a failure to communicate, I guess you'd call it. And Cutter finally got tired of it. So one day he wouldn't let me leave her shop until we talked it out."

"That's…sweet, really," Alyssa said.

"Ended up pretty darn sweet," Teague said with a grin that made Drew feel an odd sort of pang. Then Teague turned to pull his cell phone out of an inside jacket pocket. "Excuse me, I need to check in with the boss."

"I made hot chocolate," Alyssa said, gesturing to a pan on the stove. "Have some, it will warm you up."

"Sounds great," Teague said.

"Mugs are in the cupboard by the oven."

They left him to make his call. Drew followed Alyssa back out into the living room. She walked over and began to straighten the rugs out, so Drew lifted the chair back into its normal spot. It took only a few seconds to have everything back to rights.

"Small price to pay," Drew said, "for as much fun as he was having."

"Yes," Alyssa agreed.

For a moment an oddly charged silence spun out. Then, simultaneously, they spoke.

"I'm sor—"

"I apol—"

They both stopped. Looked at each other a bit awkwardly.

"You're right," Alyssa said then. "I do bait you. I'm sorry."

"And I always snap at it," Drew said. "I apologize for that."

"Maybe we need a Cutter to chew us out."

"I'd settle for just stopping it."

Alyssa sighed. "You'd think we'd learn."

Drew studied her for a moment. "Can I ask you something? Peacefully?"

She hesitated a moment, as if bracing herself, before she said, "Go ahead."

"You're a smart woman, Lyss. Very smart. You know stuff instinctively about people that I can only figure out if I sit and think about it for an hour. And even then I might not hit the right answer. Not the way you do."

She looked so startled he paused. Then, at her expression, he realized his compliments had thrown her. He wondered if it was because he said them too rarely, or simply because this wasn't what she'd expected.

"Oh, there's got to be once heck of a *however* after that," she said.

"I'm sorry," he said again. "I don't say things like that often enough, do I?"

"You don't say them," she said drily, "at all."

"I guess I didn't think you'd want it. From me, I mean."

"Oddly, I find it means more coming from you," she said. "Maybe because you don't throw out praise easily. At me, I mean."

He couldn't tell if she was using his words back at him as a jab, or if she was teasing. Somewhere along the line she'd gotten a lot better at hiding her thoughts. She was no longer the girl whose every emotion showed in her innocent face. Which no doubt had made it easier for Doug. He would have been able to tell instantly if he'd gone too far.

"Well, you are," he said lamely. "And you do."

"And you're going where with this flattery? Or do I already know?"

He kept his voice as neutral as he could manage, no anger, no snark. Resisted the urge to insist it wasn't flattery at all.

"I just wanted to know if…you ever, even once, considered that you could be wrong?"

To his relief, she didn't leap to Doug's defense. Perhaps because at the core, this wasn't really about Doug.

"You're a very smart man, Drew. I appreciate you in a way that I never would have before."

That damned word again. He tamped down the irritation it sparked. She was talking, not angrily, and he didn't want to mess that up. Not to mention that the compliments returned were nice.

"And in case you hadn't noticed, I've come to trust your judgment. And he was your brother a lot longer than he was my boyfriend. So, of course I've considered that I could be wrong."

He suddenly knew how she'd felt at the too-rare praise. Even the damned *appreciation* didn't seem so bad, added to all the rest.

And all of it seemed to pale next to the admission. At least she'd thought about it. Even if she'd rejected the notion, she'd thought about it. That was something. Not enough, true…but then, he wasn't going to ever get what would be enough.

"May I ask you something in turn?"

The formality of the way they were talking suddenly struck him. But maybe that was what they had to do, to keep it at least calm.

"Go ahead," he said.

"You went away to college when your brother was fifteen. So you didn't really live with him from then on."

"No. You two took off right after I came back." He held up a hand when she stiffened. "Not a slam, just a fact."

"This isn't my question, but…did you ever wonder why we waited until you were back?"

He blinked. "What did that have to do with anything?"

"He didn't want to leave while you were gone. He knew you'd come back, then your parents wouldn't be alone."

He opened his mouth to deny that Doug would ever think that deeply about anyone other than himself. Then he stopped himself. They were communicating, really talking calmly, for the first time in a while and he didn't want to ruin it with a knee-jerk reaction. That it was so ingrained became clear to him when he couldn't think of anything else to say. He was thankful when Alyssa turned back to her original question. Which, again, she phrased much as he'd phrased his.

"Say you were right about the Doug you knew, grew up with. Have you ever considered that he might have changed, after we left? That he wasn't the same person you remember?"

He wasn't sure how to answer that without dumping them back into the fruitless arguments of the past. He sighed, and went with the truth.

"Not really, no."

"Well, that's honest at least, if not very charitable."

"I gave to the charity of Douglas Kiley from the day he was born," Drew said. And he meant it. Doug had siphoned off everything, his parents' attention and time, then everyone else's.

Alyssa didn't respond at first, and he wondered if he'd managed to make her angry, even though his tone had been, with effort, still neutral.

"I never thought of it like that," she said after a moment. "Being an only child, I didn't have the division of attention."

He hadn't expected that. He knew she'd been the apple of her parents' eyes, beautiful, smart, destined for a success they'd never had. It must have been a shock to her when they'd turned on her so completely. "No," he said softly, "you just had it cut off altogether, when you needed it most."

Her head came up sharply. "I didn't thank you for that. Going to my parents. And what you said to them."

"For all the good it did. Your mother is...a real piece of work."

He grimaced at the memory of the woman coldly declaring to him that her daughter had been dead to her from the day she'd run off with Doug, ruining her chances at the life she'd planned for her. Getting pregnant had only sealed her fate. The woman had no interest at all in her only grandchild, had refused anything but a brief glance at a picture of Luke, which had brought on a snort of disgust and the comment that he looked just like his father.

"Yes. She is." She stared down at the pillow she'd been toying with, as if she desperately needed to do something with her hands. "That's part of the reason running off with Doug was so attractive."

"To get away from her?"

"Yes. I mean I loved him, insanely, but escape was a factor, too."

He managed not to glance at the gold pendent. And somehow reacting to the insane part seemed like a bad idea, especially when she was admitting something he hadn't known, that she'd never told him before, but that he probably should have guessed. He had, after all, met her mother.

"She always felt short-changed in her own life. So I was supposed to live the life she thought she should have had for her. Never mind what I wanted."

"I'm glad you're nothing like her," he finally said, thinking that should be safe enough.

"I try. She's a sterling example, in a backwards way."

The way she said it made him smile. She truly had come a very long way.

"And I'm glad you didn't like her. Even though she feels about Doug the same way you do."

Drew's brows shot downward. "Is that really what you think? That I'd like a mother who could treat you like that, just because of that?"

"No. No, I don't, really."

Mollified, he said, "Besides, she doesn't dislike Doug

because of who he was. She has no idea who he was. She hates him because she blames him."

"For what I did."

"He manipulated you. God, Lyss, you were just a kid. He's lucky the age of consent is sixteen here, or he could have gone to jail for that."

She stiffened. "I was with Doug of my own free will. Whatever else, don't doubt that."

"I know that." Again he felt the urge to push, to make her see. But this was the most they'd talked about it without one of them losing their cool, and he didn't want to ruin that, so he bit back the words. "And I know he cared about you." He didn't add "As much as he cared about anyone besides himself," for the same reason he didn't push, and because he'd said it often enough before.

The admission seemed to soothe her. "Can I ask one more question?"

"Lyss, ask anything you want." He meant it. They hadn't talked like this, openly and calmly, for so long, in maybe forever.

"You said your parents blamed you when Doug and I left."

"Yes."

"Why?"

Well, maybe he'd been a little hasty in telling her to ask anything. Because he didn't like the answer to this one. But he made himself answer it anyway. It seemed crucial at this moment to keep this going.

"They thought I'd always been too hard on him. Expected him to be like me. That he'd turned out the way he did because he couldn't."

"You did set a pretty high standard," Alyssa said.

Another compliment? Drew wondered. Or was she agreeing with his parents?

"For all his complaining about you," she said, "I always sensed that deep down, he respected you tremendously."

Drew snorted inelegantly. "Could have fooled me."

But his own words, about how she knew things about people, came back to him. But that didn't mesh with how Doug had fooled her. Had that been how she'd learned? By trying to read a master manipulator?

Or had her life been so crazy, so grim, that she'd had to learn that skill just to survive? That thought made his stomach knot.

"Perhaps he did fool you," she said. "Because it was clear to me that he didn't even try to live up to you because he was afraid he couldn't."

He felt an old, familiar chill. All the hope this long, quiet, even deep conversation had engendered in him died a quick, icy death. She did agree with his parents, that Doug's fate, the course he chose in life, was partly because of him. Doug had said as much after all, that he would chose the darker path because he couldn't match Drew's.

So much for compliments. He should have known. When it came down to it, Alyssa would always support Doug. Even almost seven years dead, his charming scoundrel of a brother was still wreaking havoc with his life.

Chapter 17

Cutter came out of the kitchen, appearing to be headed for the family room and Luke. His appearance reminded Alyssa that Teague was in the kitchen, and she wondered with no little embarrassment if he'd stayed in there this long on purpose, not wanting to get sucked into this never-ending clash.

On that thought, Cutter stopped. He looked over at them, then changed course and headed their way. He stopped beside the coffee table and shifted that intense gaze from Drew to her and then back again. And once more, he let out that oddly disgusted-sounding canine sigh.

"Yeah, we're at it again," Drew muttered.

"Are we?" Alyssa asked. "I thought we were calmly discussing it."

Surprise flickered across his face. They really hadn't been arguing, not like before, so why was he surprised? Because he'd been about to launch as usual, after she'd in essence agreed with his parents, but Cutter had interrupted? Had the dog somehow sensed the tone was about to change?

Apparently decided now, Cutter walked over to Drew. He sat down in front of him, practically on his feet, and stared up into his face. Drew stared back at him, but she imagined it would be rather hard not to.

A contest of wills?

She wasn't sure why the phrase popped into her mind, but it seemed to fit. The dog must somehow sense the tension, she thought. And because it apparently had been Drew feeling it—she herself had been remarkably composed given the subject—he had focused on him.

She wondered what Cutter would do if Drew got really angry. Not that he ever did, at least not that he ever let it show. In fact, other than when the subject was his brother, he was calm and level and for the most part kind and thoughtful. And with Luke, he was incredibly patient, sometimes even more than she was.

Luke.

"You know it's not really about Doug at all," she said. "It's about Luke."

Drew didn't look away from the dog. Odd, she thought. He didn't speak, either. Maybe he was still on the edge of snapping back something about Doug and instead chose not to speak at all. She took this as a good sign. And said something she'd wanted to say since the day Luke had run away, when she had called Drew and he had dropped everything to come running. No blame, no accusations, he'd just come, because Luke was the most important thing in the world to him. They shared that, at least.

"Nobody can change the fact that Doug is Luke's biological father. But you're the man who's been there for him, always put him first. The man he looks up to. The man he respects." Her voice tightened, but she went on. "The man he loves."

Cutter made a soft, whuffing sound. Drew's head came up then and he looked at her. And something in his expression was different. She wasn't sure what it was, just that he seemed…not softer, not Drew, but as if he'd been moved by something. Her words, or Cutter's stare? After having watched the dog for a while, she wouldn't be surprised if it were the latter. But either way, she'd take it.

"I'm sorry you hate your brother."

"I don't hate him. He's gone, that would be pointless."

"But you're still angry with him. Just think how it must feel for Luke," she said softly, "to know the man he loves so much feels that way about his biological father?"

Drew looked back at Cutter as he sucked in an audible breath. "I never meant for him to hear that."

"I know. Neither did I. But he did."

For a moment he lapsed back into silence. And Alyssa risked something she rarely did. "You're angry at me, too."

Drew's gaze snapped back to her face. "I'm not angry. I just don't understand."

"I was seventeen. There's no reasoning."

"Then, yes. But…later. And now."

"I told you. It's for Luke. He knows you're not his natural father. Someday he's going to be curious."

"And you want him to believe a lie?"

She sighed. They weren't arguing, not really, but they'd said all this before. "I don't want him growing up thinking his natural father didn't even care enough about him to stick around."

"Even if it's true?"

"Sometimes," she said, "truth needs to wait until someone's ready to hear it."

"Truth is," he stated again. But he was still speaking calmly, quietly. So she pressed on.

"Yes. Who believes it or why doesn't change it. But if someone doesn't believe it, you can't make them believe with a hammer, Drew."

He blinked. Looked away. Cutter made a sound that wasn't quite a whine, not quiet a growl, but some odd combination of the two. Silence spun out after that, for a long, not quite tense moment. And then, finally, Drew, let out a long, slow breath and met her gaze.

"All right," he said.

"All right, what?"

"You win. From now on, your version of Doug is the accepted one in this house."

She listened for any trace of sarcasm in his voice, but found none.

"I've sworn to myself before that I'd never fight with you about this again, and I've broken that vow too many times. But now I'm swearing to you. No more."

She stared at him. She understood the difference. If Drew Kiley gave someone his word, it was golden. He'd never broken a promise to her, and she knew he wouldn't break this one.

It was all she'd ever wanted, she'd told herself. For him to stop maligning Doug. And now that he'd offered it, now that he'd made that promise she knew he would keep, she wasn't much happier than she had been. Perversely, now that she'd finally gotten what she wanted, it wasn't enough.

"What more do you want?" he asked, as if he'd read her thoughts.

Discomfited, she admitted with no little chagrin after her own comment, "Apparently I wanted you to believe. Really believe. For Luke's sake."

Drew stood up. He shoved his hands in the front pockets of his jeans, as if he needed to keep them still.

"Funny," he said. "Because that's what I wanted. I wanted you to believe."

"I know."

He started to walk toward the family room, to check on Luke no doubt. Then, near the doorway, he turned to look back at her.

"But not for Luke. I thought, and still do, that the truth is best. But I'll grant you that maybe he's not ready, not old enough yet."

Relief flooded her. He was being more reasonable about this than he ever had been before. She didn't, as she usually would have, ask which truth he meant, she knew. She wasn't going to test his apparent new resolve so quickly.

She almost didn't ask her other question, didn't want to upset things, but she wanted to know.

"Then why?"

He looked at her steadily. "I wanted you to believe for me."

She stared after him as he went into the other room. She wasn't sure what had just happened. Wasn't even sure exactly what he had meant.

Cutter came over to her, sat at her feet much as he had with Drew. He simply looked at her, with that intensity of gaze that made it hard—no, impossible—to look away.

She reached out and petted his head. "You must think we humans are pretty stupid, huh? We have all these words, but we can't communicate as well as you can with none."

Cutter rolled his eyes. She laughed, before she could stop herself. It was impossible, of course, he was just a dog, he didn't mean it in the way a person would. He was probably just trying to look toward the family room while still facing her, or maybe he'd heard poor Teague hiding out in the kitchen. It was surely coincidence that he'd done it just then, but the timing was amazing.

"You're so darn smart, aren't you? I wish you could tell me what Drew meant by that."

Cutter inched forward, and laid his head on her knee. He nuzzled in closer, looking up at her. She went for the spot below his right ear, scratched it. The dog sighed in blissful satisfaction, as if all he'd wanted was her touch.

"Well, that would be a nice answer," she said.

And she found herself wishing that the answer to her question really was that simple. But she was sure it wasn't. Things never were, were they? And the thought of Drew wanting any sort of touch from her was dangerous territory she wasn't ready to stray into.

The other thing she was sure of was that whatever this emotion was that had welled up inside her when he'd looked at her that way, when he'd made that simple, almost plaintive declaration, it was something she'd never felt before. Something warm, flooding, and almost frighteningly strong that she couldn't even put a name to.

Something she didn't even want to think about, at least not now. Not with Baird out there somewhere, waiting, maybe watching.

She got to her feet, torn between checking on Luke herself, and going to tell Teague, ruefully, that it was safe to come out now. She opted, as always, for Luke. Teague was a smart guy, he'd figure out quiet meant safe.

Whereas she didn't know when she'd ever feel safe again. Because she had a feeling that wouldn't go away—that, Baird or not, her life was never going to be the same again.

Chapter 18

"It's okay," Hayley said as Alyssa opened the door to her. "Cutter would alert if there was anyone around. And even if someone is watching, I'm just a friend coming to visit."

"And Baird won't suspect a woman?"

"We can do things a man couldn't without drawing suspicion. A guy will automatically classify us as not a threat to him. Or so Quinn says."

"Lucky us," Alyssa said wryly, but with a smile.

She stepped aside to let an eager Cutter past her. Then laughed as the dog greeted Hayley joyously, dancing, tail wagging, a happy little whine escaping him. "And if you've come mainly to visit Cutter, I understand."

Hayley laughed as she bent to give him a thorough greeting—pets, scratches and silly talk that the dog seemed to love. "How's my boy? Keeping things under control here, are you?"

"He's quite something," Alyssa said. "More personality than some people I know."

"Yes, indeed," Hayley said. "He's very good company."

"And almost eerily clever."

"Yes, that too. And perceptive. Makes me wonder how we found people to help before he came along."

"How did you?"

Hayley straightened, and nodded as Alyssa gestured her inside. "Mostly they found us. And they still do. Not everybody has a Cutter, sad to say."

"But you don't advertise or anything."

Hayley shook her head as Alyssa closed the door behind them. "Foxworth has a reputation. And an amazing network."

"Network?"

"Since we don't charge a fee, and because the kind of people we help are usually the kind who are grateful for it and want to pay us back in some way, we have a network of willing helpers across the country. Some with some unique skills and knowledge, some just regular people who want to help somebody who's in a jam like they were."

As Hayley was taking off her jacket, Luke burst into the room at a run, clearly searching for his missing friend.

"Oh," he said, skidding to a halt when he saw Hayley. "You're not going to take him away, are you?" he asked anxiously.

Hayley smiled. "No, Luke. Not just yet. I think you need him for a while longer."

Luke smiled in obvious relief. Alyssa smiled back at him.

"I can see we may need to speed up the pace on getting that dog of our own," she said.

"Today?" Luke asked eagerly. "I mean, I'd rather have Cutter, but he's hers, and Quinn's, and I know they wouldn't want to give him up because I know how much I'll miss him, so I need my own."

Hayley laughed. "Makes perfect sense."

"Probably not today, honey, but soon," Alyssa said.

"Maybe Dad can take me. He said we should get one from the shelter, one who didn't have a home, or any people who love him."

Alyssa nodded, her throat suddenly a bit tight. "He's good at that," she said softly.

"Where is Drew, by the way?" Hayley asked, looking at her as if she understood completely. Which would be an accomplishment, Alyssa thought, since she didn't understand a darn thing herself.

"He had to go in to the office for a couple of hours, but he'll be back early this evening. He only felt he could leave at all because Liam's here, so thank you for that."

"No problem," Hayley said. "It's what we do. And I know Liam's been enjoying it." She smiled at Luke. "He likes you."

"I like him, too," Luke said. "He plays silly."

"Now there's a recommendation if ever I heard one," Hayley said with a grin, and Alyssa had the feeling Liam was going to get teased about that one.

Luke turned to the dog and said eagerly, "Let's go outside, Cutter, so we can play."

They watched boy and dog race toward the back door.

"Liam's already out there?" Hayley asked.

"Yes. He did a…perimeter check, he said? But he wanted to stay outside while it was dry."

"That's all right, then."

Alyssa didn't miss the inference, that Liam was outside so Luke would be safe. She hated that their lives had degenerated to this, that her son couldn't make a move without them having to worry about his safety so intensely. But she was even more grateful that, thanks to Cutter and the engaging Texan, Luke was blissfully unaware.

"I think sometimes Liam misses the Texas heat," Hayley said, watching as Luke yanked open the back door, ready to race outside at top six-year-old speed.

Then he stopped, looking back at Hayley as if he'd just

thought of something. "Maybe you need to find a little boy who needs a home. Like me. So Cutter will have somebody to play with, too."

Then he darted outside, leaving Hayley laughing, and Alyssa feeling a little tug of emotion; she hadn't realized Luke had been so aware that he had needed a home. She swallowed hard, and glanced at Hayley.

"He has a point," she said.

"I suppose he does," Hayley said, a touch of color in her cheeks.

"Kids in the game plan?"

"Yes," Hayley said, her color deepening, but a smile— a soft, loving smile—curving her mouth. "Quinn will be a great father."

"Yes."

"As Drew is."

Alyssa sighed. "Yes. He is."

"He loves Luke."

"Completely."

Hayley looked as if she were about to say something more, but apparently changed her mind. Alyssa wasn't sure if she was glad, or disappointed. She offered a cup of the coffee Drew had put on this morning, and Hayley accepted with a smile. She definitely liked this woman, Alyssa thought as they walked to the kitchen. And realized she had missed having friends.

"That's a sad expression," Hayley said as she accepted the mug Alyssa had prepared to her liking, and sat with her at the small table in the breakfast nook.

"Just thinking how long it's been since I've done something like this. Meaning never."

"Had coffee with a friend?" Hayley asked.

That Hayley considered them friends, even after such a short time, warmed her. And made her feel free to speak without fear of being judged. Not everyone was like her mother, after all.

"Had a friend," she said frankly. "I haven't wanted to see anyone I knew before, old friends, not after my life became such a mess. I mean, I was a walking cliché, good girl gone bad, all for a boy. And I've been so wrapped up in Luke since we got here that I haven't had time, or taken the time, to make new ones."

"Some of those old friends might surprise you," Hayley said.

"Maybe."

"It must have been rough in the beginning, coming back here."

"In the beginning I was still too weak to care. I'd been so sick, and I was so worried about Luke. I was terrified I'd never get him back, that he'd grow up in foster care, because I'd gotten sick."

"I can't imagine."

"And then Drew rode in, the proverbial knight in shining armor. He saved us both."

"And brought you back here."

She nodded. "Drew made all the decisions then, and I was glad of it. I was just too scattered."

"But when you got better?"

She smiled. "I had to convince him I was well enough to deal, before he'd give some of those decisions back to me."

"But he did. Some men wouldn't."

"Drew's not one of them. He's never tried to control me, not really."

"Some might say marrying him was a bit extreme."

She shrugged. "They weren't there. He was right, it was the quickest way to get Luke back, get him out of foster care. He was such a straight arrow, running a business, not even a traffic ticket on his record, and besides, he was Luke's uncle by blood. They jumped at it."

"I'm sure they're overloaded."

"Yes. But it could have taken forever if he hadn't stepped in."

"And you've stayed."

Alyssa stared down into her coffee mug. She didn't want to bruise this new relationship by not answering, but how could she when she didn't really know the answer herself?

"I'm sorry," Hayley said. "That's really none of my business."

"No," Alyssa said, afraid she'd offended her new friend. "It's all right. It's a good question. And I don't have an answer, not really. Except…" She let out a compressed breath. "Doug promised me the moon, a really good life, had lots of grandiose plans, but it never happened. Drew never promised anything, he just did it."

For a moment Hayley didn't say anything. She took another sip of coffee, set the mug down, then finally spoke. "There are some men who won't even take responsibility for their own kids, let alone someone else's."

"I know."

"Fortunately, there are a lot more of the other kind. The good guys. They're just…quiet about it."

"Like your Quinn?" she asked with a smile.

Hayley nodded. "And your Drew."

Your Drew.

It was startling, the little jump her heart made at those words. She knew in some senses it was true. He would do anything for Luke, and making her happy made her son happy, so it followed that he would do just about anything for her. And in fact, had. She'd never really done without much, since he'd taken them in. In that way, he'd treated her as if their marriage was real. He'd built this house, he'd consulted her every step of the way in designing it, turned the furnishing over to her, asking only that she consult him in turn. He'd built Luke a play fort that would be the envy of any kid, and had spent hours helping the boy learn to ride a bike.

But he wasn't hers in the sense that Quinn was Hayley's.

He wasn't hers in that intimate, inextricable way of genuine lovers committed to each other.

She felt a tug of longing, wondering what it would be like. She'd had a chance, maybe, back in the beginning. Once she'd been well, strong again, what she supposed had been inevitable had happened. Drew was young, strong, healthy, with the appetites of any man. And she'd felt she owed him, but had no way to pay him back.

Except one.

She had made the first move, knowing instinctively that he would not. He'd been surprised, reminded her this wasn't part of their agreement. She'd pressed on, until she'd sensed him give in.

And then she was surprised. Surprised by his gentleness, his patience, the time he took. By how he lingered—touching, stroking, kissing—in a way Doug never had.

And she'd been amazed at her own response. Her body seemed to sing at his touch, in a way that frightened her. She loved Doug so how could she respond this way to his stuffy big brother? Some part of her pleasure-numbed brain had acknowledged the fundamental difference. Doug took, Drew gave.

But she'd felt so guilty afterwards. Guilty because it had been better for her than she would have ever thought possible. Guilty because she'd betrayed Doug. And that he was dead and she—and Drew—were very much alive didn't ease it much. The only thing that would have eased her guilt would be if it had been awful. Not glorious.

And Drew sensed it. She'd fallen apart and run from him, like the silly child she'd still been.

An image formed in her mind, painfully vivid. Drew, standing in the doorway of the room she'd retreated to, sobbing. Still naked and strong and beautiful—she couldn't deny that—he'd stared at her.

"Don't ever do that again," he had said, his voice a tight, low, harsh thing. "I don't want or need your charity."

"I... It wasn't charity."

"No? Then it was in payment for charity, is that it?"

That had been close enough to the truth that she couldn't hide it.

"I don't need that, either," he had said flatly. "You don't owe me a damned thing, Alyssa. Doing this was my decision."

He'd left her there, a mass of conflict, her insides churning in confusion. She'd hurt him when that had been the last thing she'd wanted. She felt as if she had betrayed Doug, and for a moment had wished she'd died with him.

Except for Luke.

And it was the thought of her son, safe and loved, and already starting to blossom under Drew's steady care, that made her quash her own roiled emotions. She had no right to them, she told herself. Luke had to and would come first. And that meant she would do as Drew demanded.

She would stay away from him. And she had, except for a weak moment after he'd insisted on the alarm system to help keep them safe. That time had been different, at least Drew had been different after. Not angry this time, but almost sad. And she wasn't sure what had changed.

Still she had wondered what it might have been like if she hadn't fallen apart after that first time. Wondered if she had missed a chance at something. The chance to change everything. And if she would forever regret it.

And as confused, tangled, and chaotic as she was at that moment, it turned out she had been right.

Chapter 19

"What did they used to call this kind of—what did they say, 'arrangement'?" Quinn asked.

"I believe it was a 'marriage of convenience.'"

"Darned inconvenient if you're right, and now he's in love with her."

"He admitted it to me," Hayley said. "She hasn't, but I think I'm right anyway."

"You usually are," he said, earning the smile he'd wanted.

He watched her as she went back to what she'd been doing, looking over the guest list for the wedding in the few minutes before the Kileys were to arrive. He'd been a little amazed at the rate of RSVPs saying they were coming, and had the rueful feeling they should have invited fewer to begin with. Not that they'd been in control of that, of course.

"You sure you don't want to call it all off and elope?" she asked, not for the first time.

"As long as it happens, I don't much care how," he said. "But you deserve the big day."

"I just want to deserve you," she said.

Quinn shook his head slowly, one corner of his mouth lifting slightly in that bemused smile that appeared every time he thought about the wonder his life had become. He never in a million years would have guessed when that scamp of a dog had burst out of the trees that his life was about to be changed forever.

"Besides," she added, "Charlie."

Quinn sighed. "Yeah. Charlie." Then he grinned. "Hey, be thankful Charlie's not planning it. We'd have to rent the county fairgrounds."

Hayley grinned back. "They have horses there, don't they? We could escape on horseback."

God, he loved this woman.

He was still kissing her when the sound of tires on the gravel drive—kept gravel for just that reason—announced that the Kileys had arrived. With a sigh Quinn released her.

They got downstairs just as Luke and Cutter bounded out of the backseat. The dog made a beeline to them, greeting Quinn first, which was unusual.

"He just saw me yesterday," Hayley said, reading Quinn's expression perfectly, as usual. "You he hasn't seen in a couple of days."

"He's been a godsend," Alyssa said. "For more reasons than one."

Quinn guessed that she meant the dog had been a distraction for Luke, keeping him from realizing what was really going on.

"He makes himself useful," Quinn agreed.

"And then some," Hayley added as Cutter nudged her hand to get his ear-scratch.

"He's the best," Luke exclaimed as he ran up. His smile shifted quickly to a doubtful look. "I don't think we'll find a dog as good."

"He'll be different, just like your friend Dylan is different than Tran," Drew said.

"But he'll be yours," Alyssa said. "And that will make him just as good."

Admittedly, he didn't know much about kids, but it seemed to Quinn that Drew and Alyssa made a good team dealing with Luke. Whatever their differences, they seemed to pull together when it came to the boy.

"I talked to Laney," Hayley said. "She's got a couple of dogs in mind. She offered to have them at the shop for Luke to come visit, when you're ready."

"He'll want them both," Drew said drily.

Hayley grinned. "She guessed that. That's why she said one at a time. And it will save you going to the shelter, where he might just want all of them."

"I like her already," Alyssa said.

"Teague found a good one," Quinn agreed.

"Or rather, Cutter found him one, from what he told us," Alyssa added with a laugh.

"He does have a way," Hayley said, echoing the laugh.

The dog was watching and listening, his gaze shifting to everyone that spoke, as if he were actually following the conversation. If it were any animal but Cutter, Quinn would have said he was simply reacting to the occasional mention of his name, and the word dog. But he was long past making assumptions like that about this dog.

Just as he glanced down at him, Cutter's head snapped around, and the dog stared down the driveway. Quinn watched him for a second or two, then relaxed. The dog's head and ears were up, and his tail wagged. A staccato, two-note bark came from him.

"Liam," Hayley said.

"That's the bark," Quinn agreed.

"Wait," Drew said. "He's got different barks for different people?"

"Well, Liam and Teague have to share one. Rafe gets his own."

"And you two, I presume," Alyssa said, laughing again. She really was quite lovely, Quinn thought, when she was laughing and smiling instead of worried and tense.

They could hear the crunch of tires on gravel now, and a second later Liam's car emerged from the trees. Cutter trotted over as the young man got out of the vehicle.

"Hey, hound, you just saw me half an hour ago," he teased as he scratched the dog's ear. "Think I'd been taken over by aliens in the meantime?"

"It's that taking the job seriously thing," Hayley said, smiling at them both.

"Speaking of which," Quinn suggested.

Liam didn't come to attention. Unlike Teague and Rafe and Quinn himself, it wasn't trained into him. But for him he came close enough, and Quinn acknowledged it with a barely perceptible nod.

"They weren't followed," Liam said.

Alyssa looked startled, and Drew went very still. Quinn didn't ask if Liam was sure. He was the best tracker they had, and he knew when someone else was tracking. If he said they were clear, they were clear.

"Followed?" Luke asked, frowning.

"It's nothing, honey," Alyssa said quickly.

Drew tensed, and his mouth went tight, but he said nothing. And Quinn realized that just as their love for Luke made them pull together, it also drove them apart when they didn't agree. He tended to agree with Drew, that hiding the threat from the boy wasn't necessarily the best thing, but he also understood Alyssa's need to protect. It was in a mother's DNA, he thought.

It would be in Hayley's, when the time came.

He felt a little shiver that was a combination of anticipation and dread and eagerness. Hayley hadn't just changed his life, she'd changed him.

He gave himself an inward shake, ordering himself to focus.

"Hey, buddy," Liam said to Luke, "why don't we take a hike?"

Quinn managed not to smile at the phrase and it's double meaning. Liam was getting good at sensing undercurrents.

"A hike?" Luke asked.

"I'll show you where the eagle's nest is," he said.

Luke lit up. "Really?"

"Cutter can come with us." He looked at Quinn. "Unless you need him."

"I think we can spare him for the moment."

Once the trio was out of earshot—well, Luke and Liam, he was sure Cutter could still hear them—Drew spoke.

"You told him to see if we were followed?"

Quinn shrugged. "Didn't have to tell him. It's S.O.P. in situations like this."

"So, it wasn't because you had reason to think we were, then," Alyssa said, sounding relieved.

Quinn didn't want her too relaxed about it, so he gave her the truth. "Not a specific reason, just a lot of experience. When somebody like Oliver is involved, things tend to go certain ways."

"That's why Luke should know. We should show him a picture of Oliver, so he'll—"

"Be terrified?" Alyssa interrupted him. "He's six years old, Drew."

"But he's smart, and if he knows to look out then—"

"We're supposed to protect him."

"I swore I would, and I will. But—"

"You're both right," Hayley said. "Our job is to figure out the best way to do that. Let's go in and talk about it."

Just like that, peace reigned again, and Quinn thought once more how lucky he was. How lucky Foxworth was. Hayley had added a unique something, a sort of sensitivity and understanding that got people to open up to her, trust her, a way of reading people that had salvaged what could have turned into nasty situations more than once.

He didn't know how long it would last, though. What was coming in this meeting wasn't going to make Alyssa happy. He just hoped Drew was smart enough to avoid any "I told you so," afterward.

When they were seated—it was warmer today, so they went to the third-floor meeting room, where Alyssa could also look toward the woods where Liam and Luke and Cutter were—Quinn didn't waste time with niceties.

"Detective Dunbar called me this morning," he said. "He had a call in to an old colleague of his at LAPD. He was in the middle of a robbery-homicide case, so it took a while."

"Robbery-homicide?" Alyssa's voice was full of apprehension. She was many things, Quinn thought, but slow on the uptake wasn't one of them. Information coming from that particular kind of investigator wasn't likely to be good. Drew said nothing, but Quinn doubted what he was about to say would surprise the man.

"Doug was picked up as a suspect in a gas station robbery six months prior to the convenience store."

"Picked up? Not arrested?" Drew asked.

"They didn't have enough to hold him."

"So he was innocent," Alyssa said, sounding relieved. Drew sighed and gave a sad shake of his head.

"According to Brett's friend, he was guilty, they just couldn't prove it," Quinn said.

"Then he—" Alyssa began.

"Don't," Drew said. "Please, just don't."

Alyssa shot him a sideways look that Quinn thought must have singed. Then she looked back at Quinn. "What day was this?"

"December twenty-first, before he died in June."

Her brow furrowed as she tried to recall.

"Right before Christmas," Hayley said quietly.

Alyssa's head came up, and her eyes widened. Her hand

came up, slowly, and she touched the gold necklace with the tiny pendent Quinn had noticed she seemed to always wear.

"He bought me this that year," she whispered.

"Now you know how he paid for it," Drew said sourly.

Alyssa winced, and Quinn thought he saw a flicker of self-reproach in Drew's eyes. This must have been going on so long that it was a festering sore, something that resulted in a reflex reaction any time it was poked.

"Sorry," Drew muttered. "I'm sure you could have figured that out on your own."

"Assumed it, you mean?" Alyssa countered, but there was little heat in it. She was beginning to see, Quinn thought. To admit that her version of Doug might not be the real one. It had been the goal here, to find the real man Drew's brother had been, but that didn't make it any more pleasant. There was a reason Foxworth generally steered clear of these things, and he should have kept it that way.

As if Cutter would have let him.

"I said I'm sorry."

"Fine," Alyssa said, ending it with that female culmination that Quinn knew meant anything but what the word itself meant.

A rather loud jangle thankfully broke the tension. Or so Quinn thought until he saw Drew's face as he grabbed at his cell phone. It must have been an alert of some kind, and the man's expression said it wasn't good.

He looked at the screen, then at Quinn.

"It's the business alarm," he said grimly. "Somebody's breaking into the office."

Chapter 20

"Stay here," Drew said. He saw the protest about to start, so he added the one thing that would silence it instantly. "With Luke."

They had all raced down the stairs in seconds. Quinn dialed three numbers into his phone, while simultaneously stepping outside and letting out a piercing whistle. Silence reigned in the clearing. And then Cutter burst out of the trees at a head-down, tail-straight-out run. He was nearly across the clearing by the time Luke and Liam emerged. Drew wasn't sure what Liam saw, perhaps something in Quinn's posture or demeanor even from that far away, but he scooped Luke up and over his shoulder and began to run. The boy seemed to think it was a game; Drew could hear his laughter even from here.

"Alarm at Drew's office," Quinn said to Liam as soon as he had handed the boy over to Alyssa, who hurried inside with him. Hayley waited. For instructions, Drew realized; she truly was as much a part of this team as anyone.

Quinn glanced at Drew. "Do they call the sheriff?"

"They notify me first. If they don't hear from me in five minutes, then they call them." He thought quickly. "Fastest response time ever was five minutes, it's usually closer to ten, fifteen if they're busy or spread thin."

"So they could possibly beat us there." He looked back to his fiancée, still talking rapid-fire. "Call Brett."

She nodded. "You want him there?"

"His call. Just want him to know we'll be there and why, in case we run afoul of the locals." He turned to Liam. "Go. I'll be rolling in two. Channel six."

Without a word Liam nodded and ran for his car, and was gone within seconds. Quinn glanced at Hayley, who stood waiting. "You want Cutter?"

She shook her head. "I'll lock down, and we'll be safe enough here. No reason to think Oliver has any idea about us. Besides, you might need him."

Quinn didn't argue, Drew noticed. He obviously trusted Hayley's judgment in the matter.

"Rafe's due in about fifteen," Quinn said. "Text him that you're on lockdown, so he comes straight in."

Hayley nodded. "Then we'll be safer than anyone else on the planet."

"Indeed," Quinn agreed. He gave her a swift kiss and headed for the larger blue SUV parked next to where Liam's had been. Drew followed. Quinn let Cutter in the back, then stopped.

"Stay here," he said.

"No," Drew said simply. Quinn blinked. Drew doubted he was used to people saying no to him in situations like this.

"Drew—"

"Is my family safe here?"

"Fort Knox," Quinn said. "And once Rafe gets here, they might as well be on the moon for anybody who tries to get to them."

"Then I'm coming. This is my livelihood, my job to defend."

"It's what we do. What we train to do."

"In my work, I hire the best I can, then leave them alone to do it. I'll do the same with you. Besides, I've the keys to get in, and the code to turn off the alarm."

"Wasting time," Quinn muttered, and gave in.

Seconds later the SUV was hurtling down the drive at an even faster pace than Liam's.

"You'll stay in the vehicle unless I say otherwise. And if it goes to hell, you do nothing more than call for help."

"Who?"

"What?"

"Who do I call?"

Quinn glanced at him. "Foxworth first. Hayley'll deal."

"Not your detective friend?"

"Only if shots are fired. And then Rafe will deal."

Drew had the feeling he was being assessed, tested. He kept his expression impassive, and merely nodded. Apparently it was the right choice, because Quinn nodded in turn.

"He's that good?" he asked as they reached the last road before the small district whose peace and quiet had just been shattered by the claxon of the alarm.

"He's the best," Quinn said, negotiating the turn. "Failure isn't in his lexicon. He'd die first."

Quinn's voice had taken a grim turn, and Drew gave him a sideways glance. "You mean that literally, don't you?"

"That he'd die first? Yes." His mouth tightened. "Sometimes I think he's looking for the chance."

Drew didn't know what to say to that. Obviously Quinn had a deep respect for the man, and that was telling. But it was clearly coupled with a deep worry as well. There had been a time, way back, when he'd felt the same way about Doug. When he'd worried about his careless little brother, feared he'd get hurt, or worse. But the constant barrage of denigration, insults, nasty tricks, and downright sabotage had turned off that brotherly caring before he'd finished high school and escaped.

He'd wondered, briefly, if Alyssa might be the saving of his brother. She was such an innocent when he'd first met her, so good and straight and smart that he couldn't picture them together. He'd thought surely she was smart enough to see through Doug's facade. But she was also barely more than a girl, with a teenager's ability to see what they wanted rather than what was. She—

"Is there anything in the office that will give him your home location?"

Drew suppressed a shudder and said evenly, "No." Quinn glanced at him. Drew shrugged. "It's the most obvious and findable place to start, if you're looking for me or mine. So I cleared any trace out after I learned Oliver had been released."

"Smart."

Fear, Drew thought. "My people know where we live, they've all been to the house, but they know not to say anything. They're good people."

"Sometimes good, honest people are the easiest to fool," Quinn said rather grimly as he made the last turn. "They can't believe people are really that devious until it's too late."

"But if he'd accomplished that, he wouldn't be breaking into the office, would he?"

Quinn shot him a sideways glance and said with a grin, "You really do catch on fast."

Funny how a compliment from this man he'd known such a short time was so heartening.

"On scene."

His useless thoughts were cut off by the slightly scratchy but quite intelligible sound of Liam's voice; the connection must be live and routed through the vehicle's speakers for driving.

"Copy."

Quinn didn't ask for a report, or if there was any sign, or even if the alarm was still going off, although the fact that there had been no sound of it in the background—or for that matter from here in the car—sort of answered that. Obviously, he trusted Liam to do as he was trained to do. He was beginning to see just what an efficient and skilled operation Foxworth was.

Drew realized suddenly that Quinn had never asked him where the office was. No doubt, he already knew.

"You've been here," he guessed.

Quinn nodded. "We did a recon, after we knew Oliver was in the area. Just in case."

"You leave nothing to chance, do you?"

"We control what things we can, so we can save our resources to adapt to things we can't."

Quinn pulled over just before the turn onto the narrow side street. Cutter was on his feet before the SUV even came to a stop. Quinn simultaneously hit a button below the dash that activated the lift gate in the back, and a green button on the overhead console.

"On scene," he said toward the speaker Drew now saw next to the button. "With Cutter," he added.

Sort of, Drew thought. The dog had leapt clear the moment the hatch had lifted enough, and had taken off at that same dead run toward the building just as Liam answered. He wondered if the dog had been here with Quinn, then realized he'd been with them practically since they'd learned Oliver was out. Maybe he scented Liam, Drew thought. That had to be how he knew.

"Copy. Clear so far. Which way?"

"He's en route from the north. I'll come in from the back."

"Copy."

"Civilian in the vehicle," he added.

"Afraid he'll shoot me by mistake?" Drew asked drily.

Quinn was already out of the car, but he looked back. "No. Afraid he might have to keep you here."

"I gave you my word."

For a split second Quinn stared at him, and Drew had that feeling again, of being assessed.

"Then give me the keys. And the code."

Drew wasn't happy, but he didn't hesitate. "Code is 64171." He pulled out his key ring and isolated two keys. "Big one's the main door, smaller one's my office. Been locking it lately, too."

Quinn nodded and was gone.

And the moment he was out of sight, and he sat there alone, feeling helpless and useless, Drew realized the promise he'd made might be harder to keep than he'd thought.

Alyssa paced restlessly. She couldn't seem to stop it, although she'd tried several times to sit down and stay.

Luke was edgy, but not wildly so. She'd told him the burglar alarm had gone off at his dad's work, and they were going to check. His eyes had widened at that, but before he could think too much and get scared, she'd added, "It's probably some critter. Remember that big ol' raccoon that set the one off at home, checking for more pie?"

Luke had laughed at the memory of the fresh apple pie that had been cooling on a windowsill, drawing the curious—and hungry—little raider. And when Hayley had set him up with a game of birds crashing into pigs in helmets he'd settled in happily. That had been twenty minutes ago, twenty minutes punctuated by occasional yelps of triumph and groans of defeat.

And growing anxiety on her part.

"They'll let us know?" she asked.

"Of course," Hayley said. "It will be fine, Alyssa. Quinn and Liam will handle it."

"I wish Drew had stayed here."

"From what I've seen and learned, he wouldn't be much

for staying here while somebody else does what he feels responsible for."

Alyssa sighed. "No. No, he wouldn't."

"Lucky for you."

She said it evenly, not a trace of inflection in her voice. Yet Alyssa still felt as if she had to explain.

"Believe me, I see the irony of it." She smiled wryly. "All the things Doug used to taunt Drew for, the things he hated about him, are the same things that saved us, and have kept us safe and protected all this time."

"You're not looking through the eyes of a seventeen-year-old any longer," Hayley said.

"Neither was Doug. He was twenty-four when he was killed. But he never looked at Drew as anything but his pain-in-the-ass big brother, who always tried to show him up."

"Maybe," Hayley said, gently this time, "you've grown up more than Doug ever did. Having a child will do that."

Alyssa looked over at Luke, who was still engrossed in his game. "Yes. You realize life is about something bigger than just yourself."

"Maybe Doug would have, given more time."

"Maybe," she agreed. And realized with a little shock that she had somehow come to accept the immaturity of the man who had fathered her son. But then, it would be impossible not to see when she compared him to Drew.

But the rest… No, she couldn't accept that. She couldn't believe Doug had intended to just abandon her, leave her alone, broke and pregnant. Yes, that had been the end re-sult, but she clung to that hope, that his intent had been to help them, to take care of them, as if it would somehow make things right.

The memories flooded her, of lying weak and helpless in a hospital bed, trying to fight off the infection that had flattened her. Needles dripped fluid and drugs into her while, in the brief periods of wakeful lucidity, she worried frantically about Luke. The thought of her sweet little boy in foster care, or worse, in some grim government facility somewhere, spiked her worry into panic, which made it all the more difficult to fight.

"The day I woke up in the hospital and Drew was there," she said, barely aware she was speaking aloud, "and he looked at me and said it would be okay. He just held my hand and said to let him take care of everything, he would get Luke back, and I knew he meant it. And that he would. That he could, because he was so solid and respectable."

"And what did you feel then?"

"Relief. Gratitude."

"So even then, even sick, you saw the value of all the things Doug had always denied."

Alyssa blinked. She'd never thought of it quite that way, but Hayley's quiet words made it so clear she wondered that she hadn't.

"Yes." She sighed. "I didn't even find out until about six months later, when I finally worked up the nerve to call about the bill, that he'd even taken care of that. I wondered why they hadn't been sending me notices. He'd been paying them every month until it was clear."

"And he never told you? Didn't want you to worry?"

"He said he didn't want me to feel like I owed him."

"But you did feel that way."

"How could I not? He swept in like that shining knight and took care of everything. I've never felt more useless, but it was better than how hopeless I'd been feeling. And I had my son."

"So you married him."

"It gave him legal standing to do all that fast and efficiently," she said. "And it didn't matter. Doug was dead, and I was certain I'd never love anybody like that again, so what difference did it make?"

"You *were* certain? As in you're not now?"

"The only thing I'm certain of now, is that I have no idea what love really is," she said wryly.

"Except for Luke."

She glanced over at her son, still happily, determinedly playing, having successfully tuned out everything else.

"Yes," she agreed softly. "Except for Luke."

"And Drew."

It wasn't what Hayley said that threw her, it was probably a natural question. It was that it hadn't really been a question at all. She'd sounded as certain as Alyssa was uncertain. That she loved Drew as well as Luke.

"I don't… I mean, it's not like that, I—"

"Foxworth copy?"

A deep male voice issued from the unique cell phone beside Hayley. Alyssa didn't recognize it, but Hayley picked it up instantly.

Just be grateful for the timing, she told herself. And that it wasn't Quinn or Liam or Drew, calling for help.

She wondered if she would ever feel safe again, with Baird Oliver running loose.

Chapter 21

"Foxworth here," Hayley said into the phone that obviously also served as a walkie-talkie of sorts. She'd heard them call it a comlink.

"Hayley." The same, deep voice came back. "Status?"

"We're fine here."

"How many?"

"Three. Six-year-old boy and his mother. We're in the top-floor meeting room."

The Foxworth room with a view, Alyssa thought, glancing out the expansive window, finding herself watching for eagles despite everything.

"Cutter?" the deep voice asked.

"With Quinn."

"Copy."

"Where are you?"

"Perimeter."

"Coming in?"

"In a few."

The connection went silent. Hayley put down the phone. At first Alyssa had been simply grateful for the interruption at a difficult moment, but now she was curious.

"I gather," Alyssa said, "that was the famous Rafe?"

"Yes."

"Does he talk more in person?"

Hayley grinned. "Some, but not much. He's Quinn's oldest friend. They've known each other since they were kids, and Quinn says he's never been talkative. He's been in Washington, D.C., working on something…personal for us. But now he's back, and outside making sure we're secure."

"Does he do that every time he comes back from somewhere?"

"No. But he knows the basics of the situation."

"Those texts you sent."

Hayley nodded. "I knew he'd get them as soon as he got off the plane."

"I didn't hear a car on the gravel."

"Our approach alarm, you mean?" Hayley said with another grin.

"Yes." Alyssa smiled back. She had to admit, it was hard to stay stressed around this woman. She seemed so calm, so confident. But then, she supposed it would take that kind of woman to hold a man like Quinn in such thrall. Or had being with Quinn changed her into this self-assured, capable person?

If it worked that way for her, she thought with an inward grimace, she'd be a confident, straight-arrow, respected and solid member of the community, instead of Drew Kiley's quiet, reclusive and touchy wife.

"He probably parked down the road a bit. When you do hear his car on the gravel, he'll have already checked every inch of the grounds."

"And he's really…a sniper?"

Hayley's smile was understanding this time. "Yeah, it

spooked me a little, too. But if you're going to fight the good fight, you need warriors."

"I never thought you'd be needing them for this."

"We adapt as the situation changes. Quinn's big on that. He says staying locked on a plan when the rules have changed is going to leave you dead in that box you can't think outside of." Alyssa blinked. Hayley laughed. "He says it that way on purpose."

"Breaking the grammar rules to show you have to adapt to the situation?"

"Exactly."

"Foxworth," Alyssa said, "is rather amazing."

"Because Quinn is amazing." The love that echoed in her voice warmed Alyssa at the same time it set up an ache inside her, a sort of longing she'd been feeling more and more lately. "As is Drew," she added.

Alyssa tried to smile at the compliment, but they were back in that awkward place again. Although Hayley didn't seem to sense it, which was odd, considering how perceptive she seemed about everything else. But once again she was saved by that voice on the phone. She was becoming very favorably disposed toward liking Rafer Crawford, before she'd even met him.

"Coming in," the voice said.

"Copy, Rafe."

Seconds later Alyssa heard the door below open. Then, after a moment, footsteps on the stairs. And it suddenly, belatedly occurred to her that there had been a reason Hayley had brought them up to the third floor instead of staying on the more comfortable, homey first; there was plenty of warning if someone else came through that door.

She fastened her gaze on the woman with the meadow-green eyes. "What would you do if someone else was breaking in?"

Hayley smiled, a different sort of smile. "Quinn's seen to some training for me, too," was all she said. And Alyssa wondered if that was where the quiet air of confidence came from. If you were prepared for any situation, then you couldn't be scared of it when it happened, right?

She didn't have time to analyze that thought before the man on the stairs reached the top and stepped into the room.

Rafe Crawford didn't look anything like she'd thought he would. She'd expected a slight variation on Quinn, she supposed. And while he was as tall as his boss, he was leaner, rangier. And while Quinn's eyes were a cool, almost icy-blue except when he looked at Hayley, this man's were dark gray, and intense in an entirely different way that reminded her, oddly, of Cutter. But there were shadows there as well, the kind of thing she didn't think could be chalked up solely to whatever had caused the limp she'd noticed when he walked in. His face was lean, rugged, and impassive.

A hard man, she thought. A fierce one.

His arrival had distracted even Luke, and the boy was staring at him, wide-eyed. Alyssa wondered what those young eyes saw in this formidable man. The boy relaxed a little as Hayley went to the newcomer, throwing her arms around him in a welcoming hug. The man tensed instantly, but as he looked down at the woman greeting him the tension drained away visibly. And his arms came around her in an echoing hug.

"Welcome home," Hayley said, almost fiercely.

One corner of the man's mouth lifted in a tiny smile that was almost wistful. And Alyssa realized with a little shock that even that little change in expression changed her entire impression of him. Rafer Crawford might be a fierce man, but he wasn't that way by nature. He was a man who had been made that way by life. A life that probably made hers look like the proverbial picnic.

Ending the hug at last, they started across the room. Hayley watched him take a half-dozen steps before she stopped. He stopped beside her automatically. She asked softly, "Long plane ride?"

The man's face went impassive again. "It's fine."

"Uh-huh." Hayley looked at him assessingly. "Let me guess. You didn't get up and walk on the plane."

He shrugged. "More than once or twice and people start getting nervous these days."

"So your leg stiffened up."

"It's fine now."

"That's why the long perimeter check."

"Needed doing."

"And…you're angry."

Finally, his mouth quirked again. "Some would say that's a given every day."

"They don't know you. I do. And I know you'd rather he let you take care of it."

"Another week and I would have had the guy in my sights." He reached out to put a hand on her shoulder, and Alyssa could tell from her reaction it wasn't a gesture he made often. "He nearly got both of you killed."

"Believe me, I remember. But Quinn has his reasons."

"Yes." Rafe let out a compressed breath. "And I wouldn't have taken that damned order to stand down from anybody else."

She smiled up at him. "I know," she said softly.

Belatedly Alyssa realized what she was watching. Foxworth wasn't just a Foundation put together by two surviving members of a family, it was an extended family carefully built and tended. She had the feeling this man would indeed die to protect anyone Foxworth. And for a moment she envied them all.

"Besides," Hayley said, "we need you back here for the wedding."

Rafe gave her a look that was the oddest combination of smile and grimace Alyssa had ever seen. "It's not too late," he said.

"Not a chance. You're Quinn's best man and he's not changing his mind."

"The rest, okay, but he really wants to trust me to give a toast? In front of all those people?"

"It could be worse. If we'd gone with Charlie's guest list, it'd be three times as many."

For an instant Alyssa saw that wistful look flash in his eyes again, but before she could analyze that Hayley turned to her.

"I apologize," she said, "but he's been gone for nearly a month."

"I understand," Alyssa said quickly.

"Rafe, this is Alyssa Kiley." Alyssa held out her hand and, after a moment, Rafe took it. It was a strong, roughened hand, the hand of a man who worked. Hard, physical work. Like Drew's hands.

"And this," Hayley said, gesturing to where Luke was now standing beside the table where he'd been sitting, still watching the new arrival warily, "is Luke."

"Luke," Rafe said. He couldn't crouch down just now, as most men did when confronted with a small child, Alyssa realized. But he bent and held out his hand much as she had. After a split second Luke solemnly took it and shook it firmly. Alyssa doubted anyone else could see it, but she could tell her son was pleased by the adult gesture.

"What's wrong with your leg?" Luke asked. Alyssa winced at the little-boy bluntness.

"Luke, you shouldn't—"

Rafe waved her to silence. "No. It's all right. I prefer an honest question to all the sideways looks and whispered speculation." He turned back to Luke. "It got hurt, badly, a long time ago. If I have to sit still for a long time, like on an airplane, it hurts more for a while."

"Oh. Will it ever get better and not hurt anymore?"

"No."

Luke frowned. "That's bad."

"It's not good," Rafe agreed. "But they wanted to cut it off."

"Your leg?" Alyssa winced as the boy's eyes widened. But Luke had started this, so he should learn about asking questions when the answers might not be pleasant. At least, that's what Drew would say.

Rafe nodded.

"Wow," Luke said, looking down at his own sturdy little legs. "That would be really bad."

"And really bad is worse than just bad."

Luke nodded, a little fervently.

Rafe straightened. "Thus ends our lesson in priorities for the day. As you were."

"I know what that means," Luke said excitedly. "Teague told me. It means go back to what I was doing."

"Exactly."

The boy did, seemingly happily.

"That's the most I've heard him talk about it since I've known him," Hayley whispered to Alyssa.

"I'm glad he didn't get mad," Alyssa whispered back.

"At a child? No. Not Rafe."

"It was good of you to indulge Luke," Alyssa said as Rafe came back. "It was a pretty rude question."

"It was honest curiosity," he said with a half shrug. "Can't fault that." He turned to Hayley. "How long have they been gone?"

"Twenty-two minutes."

Alyssa blinked at the exact answer.

"Eight to go," Rafe said.

Alyssa wondered what the half-hour mark meant to them. Time to send in help? And had it really only been twenty-two minutes? It seemed longer. Hayley was remarkably calm, given her fiancé was out there, maybe confronting that nasty piece of work that was Baird Oliver.

But then, so was Drew.

She shivered. She'd always thought of Drew as nearly

indestructible. But even the strongest rock would eventually crumble in time. What if they lost him? She'd wondered this before, but only in the context that someday he might get tired of supporting them. That he might someday leave them, like Doug had. He was so solid, so strong, she'd never thought about something actually happening to him.

They'd be all right financially—he'd told her they'd be taken care of. She remembered something about life insurance for both them and the company. But despite her experience with being broke and living on the edge, it wasn't that that rattled her now.

She simply couldn't imagine her life without Drew there. Without Drew to help her with Luke, without him there for Luke to look up to and emulate. She'd encouraged that, even realizing she was encouraging him to take a different path than his natural father. And she wasn't sure when she'd decided the carefree and careless life Doug had chosen wasn't good enough for Luke.

She wasn't sure if she even had decided, or if it was just so obvious now that it was no decision at all. But somewhere along the line she'd admitted, at least to herself, that Drew's was a better way. A tiny spike of guilt stabbed through her. Was it a betrayal of Doug to raise his son to be more like the brother he'd hated? She quashed it. Luke was what mattered, and there was no way she could encourage him down a path that could lead to an end like Doug's.

She looked over at Luke, where he was bent over the video game. He'd already dealt with so much in his young life, and Drew had made it all seem only a bad memory. Luke had blossomed under his care, she couldn't deny that. He would be devastated to lose the man he called, rightfully, Dad.

What she could deny, what she had to deny right now, was how devastated she would be.

Chapter 22

"Thanks, Marcy," Drew said. "Sorry the alarm disturbed your evening."

"Oh, that's all right," the woman who ran the real estate office said with a smile. "Whoever set it off could have come here if it hadn't scared him off. I just wish I'd seen him so I could tell you what he looked like."

Drew opened his mouth to assure her it was nothing, then realized that perhaps she should keep on thinking it was something. He thanked his business neighbor again, and headed back toward the street. He could see the single sheriff's unit sitting down the street in front of the two-story, gray building that was the office for Kiley Construction. It was a converted house, as were all of the half-dozen businesses on the street, courtesy of his father's foresight years ago, realizing their little town was growing and would need a larger business district. It gave the area a friendly feel he and the townspeople liked.

The small green space at the end of the street drew even

more people, especially those who'd just made a purchase at the bakery on the corner and wanted to use the benches Drew and his father had installed, or look at the various sculptures they'd acquired over the years from local artists and craftsmen. It had turned out to be a good use of that oddly shaped bit of land. He was proud that had been his idea, and that his father, doubtful at first, had finally told him it was brilliant.

But it also gave a lot of cover to an intruder with burglary on his mind. Not something they normally had to worry about here. And hopefully never again, after this was over, he thought. Then he spotted Cutter trotting toward him. The dog came to a halt and sat, looking dejected. Quinn was right behind him.

"You were supposed to stay in the car."

"I did, until Marcy came outside. She runs the real estate office two doors down and was working late. I was afraid she might walk into something."

Quinn studied him for a moment, then nodded. "Good call," he said. Drew felt oddly pleased by the praise. He was out of his element, and man enough to admit it, but having Quinn agree he'd done the right thing eased the discomfiture a bit.

"No sign of him?"

"Only this, maybe. This look familiar to you?" He held out a plastic bag with a small piece of green fabric.

Drew took it, then looked back at Quinn's face.

"Where'd this come from?"

"Cutter found it on a blackberry bush just outside the back fence. Can't be sure it's connected."

Drew looked at the piece of heavy green cloth. Turned the bag over. The fabric looked different on one side than the other. Treated somehow. Waterproofed, most likely.

"It's the same color as the jacket he had on the day I chased him," he said. "But it's not a rare color around here."

Quinn nodded. "We'll hang on to it." He put it into his

pocket. "If you find something, the deputy will make a report and we'll hand this over."

"You didn't find anything?" Drew asked.

"Appears secure," Quinn answered, "I don't think he got in, but we'll need you to take a look. Deputy's just waiting for that."

They were at the foot of the walkway when Liam emerged from the trees between the office and the park. "There's a hideout," the young man said when he got to them. "He was there for a while, waiting. There's a plastic tarp there that might have some evidence on it. I left it in place."

"You mean he was watching?" Drew asked, a chill creeping over him. "From where?"

Liam gestured behind him. "About twenty feet back in. Probably waited until you left this evening. At least that's what Cutter indicated."

Drew barely blinked, such had his faith in the dog grown even in this short time. "Did he?"

Quinn nodded. "He knows who we're looking for. He ignored the old man we came across gathering downed wood, just made a beeline through the trees."

Quinn looked at Liam. "Where did Cutter lose the trail?"

"Backside of those trees. There's a stream there, with a wooden walkway next to it."

"It's a salmon stream. Protected. We built the walkway as part of the development," Drew said. "It goes out to the street below."

Liam nodded. "Cutter tracked him to the end, where there's a small parking area. One car there, probably the old guy's. Cutter cued on a spot near the road, but the way he was acting I'd say our guy was long gone."

"He probably took off the moment the alarm went off," Quinn said.

"Why would he risk it?" Drew asked. "There's a sign about the alarm out front."

"Maybe he thinks you've got that cash stashed in there," Liam said.

"After more than three years?" Drew shook his head.

"I wouldn't put a guy with his record of petty thefts, robbery and drugs in the smart category," Quinn said. "But I'd say it was more likely he was looking for something else."

Drew knew what he meant. "You mean he's looking for where we live. That's why you asked before if there was anything here."

Quinn didn't try to reassure him with a lie. "Yes."

"He's hunting us," Drew said. Anger was finally beginning to grow, thawing the chill with its heat.

"Seems likely," Quinn agreed. "Let's check the building, and then we'll go over our options."

Drew walked around the outside, checking every door and window. He was about to pronounce it untouched when he noticed a small, narrow dent in one of the windowsills.

"That's new," he said, gesturing at the depression that hadn't even quite broken the trim paint.

"And that window's alarmed?"

He nodded. "It's the file room. Permits, plans, EPA reports, going back years."

Quinn glanced around. "And it's out of sight of everyone except people in the park, whose view is obscured by the trees."

"Yes," Drew agreed, the anger uppermost now. "If I hadn't left early, if I'd been here, maybe I could have—"

"He probably wouldn't have tried at all," Quinn said. He glanced around, then pointed at the small sign with the alarm company's name. "I noticed you don't have any signs or stickers advertising the alarm at home."

"Lyss didn't want them. She thought it would just be advertising we had something worth stealing."

"She has a point. It could be a toss-up," Quinn said. "I gather you didn't tell her the real reason? That you knew Oliver was getting out?"

Drew gave the man a rather sheepish smile. "No. We'd been getting along really well, and I didn't want to mess that up."

Quinn only nodded, as if he understood. Drew doubted that; the man had a woman who loved him so much it made the air between them practically crackle. Envy spiked through him. He didn't like the feeling.

"Would paying him get rid of him?"

Drew's blunt question was the first thing he'd said since he'd told Alyssa what had happened at the office. They'd been there awhile. Quinn had explained once the deputy had seen the hide Cutter found, and the pry mark Drew had spotted, he'd become seriously interested and obviously moved it out of the category of false alarm to attempted burglary. A call from Detective Dunbar had only cemented his attitude.

"Dunbar seems to think we know what we're doing," Quinn had said. Now he answered Drew's question. "For a while. But judging by my experience, if he gets easy money out of you once, he'll be back."

Alyssa sighed inwardly. Quinn was right, she knew. Baird would never give up an easy source of cash. Easier than robbing convenience stores, anyway.

Drew walked over to the window and stared out across the clearing toward the trees. She watched him, standing there, tall, strong, determined. Then he turned halfway back, and the light coming through the window washed over him, and she saw the tension in him, the tightness of his eyes, his jaw.

She'd done this to him, she thought. It was her life, her past coming back to haunt him, to drive him.

"I'm sorry," she whispered, almost unaware she'd said it out loud.

Drew spun around the rest of the way.

"What?"

"This is my fault. I brought this down on us. On you. I—"

Drew was there in an instant, crouching before her. "You did not. This is Doug's doing. He hooked up with this guy. If anybody brought this on us, it's him."

For once she didn't argue with him. She realized it was because she was so relieved he didn't blame her, in fact was defending her. And that realization made her...not uneasy but aware that something fundamental had changed. When had Drew's opinion of her become more important than preserving Doug's memory?

He put his hand over hers, and only then did she notice hers was icy cold. Instinctively she curled her fingers around his, realizing only now the strength she always took from his touch.

"Drew," she whispered.

His head came up as she spoke the name. His expression changed, shifted as if under a whole new kind of tension. She felt something odd, some tenuous connection between them, new and strange.

"Options," Quinn said briskly, snapping her back to the matter at hand.

Drew seemed as reluctant as she to give up this tentative link. But after a moment he moved. But he sat beside her this time, not the usual two feet away. That change alone somehow had the power to rattle her.

"First option," Quinn said, "you leave town. Go someplace safe until we or law enforcement round this guy up."

"Good idea," Drew said. "You and Luke can...take a vacation somewhere."

She was considering it, picturing selling it to Luke as a family trip, until he said it that way. "What about you?"

"I'm not going anywhere until this is resolved."

"And we're not going anywhere without you."

Drew blinked. Looked surprised. She was a little surprised herself at her own vehemence. The tenuous new bond she sensed grew, tightened. He was looking at her so intensely she found herself scrambling for something, anything, to say.

"Luke feels safe with you."

Something changed in his expression then, the bond between them seemed to evaporate. She didn't understand; he loved Luke as if he were his own. But somehow saying that then had been the wrong thing.

Or the right thing, she thought, if she wanted things to stay as they were.

But did she?

"If Luke's welfare is our primary concern, which it is," Hayley said, "then I agree you should all stay together. Luke needs his father with him. He needs his family. So if you go, you should go together."

Drew scowled. "I want them safe. But I want to help take this guy down. He's threatening my *family,* damn it."

Drew, she realized, was angry. More, he was furious. He so rarely got angry, really angry, it startled her to realize he was there and had been for a while now.

"Well," Quinn said, rather mildly after Drew's outburst, "I did say that was option one. Option two is we continue as we are. We've got Rafe back in the mix now, and as soon as Teague's back from checking on that rental car, that's full coverage 24/7, with somebody left to go hunting."

Drew perked up at that. "About time he was on the receiving end," he muttered.

"Agreed. We can see to that." He looked at Drew consideringly. "If we don't turn him up, then we may have to go to option three."

"I was wondering if there was one," Drew said.

"Option three is we keep Luke someplace safe but local—with Cutter to rip the throat out of anyone who tries to hurt him—but you keep to your normal routine, maybe even become a bit more visible, see if Oliver makes a move."

Drew didn't even blink, just nodded calmly. Alyssa

stared at him, then looked back to Quinn. With an effort she kept her voice level.

"This is my responsibility," she said. "If anyone's going to act as bait to lure Baird out, it should be me."

"I told you, Lyss, this is not your fault," Drew said, somewhat urgently.

"If not for me, Baird Oliver wouldn't be here."

"You don't know that. He's blaming Doug for losing his share of the money, maybe he would have decided to come get it out of me anyway."

She hadn't thought of that. And from what she knew of Baird, it wasn't an unlikely idea.

"But he'd be more likely to come after me. I'm just a helpless female, after all."

"Helpless my ass," Drew said. "You'd take on a wolverine with a feather duster to protect Luke."

Alyssa blinked at the outlandish analogy. And stared at him, feeling impossibly warmed by not only his words but the confident tone of them.

"Yes, I would. But he doesn't know that. He knows only who I was, the quiet, submissive shadow of Doug's, who always did what he said, even if it got me into trouble." She met his gaze straight on. "He has no reason to think I've changed."

"Whereas I know you have."

In that moment she wanted more than anything else to throw her arms around him and hug him with the fierceness that was welling up inside her at his defense of her.

And she realized, not with fanfare or shock, but with a quiet awareness, as if it had been there for a long time just waiting for her to notice, that the good opinion of Drew Kiley meant more to her than anything except her son's love.

Chapter 23

They compromised, in the end, on a combination of two and three. They would continue as they were for forty-eight hours, and if by then they didn't have Oliver wrapped up, they would move to option three.

Drew wasn't happy, but he knew there wasn't much he could do about it. His will to keep his promise to let Foxworth do what they did was beginning to fray. And he was having a little trouble balancing the urge to break it and hunt Oliver down himself, and the urge to do as Quinn had first suggested and take Alyssa and Luke and get them out of there.

He'd never wanted to run from trouble before.

But he'd never wanted to protect anyone so much before, either.

It had been a long day. An unsettling day. He was still wrestling with the decision of whether to keep the office open at all. They only had one project going at the moment, a large one down in Port Orchard, far enough away that people weren't coming into the office first as they usually did. His crew didn't know exactly what was going on, but they knew he was dealing with something, and had stepped up to give him the time he needed.

First thing he was going to do when he got back to work when this was all over was look and see if he could afford to give the guys a bonus. But right now, he was just wishing that moment would come soon. Real soon.

Alyssa was upstairs organizing Luke's bath, under the watchful eye of Cutter. While the entire house was under the watchful eye of Rafer Crawford. Now that was a guy who'd make you think twice before doing damned near anything, Drew thought. Unlike Quinn and Teague's brisk, military sharpness, or Liam's boyish, Texas charm, Rafe's demeanor was quiet, almost withdrawn, and yet he managed to unsettle you with just a look. The man had seen things, done things, that Drew could only imagine. He wasn't even sure how he knew that, but he did. He would not want to cross Rafe Crawford.

And he was very glad he was on their side.

The man had declined the offer of shelter inside. It was dry enough tonight, and he worked better with some room around him, he'd said. Drew suspected he just preferred not to be that close to people, although he was polite enough, and good-humored with Luke.

As long as he kept his family safe, Drew thought, he'd put up with a lot worse than the man's reticence. Liam would take over early in the morning, Quinn had said, until Teague arrived. Drew noticed Quinn didn't say who would then become the hunter he'd mentioned.

Too restless to settle, Drew went upstairs. Cutter was stationed in the hallway outside the bathroom door, lying upright, watchful. The dog looked over his shoulder at him, but went back to sentry duty immediately. Drew could just glimpse Luke, half into his pajamas, protesting as Alyssa dried his hair with a towel.

"Don't rub so hard, Mom!"

"Sorry, sweetie. I didn't mean to."

It was the simplest of exchanges between a mother and son, yet it filled Drew with an emotion that was almost painful. He loved them so much. Both of them. And the thought of them in danger was beyond wrenching.

He wondered if her parents would change their tune now, knowing she and the grandson they'd never met could be in trouble. Probably not, he thought. They'd probably say she'd brought this on herself, by hooking up with the likes of his brother. There had been a time when he would have said that himself.

As if triggered by his thoughts, Luke spoke again, abruptly.

"Why is all this weird stuff happening?"

Drew tensed. "Weird?" Alyssa asked.

"It's because of my father, isn't it? My real father?"

Drew had thought he was long past the jab of pain when Luke said that phrase. *My real father.* The boy had no idea how it stung. He was just a kid, he had no intent to hurt.

Quit whining about your feelings and focus on what mattered. How had the boy put that together? He was smart, Drew knew that, but they'd been careful. How had he realized that this upending of his life had something to do with Doug?

Alyssa wrapped the towel around her son and pulled him close. "Your *real* father is here in this house, Luke Kiley. The man who's given you—and me—everything, the man who saved us, the man who takes care of us, who's there for us every step of the way."

Drew felt nearly weak in the knees. He'd never heard her say anything like that to Luke, she had always responded to his remarks about his father with a defense of Doug. Never him.

"Because he loves us," Luke said.

Drew held his breath. Waited. Did she know? Had he betrayed it in these crazed, up and down, terrifying days?

"Don't ever forget how much he loves you," Alyssa said after a moment, dodging the plural as she helped the boy pull on the top of his pajamas, emblazoned with images of his favorite comic superhero. "He's your father in every sense of the word but one, and that's the one that matters least."

Drew almost stepped back, out of sight. But something made him stay, and when Alyssa stood up and turned, the sudden color that flooded her cheeks told him she knew he'd overheard. There was a look in her eyes, something that pulled at him, made him glad he'd stayed. And something else, he noticed with a little shock.

She wasn't wearing the necklace.

He shoved down the surge of hope that rose, hope he'd thought long dead.

They put Luke to bed together, something that pleased the boy so much he went to sleep with a smile on his face. Alyssa left the door to his room partly ajar, just enough for Cutter to get in and out.

"Not that I'm not convinced he couldn't open it himself if he had to," she said.

Drew laughed. "Me, either. That's the most undog dog I've ever seen."

"Hayley says every time she gets to thinking he's some mystical spirit in a dog's body, he rolls around in some mud or something dead to remind her he's just a dog."

He chuckled.

"They're quite something, those Foxworth folks," she said.

"Yes."

"Makes you wonder, doesn't it? If it was just by accident they found Luke that day?"

"I'm just glad they did."

They'd reached her door to the master bedroom, which

he'd given her from the beginning. It was always an awkward moment, one he usually tried to avoid by staying up later than she, or if he was tired, going to bed earlier in the room down the hall. Here they were, a couple married for three years, going to separate bedrooms, as they always did. The two times they—mostly he—had lapsed and had what he'd sourly thought of as obligation sex, it had been downstairs, in a hurry, almost furtively. They'd never shared a bedroom or even a bed.

He'd known that was what it was even as it happened. The first time it had caught him off guard. The second time he'd known full well she was only offering because she felt she owed him, and he'd been angry with himself for not being able to resist. But by then he'd admitted he was falling for her, this woman who was so different than the moonstruck girl he'd remembered. And his resistance had crumbled.

It wasn't that it hadn't been good. It had been very good. At least, as good as it could be when they were doing it for all the wrong reasons. But he hadn't liked the way he'd felt after, and had sworn from then on he'd not weaken again.

"I meant what I said in there, Drew," Alyssa said softly, snapping him out of thoughts that had perversely managed to arouse rather than quash his response to her presence and the proximity of a choice of beds.

He didn't know what to say, so said nothing.

"You are his father. In every sense that matters. That's never been clearer than now."

"Is that what this is about? What's happening now?"

"No. It's about who you are. And who Doug wasn't."

Drew sucked in a breath. He'd given up hoping to ever hear something like this from her. Had Foxworth accomplished what he'd never been able to?

She was looking up at him, studying him with an intensity that set him on edge. What was she seeing, thinking? Sometimes he felt like he'd spent most of his damn life trying to figure that out. If crisis brought out the real person, then maybe he had no idea who she was after all.

"Drew?"

"I don't know what you want me to say." He felt helpless, a little lost staring down into those wide blue eyes. And he was damned tired of feeling helpless. "I don't know what you want, period."

"I do. For the first time in a long time, there's something I want, something more than just my son's well-being."

Drew swallowed tightly. "What?"

"You."

Chapter 24

It wasn't particularly flattering, Alyssa thought, that his first reaction was wariness. Oh, the fire was there, she could see it deep down in his eyes, but he kept it so at bay it was barely visible.

And why not? she told herself. She was the one who'd insisted on this sexless arrangement. The two times it had happened had been practically accidental, a sort of collision at a weak moment for both of them, and she couldn't blame him without blaming herself. For the most part, he'd kept his word.

Of course he had, he was Drew. He always kept his word. It had taken her a while to see that. She had assumed she'd have to be fighting him off even as she laughed at the idea of anyone wanting the thin, sickly-looking thing she'd become.

But she'd wondered, in the two years since she'd been completely well again, since she'd regained her strength—under, she added silently, Drew's careful tending—why he'd never tried. At first she thought he still saw her as weak, sick, and he wouldn't take advantage.

Doug would have. That had been the first shocking realization of the upside to the differences between them. Doug would have wanted what he wanted. He would have been more careful than usual, perhaps, more gentle, but in general Doug was a lover who took.

While Drew kept his word.

She wasn't sure what he'd done, he was a young, strong man with a man's appetites, but he'd kept to their agreement. Once that had been a relief to her, the thought that he'd gone elsewhere for those needs. Now, the idea was painful, something she knew she had no right to feel. And that alone should have been a clarion call of warning, but she had stubbornly clung to the idealistic vision of Doug as her soul mate, the only one she would ever have.

While Drew was just the man who kept his word.

The moment of realization had sliced at her like a double-edged blade. She hadn't wanted to come back here with Drew because he was everything Doug hated, yet those very things were what kept her and Luke safe. She'd been too weak and sick to have any other choice at the time, but now that she did, she couldn't imagine leaving. And if she was honest with herself, it wasn't just for Luke.

She'd been so young and foolish with Doug. Only after they'd run off together had she realized there was always a cost for that kind of life, and she had usually been the one to pay it. Someone had to bring in money, so she was the one with a part-time, low wage job. Someone had to make the little money last, so they could eat, had a roof, and the task always seemed to fall to her.

Sometimes Doug would bring home a wad of bills that always seemed to look like more than it was when counted. He would give her part of it, in a great show of generosity, although he kept most of it for himself. "A guy's got to have some fun now and then," he'd told her.

Her fun had never been mentioned. It was Doug's life-style that had to be maintained. And now she didn't just shudder to think of what he'd spent that money on, she shuddered to think how he'd gotten it in the first place.

"Don't," Drew said, snapping her out of her painful memories. "Don't say things you don't really mean."

There was an undertone of something in his voice that made her breath stop. A tightness, an edge, something.

Heat. That, too. In his voice, and in his eyes as he looked at her.

"But I do mean it," she said softly. "I've only just realized I've meant it for a while now."

"Lyss—"

She put a hand on his chest, over his heart, and his words cut off as if her action had sucked the very air out of him. She could feel the thud of his heart, felt a skip in her own heartbeat as his accelerated at her touch.

"Drew," she said, not sure what more to say to convince him.

And she was going to need to, she thought when he found his voice again. "You're just reacting to this, all the stress. It's fogging things up."

"In a way, it is reaction," she said, not denying it. "But sometimes stress has a way of making you see what's really important."

"You're scared for Luke—"

"I am. But he feels safe with you." She drew in a deep breath. "And so do I."

He made a low sound, almost a groan. It rumbled up from down deep in his chest, and she could feel the vibration of it under her fingers. She moved, stroking the taut muscles beneath his shirt.

"It's the circumstances, Lyss," he said, sounding almost desperate now.

In fact, this growing need was driven by so many factors, she didn't know how to deal with it. Maybe the circumstances were one of them, but they weren't the most important. She was sure of that.

"No," she said. "It's more like how you know what to grab when a fire's coming. You know what's most important. Sometimes it takes that kind of stress for you to realize."

"Lyss."

He said it softly, but he was shaking his head. She gave herself a moment to take pleasure in the nickname only he had ever used; to Doug she had been the more common Ally, which he too often linked with "cat" in a way that made Alyssa wonder if he'd really meant it as a compliment.

And then she took matters into her own hands.

She'd known she would have to. He would never assume—she would have to make it clear she wanted to change the rules. She knew she was risking the quiet peace they'd achieved until the morning the old tensions had flared up and sent Luke running. That nothing would ever be the same after this.

But nothing would ever be the same if she didn't.

"I never thought I would want again, Drew. But I want you. Now."

She sensed the moment when he gave in. She felt a fleeting sense of triumph as his arms came around her; she had breached the will of the strongest man she'd ever known. She nearly laughed with the joy of it as he pushed through the bedroom door and shoved them closed behind them.

But then he was kissing her, and all thought of any sort of victory was shattered. There was no finesse in this, none of Drew's usual reticence. His mouth was on hers, demanding, as if her words had breached not his will but a dam that had been holding this back for years.

Her last sane thought before the fire erupted, sweeping her up in the inferno with a speed that left her breathless, was to wonder if it could really make that much difference, coming to this willingly, even eagerly, as opposed to the sense of obligation she'd felt before.

The answer came to her in a wild leap of heat and sensation, surging through her so fiercely she could feel every muscle ripple as it passed. Everything she'd known, everything she'd thought she knew about this was blasted into irrecoverable pieces. She'd known nothing, she'd had no idea, no clue that it could be like this. Whatever she'd had with Doug, it was nothing, absolutely nothing compared to this. That was silly, girlish fantasy, often disappointing. This was raw, utterly real, and she was going to die if she didn't have him right now.

She clawed at his shirt, wanting him naked against her in a way she'd never thought herself capable of. For an instant he stopped, going rigidly still.

"Be sure, Alyssa. Be damned sure before we go one step further."

She took a half step back. Saw the first flicker of resignation begin in his expression. He thought she was changing her mind.

Instead she reached for the hem of her sweater and pulled it over her head. Saw the heat flash again in his eyes. And when she reached back to unfasten her bra Drew groaned, audibly this time.

He cupped her breasts as the bra slipped away. Lowered his head and kissed them. She forgot to breathe. She wanted more, she wanted it now, but she didn't have the breath to ask for it. As if he wanted that skin-to-skin contact as much as she did, he yanked off his own shirt.

He picked her up, easily, as if she weighed no more than Luke. She clung to him, kissing whatever she could reach, and the feel of hot, sleek skin over taut muscle was more than she could have imagined. Everything about this, everything about being with Drew was more than she could have imagined.

It made no sense that serious, solid Drew Kiley could

have this effect on her. She'd thought herself in love with his flippant, glib, smooth-talking brother. If that was true, if she'd been in love with Doug, she had no idea what this was. Except hotter, fiercer and more consuming than anything she'd even known.

And then they were on the bed, the bed she didn't think she could have reached on her own. It was suddenly so much smaller than it always seemed when she was here alone. She always told herself, on those long nights, that it was Doug she was missing.

Now she had the feeling it hadn't been that at all. It hadn't been that she was missing someone. She'd been wanting someone.

And he was with her now, and as with everything with Drew, it was different. As he'd made her feel safe and secure in life, he was teaching her something new here as well. Teaching her that she'd been sadly unaware of the heights her own body was capable of. His hands, his mouth, took her over. She thrilled to it, savoring every touch, every caress, until her body was fairly writhing, on the edge of overload even as she wanted more, ever more. And he gave her more, moving over her as if he were determined to commit her to memory, as if every curve, every line were crucial to his next breath.

She'd never felt so cosseted, and yet so ready to fly at the same time.

And he was ready. She could feel every masculine inch of him, hard, eager. Yes, he was more than ready, but held back. For what? she wondered foggily. Why was he waiting when her body was screaming for him?

Then she realized. This was Drew. Drew who gave, not took.

She reached for him, trying to pull him even closer. She tried to get enough air to speak, but a low moan was all that came out.

"Now?" His voice was harsh, almost as if he was in pain. If he was feeling as she was, she understood.

"Please," she whispered, the only word she could manage.

He moved, probing, and she reached to guide him. She felt her own readiness at the ease of it. And then he was there, sliding into her, filling her, and she cried out at the full, hot pleasure of it.

Drew groaned, a deep, rough sound that she felt even before she heard it. It sounded as if something had broken, snapped, deep inside him, some long-held tension or pain.

He sounded like a man who, after years of struggle, had finally made it home.

He sounded exactly like she felt.

She shifted, lifting herself to him, opening further for him, wanting him deeper. She wanted him so deep she would never really be without him. And then he was moving, stroking, driving, giving her what she hadn't had the breath or the words to ask for.

And as her body convulsed around his she cried out his name, heard her own breaking harshly from his throat, she realized she'd once more learned an important lesson from this man.

Solid reality was sometimes better than any fantasy.

Chapter 25

That damned dream.

Again.

Why did his mind choose now, when things were in chaos, to torture him? Or was it because things were in chaos, with Lyss in danger, that his subconscious was taunting him with things beyond his reach? Maybe if he just didn't open his eyes. But then he might fall back asleep and it might start again. It was early enough, the light was very faint.

No, he should just get up and take the damned icy cold shower he always did when he woke up aching for a wife he couldn't—

The light. His eyes snapped open. If he were somewhere else he might be disoriented, but he'd built this house from the dirt up, and he knew how every window was placed and why. It didn't matter that the room was still practically dark, didn't matter that this time of year the sun rose so late it could be almost eight already. What mattered was that what faint light there was was coming from the wrong direction.

He processed this in a split second before the reality hit.

It hadn't been a dream.

It hadn't been just another in the string of long, sleepless nights when his recalcitrant mind, freed from daily restraint, took him to the one place he never allowed himself to consciously go.

Alyssa was beside him. In fact, she was wrapped around him, one long, silken leg thrown over his. In her bed. In the room he'd built but never slept in.

Until now.

It hadn't been a dream. That long, explosive night hadn't been a dream.

He was afraid to breathe, let alone move. He didn't want to wake her, didn't want to face the sad likelihood that she would regret what they'd done. She would think of Doug, and wish she'd never touched his boring, staid brother. She would surely wish she hadn't been the initiator.

He'd never been one to run, to bail out on uncomfortable morning afters, what few there had been. But there had been a time or two when sneaking out before a partner awoke had been a tempting solution.

Never had it been as tempting as it was right now.

At the same time, he couldn't move. Wouldn't move. Not while there was one last moment to savor, with Alyssa naked in his arms.

He wanted her, as fiercely as if last night hadn't really happened. He wanted nothing more than to wake her with a kiss, then more kisses, wanted to explore every inch of her again, and again, then bury himself in her so deep she would make that sound again, that moan of pleasure that had driven him over the edge last night. That moan that had coalesced into his name, telling him that this once, at least, she wasn't thinking of his brother.

But she needed sleep. It had been a rough—no, far beyond rough—few days, and she'd been so worried about Luke, he doubted she'd slept much more than he had.

Leave her alone, he ordered himself silently. *You'll survive. Maybe.*

He wondered who was outside now. They'd never even heard Rafe last night, but they'd known he was there. He supposed Liam was back now, Quinn had said they'd change off at midnight. He wondered briefly if the extra sense of security their presence gave her was behind Lyss's behavior last night. If feeling safe was why she had turned to him for solace.

It's more like how you know what to grab when a fire's coming. You know what's most important.

Her words echoed in his head. Did he dare hope she meant them, in the way he wanted her to mean them? The way he desperately needed her to mean them?

The need rose in him again, and this time all his lecturing on letting her sleep was seared away. To his surprise, she woke quickly, responded eagerly, so eagerly it took his breath away. Somewhere in the back of his mind he had the idea that it was only because it was still dark enough, that if she realized how close it was to morning she might change. He redoubled his efforts; he wanted her too hot, too aroused, wanting this—and him—too much to even think about changing her mind. A few minutes later, when she practically begged him to finish it, he knew he'd succeeded.

He hadn't expected to be half out of his mind himself.

When he slid into her slick, welcoming body, he knew he was too close, he'd pushed it too far. He wouldn't be able to hold back, not long enough. Not the way she was responding to every stroke, not the way the pressure was building until he thought he would die from it.

She wrapped her arms, then her legs around him, driving him deeper. And in that instant he heard her cry out, felt the first, fierce convulsion of her body around his. The sound of his name coming from her in that tone of hot, aroused wonder was his undoing, and he let himself follow her over the edge.

When he woke up again, she was gone.

He was berating himself for falling back asleep when she came out of the bathroom, showered and dressed. He sat up, rubbing a hand over his eyes. "You're up," he said, sounding inane even to himself.

"Yes. It's time to get Luke to school, and I want to be there early enough to find someone I trust on the staff to hand him off to."

"Sorry." They'd discussed that last night. He swung his legs over the side of the bed, grabbed at his jeans. "And sorry I…crashed on you."

She smiled, a shy little smile that made his heart turn over in his chest. "It was worth it," she said softly.

Hope, pure and unadulterated, slammed through him.

"It was, wasn't it?" he said.

"Yes. Even if things are…more confused now."

Confused? The hope wobbled. "I thought things were unconfused for the first time in three years."

She sighed. "You're such a guy, Drew."

"Well, yes."

"We know each other so well, and yet not at all. Not in the way a normal couple together three years would know each other."

This was what he'd been afraid of, one of those morning-after analyses that ended up destroying everything.

"Try me," he said, an edge he couldn't help creeping into his voice.

"I just mean—"

"I know your favorite color is green, you like your bacon crisp, you have a weakness for caramel, and you'll read the back of a cereal box if that's all that's handy to read. I know you like to sit on the deck where you can smell those white flowers you planted, that you can instantly recognize the sound of an eagle's call, and that you want to learn to knit someday."

About halfway through she was staring at him, a touch of surprise in her expression. Good, he thought, and charged on.

"I know you worry about not getting enough exercise. I know you feel guilty about letting Luke have those cookies he loves. I know you're the best mother I've ever seen."

"Drew—"

"I know you have regrets about not finishing your education, but you wouldn't trade having had Luke for anything. I know you wanted to be an artist, but decided you weren't good enough. You were wrong, by the way. I still contend that."

"You're shaming me, Drew," she said softly.

He stopped, startled by her choice of words. "What?"

"I never realized. How much attention you paid."

"I may be 'such a guy,' as you put it, but I'm not blind."

"I only meant…thinking great sex was going to fix everything."

He blinked. Realized he was no doubt going to prove her point, but was unable to help himself. He grinned sheepishly. "But it was great."

For an instant she just stared at him. Then, to his immense relief, she smiled. That same, shy little smile that had tightened his chest moments ago. "Yes," she said softly. "It was."

She was having, Alyssa realized to her chagrin, trouble concentrating. Her mind kept slipping back to last night. She refused to second-guess her decision; she'd been clear-headed and thinking straight when she'd made it, and being uncertain how to feel about it now didn't change that. Drew hadn't been the instigator last night, she had. True, once she had opened the door he'd charged through like a thoroughbred from a starting gate, but she had opened the door.

It never would have happened otherwise. She knew him well enough to know that.

And he, amazingly, knew her better than she'd ever imagined.

She'd been blown away by his little recitation this morning, and she still was. Knowing her favorite color and how she liked her bacon cooked, that was one thing, simple things anybody could pick up. But the other things…how had he known she still had wishful thoughts about being an artist? She hadn't even tried since Luke had been born. The last thing she'd done was that nighttime painting of the Sound, with the dark hills of the land and the gleam of glassy water setting off the brilliantly lit ferry. She wondered where it was. Probably in ashes, along with everything else she'd left behind. Wasn't her entire life in ashes, except for Luke?

"No," she said aloud to the empty room. Thanks to Drew, the answer was no. She had a life, a life many women would envy. A life she hadn't appreciated nearly enough. What if Drew hadn't been who he was? She would have gotten out of that hospital broke and weak, and ended up who knows where. And Luke. She would have lost Luke forever.

And now, if Drew wasn't the man he was, he might have decided they were both too much trouble. That they'd brought this mess into his life, and they could take it right back out again.

But he was the man he was.

And thanks to Drew, she would never, ever think of sex the same way again. With Doug, her pleasure had come from pleasing him. With Drew…

With Drew he made her climb the walls, hungry with need. Made her a demanding, eager thing she barely recognized.

Made her scream.

She wished he was home right now.

The images that played out in her head then had her up on her feet and pacing. She crossed the living room, then turned and walked back toward the kitchen, feeling she was going to fly apart at any second. She reached the opening to the kitchen and started to turn again, even knowing it was pointless, nothing was going to help her get this under control. Nothing—

Cutter barked from behind her. She jumped. She still wasn't quite used to having a dog around, although she had to admit he was remarkably well behaved. She turned to look at him. He was sitting by the front door, looking over his shoulder at her. He'd just been outside twenty minutes ago, so she didn't think it was that.

As she turned to walk back toward him, something caught her attention. The clock on the oven glowed quietly green at her. And she came back to earth with a thud. Luke. Luke was going to be out of school in five minutes, and it was going to take her ten to get there. Panicked, she grabbed up her keys and her phone, hitting her contact list as she did. Drew's number came up first, and she dialed as she ran for her purse. He'd gone in to deal with some permits that had finally come through after months of bureaucratic delay.

"Are you still at the office?"

He seemed to pick up on the rushed note in her voice. "Yes, why?"

She opened the door and walked as fast as she could for her car, Cutter at her heels. "I'm…running late. For Luke."

Without hesitation he answered, "You want me to get him?" He was that crucial five minutes closer.

"Can you just be there when he gets out? Then I'll take him."

"On my way. You okay?"

"Fine. Just…distracted."

There was a split-second's pause, one she might not

have noticed had it not been for the deep, husky note that had come into his voice when he said, "I think I like that."

The images slammed into her again, and by the time she disconnected, got Cutter in the car and actually got the car started her body was humming with the same crazy need he'd roused in her last night.

The initial worry that no one would be there for Luke when he came out eased, she took a moment to call the school. Not that it was unusual for Drew to pick him up, but there were new people this year, and some might not know him on sight. The school was pretty careful, someone always waited with stragglers, but the current situation was hardly normal for Luke.

She reached a familiar voice, Mrs. Martinelli, one of the school volunteers. She was a retired nurse who'd never had children of her own, and had been volunteering at the school for years.

"Oh, that's all right, Mrs. Kiley. Don't rush. The kids are having a fine time. I'm told we have puppies visiting."

Cutter woofed softly from the backseat, as if he'd not only heard the word, but understood it. Alyssa laughed in spite of herself.

"Oh, dear," she said.

"Yes, it's been quite chaotic, but the children are running all over with them. You know little ones of all species love to play with each other."

"I can't wait," she said with another laugh. "My husband will be there first, though, I just wanted to let you know."

"Thank you. Always nice to have a good-looking man around."

The woman's voice was teasing, but sincere. "Yes," Alyssa said, those images of Drew still fluttering through her mind like overheated butterflies. "Yes, it is."

And Drew was there, as promised. Of course. She saw his car the moment she pulled into the parking lot. Cutter was on his feet, eager to see his little friend. And then the dog's demeanor shifted, changed. He went from friendly, slightly goofy playmate to guard dog in an instant. A low, rumbling growl came from him as he stared toward the school. As she got out of the car it escalated into fierce snarl.

Alyssa didn't know why. But it was scaring her.

He was staring toward the main school building. No, she thought, toward the playground.

The empty playground. Hadn't Mrs. Martinelli said the kids were playing? Were they inside with the puppies? It wasn't raining, but—

Movement caught her eye and she saw Drew running— not walking fast, not trotting, but flat-out running—toward her, and her heart leapt into her throat.

She scrambled out of the car. Cutter, not waiting for his own door to be opened, wriggled between the front seats and jumped out after her. The dog took off toward the playground without a backward glance, and something about the intensity of his focus only heightened her dread.

"Drew?"

Her voice sounded tiny even to her as he came to an abrupt halt. He reached out for her, pulled her against him.

"Oh, God," she breathed.

"Lyss," he began, then stopped as if it was too hard to speak.

"What? What is it?"

She felt him shudder, and the thought of what that would take terrified her.

"Drew, tell me!"

"It's Luke. He's gone."

Chapter 26

Drew held on to her, hating the way she was shaking in his arms. He tightened his arms around her, thinking she might fly apart if he didn't. He didn't blame her, he was about to go airborne himself. He forced his voice to calm as he explained.

"He was with the kids on the playground. Something about puppies running loose. And then he wasn't there."

"But I talked to Mrs. Martinelli not ten minutes ago!"

"I know. She said so. She's really upset."

"*She's* upset?"

"I know, I know. We have to find him. Damn it, I trusted them to keep him safe here."

"Maybe he's just hiding somewhere. Playing."

She sounded desperate to believe a simpler answer, and he couldn't blame her for that, either.

"If so, then Cutter will find him," he said.

That seemed to help her get her panic under control. She nodded, and her voice was steadier as they headed after the dog.

"What's being done?"

Glad she was thinking again, he said quickly, "There's a sheriff's deputy on the way. All the other kids are inside with adults. They'll be interviewed, according to school protocol. I called Quinn. He's on his way. And Liam."

"I forgot to tell him I was going," she said. They usually checked with whoever was watching before they went anywhere, but it hadn't been long enough to become an engrained habit yet, and being late had made her forget all but the essentials.

"He figured it out."

"How did this happen?"

"That," he said grimly, "we are going to find out."

Cutter had headed onto the playground. He paused there, sniffing the ground, then lifting his head into the slight breeze. After a moment he took off at a steady trot, nose down, toward the far side of the playground. They followed quickly. The dog had more than proven himself, and if his abilities seemed a little uncanny, well, maybe that was exactly what they needed right now.

Cutter's raised tail brushed one of the empty swings as he passed, setting it moving, a sight Drew found oddly ominous. Seconds later the dog picked up speed, and then he dived into the thick hedge, clearly intent on something.

Thinking it would just be a perfect capper to the day if Cutter had simply spotted an animal in the brush and was after it like any normal dog, Drew ran to the spot. Cutter was clawing at something in the juniper, just above the ground. Just as Drew got there, he came up with it and spun around.

It was a shoe. A small, boy-sized shoe.

He heard a muffled cry, looked up to see Alyssa standing there, staring at the shoe the dog held with her hand over her mouth as if to keep from screaming. Drew took the shoe from Cutter, who released it easily.

The shoe looked all too familiar.

Only when Cutter's head came up sharply did Drew realize Quinn and Hayley had arrived, with Liam right behind them. Quinn paused to talk with the school personnel, but Hayley and Liam headed straight for them.

"Cutter found this," Drew said, dispensing with any niceties under the circumstances, "right there."

He gestured at the spot where Cutter still stood, looking as if he were about to explode into movement again, his intense gaze now fixed on Hayley as if awaiting orders. The dog hadn't even gone to her, Drew realized vaguely. As if he somehow knew nothing was more important than the matter at hand, not even greeting his beloved mom.

"You're sure it's Luke's?" Hayley asked.

"Yes." Before she could point out they were at an elementary school and any kid could have lost it, he added, "The laces. Lyss did that to make it easier for him to learn to tie them himself."

He'd thought her nothing less than brilliant when he'd realized the reason behind what he'd at first thought odd. She'd divided the lace in half and colored one end blue with a marker, leaving the other end white. But when he saw how easily Luke learned to tie them, because the different colors made it so clear what went where, he'd congratulated her profusely on the idea.

Staring at the shoe Hayley now held, Alyssa held her hand out to him, reaching. He took it, tugged her gently closer. When she leaned into him, obviously seeking support, he felt a burst of warm pleasure that she had turned to him, apparently instinctively. But she was clearly terrified, and he could feel it hovering over him as well, but he refused to let himself think of worst-case scenarios.

"You were right. We should have pulled him out of school, kept him at home," Alyssa said, her voice so tiny it ripped at him.

"Never mind that now. We have to—"

Cutter made an odd sound, a combination growl and yip

that made them all look. The moment he had their attention he moved again, this time down the slight slope along the juniper hedge.

"Trail doesn't end here," Liam said, and went after the dog. Past the hedge the dog turned and, nose still down, started along a narrow track through the trees. Barely even an animal path, they had to follow in single file to get through. Within a couple of minutes Cutter broke out of the trees and led them to a spot a few yards off the paved road below, where grass and brush were flattened in a telltale pattern. He cast around for a moment, then sat down and let out a heavy sigh, clearly indicating this was where the trail vanished. Even Drew figured that signal out.

"Probably was a car parked here," Liam said.

Which meant Oliver could have taken Luke anywhere, Drew thought grimly.

Liam took the dog and began searching the surrounding area, although from Cutter's actions it didn't seem promising.

Drew knew Alyssa had to realize that, but instead of panicking again, she seemed to have a tighter grip on herself. No wailing and useless shrieking for her, he thought with no small amount of admiration.

While Liam and Cutter searched, Drew and Alyssa went back to the school. Quinn approached them immediately.

"You want the official version?"

"I'd rather have yours," Drew said shortly. "They'll be covering their backside."

Quinn nodded. "Kids were playing, waiting for parents to arrive. One of them saw a puppy, over by the hedge. They all descended. Then another puppy over there." he gestured toward the swing set further down. "And finally, one down there, near the service road. That's the one—"

He broke off as the sheriff's deputy pulled into the school parking lot. Drew glanced at his watch, a little stunned to realize less than ten minutes had passed. Drew saw immediately that the deputy had been expecting to find Quinn there.

"Detective Dunbar called me," he mentioned. "Said you were working a possible threat that could be related. That it might be a kidnapping."

"Yes," Quinn said, his voice flatter than Drew had ever heard it. The man was angry, he realized. Good. So was he. And hearing the word *kidnapping* out loud added a layer of terror to the anger. It was not a pleasant combination.

Quinn introduced them as Luke's parents. The man, whose name tag read "R. George," was respectful and reassuring. And got right to business, which Drew appreciated.

"Juvie detective is on her way, but I'll get started."

"There are several kids involved, possible witnesses. It'll take some finesse, they're pretty young," Hayley said.

An hour later, they had a picture, albeit incomplete, of what had happened.

It was Alyssa who found the key, when one little girl who recognized her as Luke's mom said she'd seen Luke talking to the man who had kept one of the puppies from "getting runned over" by an arriving school bus.

"He was a nice man," she repeated. "He saved the black-and-white one."

Drew's heart sank. For all the warnings about bad people using animals, it was only natural to a six-year-old that someone who saved a helpless puppy had to be good. Innocents just didn't think that way, which was why it worked so often.

"Was he somebody's dad?" Alyssa asked.

"I don't think so."

"Have you ever seen him before?" Drew asked.

Everyone expected a no, and froze when the wide-eyed girl slowly nodded. Drew wasn't sure if she was wide-eyed because of what she was saying, or because he was asking and he was so much bigger than she. He left it, with effort, to Alyssa, as did the deputy, who merely waited as she reached out and took the child's hand. The tiny fingers curled around hers. Drew wondered if it was just Alyssa who was able to elicit such instant trust, or if it was something that somehow came with motherhood.

"Where?" she asked gently.

"Over there," she said, vaguely gesturing toward the thick juniper hedge that served as the playground's fence. The hedge where Cutter had found Luke's shoe.

If her heart had kicked into overdrive as his had, Alyssa managed to hide it, keeping her tone even and casual with the already nervous child.

"When did you see him?" she asked.

"Couple times."

"Lately?"

The girl frowned. Alyssa tried again. "After Halloween or before?"

"After," she said confidently. "But today he was still carrying his pumpkin bag. Silly. Halloween was way long ago."

Drew sucked in a sharp breath. "What kind of bag?"

She looked at him warily, telling him he hadn't been as successful as Alyssa in keeping his tone level. But she answered.

"Pumpkin. You know, like you fill with straw and stuff and it looks like a big jack-o-lantern."

The girl held her arms out in a big circle. Drew knew, all right. They were a frequent sight in yards all over for that spooky holiday, black garbage bags with orange pumpkins with carved faces printed on the sides.

Large bags.

Large enough to stuff with a six-year-old boy.

Chapter 27

Alyssa sat on one of the chairs in the principal's conference room and stared down once more at the text message displayed on her phone's screen. It seemed a mocking parody, the grim words in the stylish font she had chosen just because she'd been bored with the standard one that had been preinstalled.

The message had come in nearly an hour ago, but still she stared at it unbelievingly.

Price has gone up. A million bucks if you want to see the kid again. Instructions to follow.

"Whatever he wants, I'll pay it," Drew said flatly. "I don't care what it costs, what we have to sell or put up as collateral. We'll worry about him coming back for more after we have Luke back safe."

Alyssa ignored her own trembling. It was pointless, useless, accomplished nothing. She focused on Drew's voice, on the determination there. He'd never not followed through, and he would now. He would get Luke back, somehow. She had to believe that.

"Oh, he won't be coming back for more," Quinn said, with a conviction Alyssa appreciated, although it didn't give her the same feeling as Drew's determination. Not that she didn't think Quinn equally capable of follow through, but Quinn was working on the principle of a missing child he wasn't connected to.

Drew was looking for his son.

It hit her then, just how true what she'd said—had it truly only been last night?—had been. Drew was her son's father, in every sense but one, and that one seemed, in this moment definitely the least important.

Other memories crowded in then, hot, potent memories of the rest of last night, of how she'd turned to him, what he'd done to her and she to him, after she'd intentionally lowered her defenses and taken that step she'd known even then could well be irrevocable.

She fought down a flood of guilt, her panicked heart clamoring that this was what she got for that, that there was, of course, a price to be paid for the sweetness she'd found in the dark. Wasn't there always? It had been fine when it had been an obligation response, a cold sort of payback. Something she'd done only because she felt she owed him.

You couldn't be hurt if your feelings weren't involved, right? At least, that's what she'd always told herself. She wasn't so sure anymore. Either that she couldn't be hurt, or that her feelings weren't involved.

But this time she had known. She had known and she had wanted it anyway. More than she could remember wanting anything in her life. Or anyone. Including Doug.

For an instant she felt as if Doug himself had orchestrated this, from beyond the grave, that he was somehow paying her back for turning to his brother.

For wanting his brother.

For enjoying it far more with his brother than she ever had with him.

And that was something she never would have thought possible. But then, she hadn't known sex could be like it had been last night, with both of them willing and for, if not the right reasons, at least better ones.

"Liam says there was no other trace of Oliver in the woods," Quinn said, yanking her back to the present, moving on as if Drew hadn't spoken about simply paying the ransom. "Cutter didn't cue on anything."

Drew's brows lowered slightly. "Would he have? I mean, he was tracking Luke."

Quinn nodded. "Cutter would have known, made the switch from tracking Luke to Oliver. To him, the site where Oliver grabbed him would have had both scents mixed together, so he would have connected them."

"Amazing," Drew said, glancing at the dog who was once more getting up to pace the room. Alyssa had noticed the pattern. Up, down, trying to rest then getting up to pace again—the dog was acting as she felt, edgy, nervous, wanting to do something, anything, but not knowing what.

"He doesn't wait any better than we do," Hayley said. "He'd rather be doing. Something. Anything. Just as we would."

Alyssa let out a compressed breath at the acknowledgement of frustration. Just sitting here when Luke was apparently in dire trouble seemed so wrong. She watched the dog for a moment, remembering his certainty as he'd tracked through the woods.

"Are we really sure about what happened?" she asked tentatively. "I mean, we're assuming it's Baird because that's the only thing that makes sense, but do you really think he—" She stopped, gulping in air that suddenly seemed in short supply. Then she tried again. "Do you really think he put Luke in a garbage bag?"

"It's a lot of surmising," Quinn agreed, "but not without foundation."

Alyssa felt a shudder go through her. Guilt rose up again, in a different form this time but even more potent.

"We should have pulled him out of school," she said again, looking at Drew, feeling somehow she owed him this, on top of everything else. "You were right. I was worried about him being scared, and now I know he should have been. Then maybe he…"

Drew didn't gloat, but then he never did. She was Luke's mother and he'd let her win that battle because of that. "Later," he said. "That doesn't help get Luke back now."

He was right—again—she thought. She was being self-indulgent, placing blame when it couldn't help, when it didn't really matter. What really mattered was finding Luke. She nodded once, sharply, decisively.

"It was a mistake to trust anybody but ourselves," Quinn said grimly.

"What do we do now?" Alyssa asked. "Just wait?"

That seemed beyond her, to just sit and wait while Luke was out there, terrified and maybe even hurt. She'd thought the day when a cop had shown up at the door of the run-down trailer they'd been living in and told her Doug was dead would forever be the worst of her life.

She'd been wrong.

"I have no intention of just sitting around waiting for this piece of debris to call," Drew said.

"Nor do we," Hayley said. "The sheriff's office is handling the rest of the kid and staff interviews. Liam and Teague are going door to door down the street where Cutter led us. We've got more faith in him than the deputies do. If anybody saw the car that was parked there, we'll find them."

"Then what?" Alyssa asked, trying to find hope in that.

"Then we have something to work with," Quinn said.

"The school's being very cooperative," Hayley said. "They know their reputation is at stake."

"Not to mention their liability," Quinn said drily.

"I don't care about that right now, either. Once Luke is back, I'll build them that new playground they want gratis, as long as he's okay," Drew said.

"But a million dollars…can we come up with that kind of money?" Alyssa asked quietly.

"The business is worth more," Drew said. "The big fish are always looking to buy us out. I'll come up with it somehow."

The business. The business his great-grandfather had begun, the business four generations of Kileys had built and saved through tough times. Yet he talked of selling as if it were nothing.

To him it was, next to Luke.

"You won't have to," Quinn said in response to Drew's words.

"What?"

"Foxworth will cover it, if it comes to that."

Drew's eyes narrowed. "A million dollars? Are you kidding?"

"No," Quinn said calmly, as if his family's foundation handed out that amount every day. Who knows, Alyssa thought, maybe they did.

"It's part of the deal," Hayley explained. "If we take on a case, we take on all aspects of it. That's why we're so selective."

"Maybe you should have stuck to your no domestic cases rule," Drew said.

"But it didn't stay that kind of case, did it?" Quinn said.

"We should have known that would happen when Cutter insisted we get involved," Hayley said.

The door to the small room opened. Alyssa's heart leapt. A tall, lean man with dark hair touched with silver at the temples stepped into the room. Hayley smiled, a wide smile of welcome; obviously this was someone she knew and liked.

Quinn stood. "Brett," he said, holding out a hand.

The other man took it, nodding as they shook hands. "Hayley," he said with an answering smile as he acknowledged her.

Quinn turned back. "Meet Drew and Alyssa Kiley. Luke's parents. This is Detective Dunbar."

Alyssa studied the man for a moment. He looked lean and fit, his face and body looked much younger than his hair and eyes would suggest. She guessed those eyes had seen a lot, much of it unpleasant. There was nothing openly hard-line or hard-hitting about him, but she sensed it was there, under the surface, to be called upon if need be.

She was surprised he was here, Hayley had said he wasn't a missing-persons detective.

"Didn't expect you in person," Quinn said, echoing her thoughts.

The man shrugged. "I heard the call go out. Seems like your case suddenly turned into something else."

"Yes," Quinn said, and gave him a quick rundown.

Alyssa watched the man as Quinn explained their complicated situation, explained that Luke's biological father was Drew's brother, but they were now married. He glanced at them then, but if he was making any judgments it didn't show.

There was a lot of respect between the two men, that was clear. Somehow that reassured her. She had the unexpected thought that she was sitting in a room with three examples of the strongest kind of men, different, yet all quintessentially male. Quinn, with his air of command, now Dunbar, with that quiet power just beneath the surface. And of course Drew, with his strength and steady, unwavering dedication to doing what was right.

She glanced at Hayley, who wore a tiny smile as if she were thinking the same thing. Hayley glanced her way and the smile widened slightly, and Alyssa knew she'd been right. That expression said "They're really something, aren't they?" as clearly as if the other woman had spoken.

A muffled voice Alyssa still recognized as Liam's issued from the phone Quinn had put down on the table.

"Boss?"

Quinn picked it up. "Go, Liam."

The phone crackled, but she heard the words anyway.

"Got two wits with matching info. I think we've got an ID on the car."

Alyssa's heart leapt, her pulse picking up speed. She sensed Drew's sudden stillness, knew if she touched him his every muscle would be taut, ready.

"Plate?" Dunbar asked instantly.

"Agreement on all but the last two digits," said another voice, Teague this time. "But we've got agreement on the make and color."

Quinn looked at the detective. "Enough for an Amber Alert?"

Alyssa's breath caught. The idea of Luke's description being broadcast on police radios all over, and showing up on the many informational signs along the highways, both reassured and horrified her. Reassured her that it was being done, and horrified her that it was necessary. She hoped she never saw one of those signs, the image would never leave her.

"I'll make sure of it," Dunbar said. "And I'll get somebody working on coming up with the rest of the plate."

"I'll put Tyler to work on that, too," Quinn said, then added, "With your permission."

Dunbar flashed the other man a wry look. "As if that would stop you. But I appreciate the courtesy."

"Which," Hayley put in, "he doesn't extend to just anybody."

Dunbar looked at Hayley, and Alyssa thought she saw a

flicker of something in the man's eyes. Sadness, longing, or something she couldn't put an exact name to.

"I'm honored." Alyssa sensed there was a solid core of truth under the dry words.

Drew spoke for the first time since the detective's arrival. "The ferry cams," he said. "Where that car was parked was between two of them. If he went east or west on the highway…"

"They would have caught him," Quinn said, getting there instantly. "And if they didn't, that narrows it down to side streets. Great call. Brett?"

"I'll call DOT," he said, "but from past experience I'd say it'll take them half an hour just to get started."

"Tyler can do it faster," Quinn said, "but he might have to…"

"Yeah. I didn't hear that," Dunbar said.

"I'll get him started," Hayley said, walking off to one side with her phone in hand.

Alyssa took a deep breath. Crazily, now that something was finally happening she felt more wound up than she had been when they'd been sitting here doing nothing.

They would find the car, they would find and deal with Baird, and they would find Luke. He would be fine, and they'd take him home and work on forgetting this had ever happened. That was how it had to be.

Anything less was unfathomable.

Chapter 28

It went against his instincts to leave the place where Luke had been last, and Drew had to pound home the logic that he was gone, and that hanging around there wasn't accomplishing anything. The juvenile detective had arrived, a young woman Dunbar assured them would get whatever remaining information there was to get. Drew had still hesitated, but Dunbar trusted the woman, and Quinn fully trusted Dunbar. And he had the distinct feeling Quinn didn't bestow his trust lightly. And that he was able to pick good people was obvious; they were all around him.

Still, it took all he had to stop himself from driving all over town, searching. Except that if Oliver had a car, he could be anywhere by now. The sheriffs were looking. The info was out to the State Patrol. Law enforcement was in motion, doing what it did.

But to them, a missing child, while critical, wasn't personal. For all their dedication, Luke wasn't their child. Although Dunbar had acted as if he were, Drew had to admit that.

And so did Foxworth. Liam, Teague and the formidable Rafer were actively searching, and unlike the sheriff's office, which had other things to deal with, they were doing it to the exclusion of all else. Drew knew their best hope was Foxworth, with the resources he didn't completely understand yet.

One of those resources, Cutter, was not happy. As they arrived at the Foxworth building, that anonymous three-story green building that housed this remarkable operation, the dog looked exactly as Drew felt, downcast, head lowered, tail dragging.

"It wasn't your fault, Cutter," Alyssa said gently, patting the dog. "You weren't even there."

Drew felt his heart lurch, that even now she felt concern for another creature. But one of the many things Alyssa had in abundance was empathy. Maybe that's what had gotten her into that mess, back in the day, if Doug truly had been struggling against comparisons to his big brother. He didn't want to think that, didn't want to have to deal with the responsibility that came with it, didn't have time to deal with it right now.

Later, he told himself, even as he cringed inwardly at how many times, in how many situations, he'd used that word to put things off. He would never allow that in his business, yet in his personal life it seemed to have become a mantra. Later, always later. Don't talk about Doug now. Don't rock the boat now. Don't ask for more now.

He gave a sharp shake of his head as Hayley responded to Alyssa's words. "He still feels badly. He knows something's wrong, and that we're all upset."

"He keeps looking at us," Drew said as they settled into chairs in the meeting room.

"It's like he knows Luke's missing," Alyssa said, her voice breaking on her son's name.

"He knows who's not here," Hayley said gently. "He's a very smart dog. To him, his job—besides finding work for us—is to take care of us. And right now that us includes you. Especially Luke. He started this whole thing because of Luke, and he won't be happy again until he's back."

"And he will be back," Quinn said firmly as he picked up a small remote on the table and aimed it at a flat screen on the wall. Drew had noticed it there before, but wondered why on earth Quinn would be turning a television on now.

As if he'd sensed the question, Quinn looked back over his shoulder. "We just got this hooked up to our network system, so we can talk to Tyler in St. Louis on something bigger than a laptop screen."

"You think he'll have something already?" Alyssa asked.

"Or nothing," Quinn said. "Either of which will tell us something."

The image came on of a young man who looked barely old enough to be out of school—thin, wiry, with sandy hair that stood up in a spiky sort of way, either by design or because he ran his hands through it a lot. There was a small upside-down triangle of beard below his lower lip, looking a bit sparse.

"Tyler, these are the Kileys, Alyssa and Drew," Hayley said, then gestured at the screen. "This is our resident genius, Tyler Hewitt."

The young man grinned, waved, then seemed to suddenly remember why they were here and that good cheer might not be appropriate and abruptly stopped. "Sorry," he muttered.

"Dive in," Quinn suggested. "Conclusion first, we're a little antsy here."

"Right. The car dropped off somewhere between the last and next to last ferry cam, headed west."

Drew let out a breath. "So he wasn't headed for the ferry?"

"No," Hewitt's voice came back. "And he never showed up in the holding lanes, at least not within the hour after he was on the move again. That's as far as I've had time to check so far."

"That's good, isn't it?" Alyssa asked. "It would be harder to find him in Seattle, right?"

"Much," Quinn agreed.

"So if we know he left the highway somewhere between those two cameras, then we have a place to start," Drew said.

"Already started," Quinn answered. "Right, Ty?"

"Yes, sir. I flashed the data to your comlink the minute I had it, so the guys knew even before you came up on comm here."

Drew felt a bit calmer now. Clearly Foxworth was just as efficient as it appeared, and the thought that the three men searching had known where to look even before they did was reassuring.

"Good job," Quinn said, and Drew thought he saw the young tech guru fighting a smile. Obviously Quinn's approval meant a lot to him. "Okay, details? From the beginning."

With a quick nod Hewitt began. "The car showed up passing through the first cam at fourteen hundred hours."

"That's an hour and forty-five minutes before school lets out," Alyssa said.

The image on the screen suddenly split, and the slightly distorted ferry-cam images popped up on the left. The four scenes were familiar to Drew, since he often checked to see if they needed to leave early for a trip to the other side, or to see the road conditions up on the highway in winter. But while they were familiar, today they weren't at all comforting.

"Sorry," Tyler said as he started the images in a sort of stop-action sequence. "It's a bit jerky, their shortest refresh time is fifteen seconds. And the cam's across the street, so it's not real clear. But you can see here—" he did something on his end and froze an image in the middle frame, then it zoomed to fill the screen "—there's nothing, and in the next image there's a vehicle starting to pull over, and in the next he's on the shoulder, and then he's in that little clear spot."

"Car looks like a match to our witness statements. Can you enhance the image? Enough to see a plate?"

"Just sent you a copy of the clearest I can get it. At least the letters match. But the lighting's not the best there, with the big trees and all, so it's hard to be sure on color. Looks silver, though. Can't see the driver at all, first the reflection then the shadows."

"That has to be it." Drew stared at the screen, at that last frozen image and what he could see of the back of what appeared to be a small, nondescript, four-door sedan.

"Agreed. What about the next image?" Quinn asked.

"You can't see a thing," Tyler said, "between the trees, the shade and the angle, you wouldn't even know a car was there unless you already knew it was there."

The young man seemed to grimace at his own awkward phrasing.

"So we can't see him getting out of the car?" Drew asked.

"Sorry, no. Or back in. He's completely out of view."

"Do you think he knew about the cameras?" Alyssa asked Quinn, her voice very quiet. Somehow this was making it all the more real. Denial was no longer an option.

"They're not hidden," Quinn said. "But if he was that detail-oriented you'd think he would have found a road less traveled. There's a lot of traffic up there, since it's the route to the ferry."

"Unless getting out of there fast was his priority," Drew said grimly.

"And he wasn't really visible once he got off the road," Hayley said.

"Go ahead, Ty," Quinn said.

"Right. He was there for a long time. Or at least the car was. It didn't move again for nearly two hours."

Drew felt his chest tighten and his stomach lurch as the images sped forward. It was like some bizarre stop-action nightmare, the edges changed, but the center of his focus, that spot in the trees where the car had vanished, never changed. The time marker in the corner of the image jumped ahead. When Hewitt stopped the progression, it read as he'd said, nearly two hours later. Just enough time to get there from the school.

Carrying a jack-o-lantern bag.

For two hours that slime had skulked around, spying on the school, on Luke, waiting for his chance?

"Do you suppose," Alyssa said, her voice tight, "that *he* brought the puppies and turned them loose at the school?"

Drew's head snapped around to stare at her. He hadn't thought of that, but now that she'd said it, it made perfect sense.

"Puppies," he said under his breath. "The perfect lure. Especially for Luke right now."

"Definitely a possibility," Quinn agreed, nodding at Alyssa. "Maybe even a probability." He turned back to the screen. "Continue, Ty."

Hewitt nodded. He put the still frames back into that jerky motion.

"Here's where it moves again. You still can't see the driver, or—" he swallowed audibly, it sounded amplified over the speaker "—if there's anybody in the car with him."

Even as he was frustrated by the lack of visual confirmation, Drew appreciated the kid's apparent realization of what they were dealing with. He watched with a growing feeling of nausea in the pit of his stomach as the car pulled out of the trees, skidded slightly on the shoulder, corrected, and whipped out onto the state highway at a fast pace.

Oliver was in a hurry. Because he had his prize. Drew knew it, deep down. That bastard had Luke.

"He continues west," Hewitt said, "but somewhere between here and the next ferry cam, he's gone."

Which could mean either he was trying to get out of view of the cameras, or…he was staying local. Drew hoped beyond measure it was the latter. As long as Luke was close, they'd find him. It made sense, though. If he'd wanted to get lost, he would have headed to Seattle, or its sprawling, well-populated surroundings.

"Keep watching," Quinn ordered Hewitt.

"Yes, sir. I'm recording it all. If that car shows up on any of those cams again, you'll know it. And I'm watching the others, too, not just ferries but every cam I could find in the county."

Quinn drew back slightly, then smiled and nodded. "We'll get you some help. I'll call Charlie to arrange it."

The kid's eyes widened. "I— No, I—"

Quinn's mouth quirked. "Don't worry. I'll make it clear you don't need Charlie's personal help."

Hewitt seemed to breathe again. This Charlie must be something else, Drew thought, to inspire such instant fear. Or awe. Whatever it was.

When the screen went black, Drew felt oddly cut off, as if the images had somehow been his last connection to his son. But he was quickly distracted by Quinn's action, to take his phone and signal the three Foxworth men in the field.

"He was headed west," he told them. "Let's work for now on the higher likelihood he turned from that side of the road, to the north. It's less populated, less probability he'd be seen."

Drew heard a series of clicks he assumed was their method of acknowledgment.

"Teague, cover the south side, Liam and Rafe the north," Quinn said. "I'll head that way in a couple."

"Bring Cutter," came a voice over the phone's speaker,

Drew wasn't sure who it was, but from the conciseness of it suspected it was the laconic Rafe.

"Planned on it," Quinn answered. "We'll connect when I'm in the area."

Again the clicks.

"I'm going with you," Drew said, getting to his feet.

Quinn turned to look at him. Again Drew got that feeling of being assessed, although flatteringly it wasn't as long this time before Quinn nodded. Alyssa stood up, and Drew was sure she was determined not to be left behind. He didn't blame her, he knew how he felt, if he didn't do something, anything, he was going to explode.

"Alyssa, Drew." Hayley spoke quietly, but something about her voice got his attention as if she'd shouted.

"What?"

"There's something else. It's not crucial right now, but it's something I think you both—" she glanced at Alyssa "—need to hear."

He glanced at Quinn. "Stay, listen," the man said. "Call me when you're done and we'll meet up and continue the search."

Since he didn't seem intent on using this to cut him out of the search, Drew nodded. Slowly, since he wasn't sure if he should be anxious, excited, or simply dreading whatever Hayley had to say. He sat back down at the table. Alyssa sat in the chair beside him. A united front, he thought. On this, they could be nothing less, and it was clear Alyssa knew that.

Hayley slid a paper across the table to them. It was a photocopy of some kind of receipt. Then she added another, this time a copy that looked like a photo print of a very old, worn, even torn in places, timetable of some sort.

"This," Hayley said, indicating the first page, "is a copy of a receipt that was in Doug Kiley's property after the accident."

Drew heard Alyssa suck in a breath. Instinctively he

reached out to take her hand, steady her; no matter how he felt about Doug, she had loved him and this had to feel like a touch from the grave.

"You'll notice it's a simple register receipt, indicating the purchase was made with cash."

Drew went still. Was she going to tell them he'd bought something with the stolen money? Something that might be a clue to where it had ended up?

"There's a dog on it," Alyssa said, frowning.

"It's a receipt from a bus line," Hayley said.

So that was it. They'd managed to track down how Doug had been going to run. He'd been going to get on a bus out of town and leave his nineteen-year-old pregnant girlfriend behind. The old bitterness about his scapegrace brother rose up anew.

"This," Hayley said, "is a copy of the bus schedule and fares that were in effect at the time. And the destination codes that we matched to the receipt."

Belatedly he realized Alyssa's fingers had gone tense beneath his. She was going to feel even worse, now face-to-face with proof Doug had been going to abandon her and her unborn son. He wished Hayley had waited until Luke was safe to reveal this, even if it was going to prove him right. Alyssa didn't need this right now, and—

Her voice gentle, and with a glance at him that Drew thought a bit odd, she finished it.

"On the morning before he was killed, Doug bought two bus tickets."

Drew frowned, but Alyssa gasped.

"Two?"

"Yes," Hayley said, her eyes fixed on Alyssa now. "Two."

"To where?" Alyssa asked, her breathing audibly quicker now.

"Seattle," Hayley said. "He was going to bring you home."

Chapter 29

Drew felt a little numb. Alyssa said nothing, but silent tears trickled down her cheeks.

All this time, all the fights, the arguments, his wishing that she would open her eyes and see the truth about Doug...all this time and she had been right, it had been he who was wrong, who had misjudged his brother even in death.

He'd been going to bring her home.

It didn't matter that he'd been that ne'er-do-well all his life, that he'd been careless and slipshod, relying on looks and charm to get him through life the easiest way possible every day of his twenty-four years. It didn't matter because apparently, when the chips were really down and reality was staring him in the face, he'd done the right thing.

He would have been surprised even if all Doug had done was buy Lyss a ticket home. But he'd bought two, and there was only one explanation for that; he'd been going to bring her home himself. He had no idea what Doug had planned after that, if anything. There was no way to know.

But there was no way to deny what those two pieces of paper proved.

"Thank you," Alyssa said, her voice thick with the tears that had finally slow. "Thank you for finding that."

"It's what you wanted us to do in the first place," Hayley said. "Find the truth about Doug. And the truth is that whatever he was before, in the end he was going to step up."

Still wrestling with the revelation, Drew wasn't sure that Doug hadn't planned on bugging out again the minute he got her home, but he wasn't about to say that. Besides, if he'd been so wrong about this, maybe he was wrong about that, too.

But there was no way to deny that at least this once, he'd been going to do the right thing. For Alyssa and for his unborn child. For Luke.

Luke.

He sucked in a deep breath. For a few moments, he'd been shocked out of the present. But what he'd just learned didn't change what was now. Luke was missing, in the hands of a man Drew feared would stop at nothing. That was what he had to focus on now. Not whether his little brother had, in the last hours of his life, finally grown up.

He would deal with the shattering of his entire image of his irresponsible brother later. He knew his ability to compartmentalize, to set aside one problem to work on another sometimes drove Alyssa crazy, but Luke was so much more important than finding out he'd been wrong about Doug.

He looked at the papers once more, the evidence he'd never thought he'd see, proof that Lyss had been right. He owed her for that, he thought. But *later*.

That damned word again. It was getting to be right up there with *appreciate*. If he kept this up, the whole language was going to drive him crazy before long.

Which was his problem, not hers.

He stood up abruptly. "We need to be looking for Luke."

Alyssa stared up at him. "That's it? That's all you can say?"

"Isn't it the most important?"

"Of course it is," she snapped.

Drew shoved his hands through his hair, lacing his fingers at the back of his head, pushing back against them as if that would somehow relieve the tension. Hayley rose quietly and left without a word, giving them space. Wise woman, he thought. Cutter, on the other hand, stayed put. Drew wondered if he'd nip one of them if they didn't straighten this out soon. He wouldn't put it past him. The dog seemed to understand more than a lot of people did.

"I'm sorry," he said after a moment. "You're right. You've been right. Is that what you wanted to hear?"

"Not if you don't mean it."

"I'm not blind, Alyssa." He gestured at the papers. "I know what that means."

"It's that hard for you to admit you were wrong?"

"What, do you think I'm mad because I was wrong, at least about what Doug was going to do? Do you think I'm not glad that in the end, he did the right thing?"

"I don't know. You hate him so much—"

"I don't hate him, I've never hated him," Drew exclaimed.

"Could have fooled me."

"I've been disappointed in him, angry at him, furious in fact, but I've never hated him," Drew said, knowing he owed her this and more, but hearing the clock ticking as Luke was out there somewhere, alone, scared.

"He was trying to help us. You admit I've changed," she said. "Why can't you give him the same benefit? Admit that he changed?"

In some part of his mind Drew realized what she was admitting, that Doug had been the irresponsible taker Drew had always said he was.

"I'm not sure one good deed makes up for the rest," he said.

"Even dead you can't forgive him. If that's not hate, what is?"

He stood up, needing to move. "What I hated," he said, "was what he did to you. Doing something so stupid, getting himself killed, and leaving you to deal with everything by yourself."

An odd expression came over her face. "It's not his fault I couldn't deal."

"You were nineteen years old, pregnant, you'd left school for him. What were you supposed to do?"

"I was twenty when he was killed," she said.

"And that makes a difference?"

"It sounds older." She shook her head, and stood up herself. "What makes a difference is that Doug was going to bring me home."

"And then what?"

She frowned. "What do you mean?"

"When you got here, what did he expect you to do? Go to your mother for help?"

Alyssa paled at the very thought. "I would have given Luke up before I would let that woman have anything to do with him. He would have spent his life paying for my mistakes."

"Exactly."

She turned, walked over to the window, looked out over the clearing where not so long ago Luke had been playing with Cutter. "She would have made him pay horribly for my mistakes. Especially because he looks so much like Doug."

"Yeah, I noticed," Drew said drily.

Alyssa went still, then slowly turned to face him. "That's part of it for you, too, isn't it? That he looks so much like Doug?"

"I've never held that against him," Drew protested.

"Oh, I know that. But...that's part of why you're so good

with him, isn't it? Why you work so hard at it? You think on some level if Luke comes out all right, it will make up for your brother."

He stared at her. Opened his mouth to deny. But the words wouldn't come. With that knack she had for getting people, for understanding them, she'd somehow put her finger on something he'd never realized.

"Maybe," he muttered, turning the idea over in his head.

"I think," she said slowly, "Doug would have come to you."

"Please. He really did hate me."

"No. He admired you."

"Admired?" Drew asked, incredulous.

She nodded. "He'd had you held up as an example his entire life. An example he knew he could never match. That doesn't mean he didn't admire you. He just knew he couldn't be you."

"So, the way he was really was my fault, is that what you're saying?"

"No. It was his. He never saw that he didn't have to be just like you, that he could have been his own man."

He stared at her again. She'd come a long way in the past two weeks. And something else struck him, something he should have noticed before.

She still wasn't wearing the necklace. The one Doug had given her. The one she'd so rarely taken off. In fact, she hadn't worn it since that night.

He tried not to read too much into that. Something out the window caught his eye. Large, brown and a flash of white as one of the eagles swooped down for a wings-out, gears-down landing in the large maple tree. He thought of Luke's fascination with the majestic birds, and how excited he'd been when Liam had taken him back through the trees to show him the huge nest.

Luke. None of this mattered, not now, not when Luke was out there in trouble.

"Now's not the time for all this. We need to find Luke."

"Yes. We do." She looked at him steadily. "And when we do, you need to tell him that you were wrong about his father. He needs to know that Doug didn't intentionally abandon him, that he didn't purposely desert him before he was even born."

"He's a little young to be thinking like that, isn't he?"

"He ran away because he thought like that, didn't he?"

"I thought he ran away because we were fighting."

"And what were we fighting about?"

Drew threw up his hands. At this point he'd say whatever it took to get out of here and back to searching for his son. "All right. You got what you've always wanted, and you'll get this. I'll tell him I was wrong."

"It has nothing to do with what I want," she said, getting to her feet and facing him down. "This is about Luke. It's always been about Luke." That had never been in doubt, at least not to him. For her, Luke was the center of the world. "I don't matter, Luke does."

You matter to me, he thought. But said only, "Then let's go find him."

At that moment Cutter leapt to his feet. Responding to the words "let's go," Drew assumed. Then realized he'd probably heard Hayley, who just then stepped back into the room.

"They found the car," she said.

Chapter 30

"Sometimes," Quinn said, "all the tech in the world can't take the place of boots on the ground."

Alyssa could hardly argue, not that she would have. Not when they'd found the car that Baird was driving when he took Luke, in less than two hours of searching.

At least, she assumed it was Baird. As Quinn had said, it was the most likely possibility. He didn't believe in that much coincidence, and in this case, neither did she.

Within moments of Hayley stepping back into the room with the news, they'd all piled into her small SUV. Including Cutter, who'd sensed something had happened and beaten them all down the stairs and out the door, opening it himself by batting at the handicapped access control.

"Oh, yes, my boy," Hayley crooned to him as she opened the rear lift gate to let him in. "We're going to need you. If Luke's anywhere close, you'll let us know, won't you?"

The dog swiped a pink tongue over her chin. Alyssa wondered if they had gotten Luke his own dog, if he'd have been as susceptible to Baird's trick with the puppies. Probably, Luke was a loving kid. He still would have worried about a puppy in danger.

Silence reigned in the car once they were moving. Hayley drove with a smooth competence, obviously knowing where she was going. Alyssa opened her mouth to ask where that was, then stopped. It didn't matter now, and she'd find out soon enough.

Quinn's voice came through the speaker on the overhead console, asking their location. Hayley's car obviously had the same comlink system installed as the others. When Hayley told him where they were, he instructed her to take the gravel road to the left after the next bus stop. They were almost on it, so she slowed immediately and made the turn.

"Down past the blue house there's a wide area. Park there. And keep Cutter in the car for the moment."

Hayley reached up and touched a green button. "Copy," she said.

Liam, wearing a heavy black nylon vest with a lot of pockets and a holstered weapon on his right hip, was there waiting when they reached the spot Quinn had mentioned. Alyssa wondered if the vest was also bulletproof, and suppressed a shiver at the thought. When they were out of the car, except for an anxious Cutter, he included them all in a nod and got right to it.

"There's what looks like an abandoned house back there." He gestured with a thumb over his right shoulder, toward a rather overgrown area at the end of the gravel road. "The car's parked in a carport behind an old shed about fifteen feet behind it."

"Luke?" Alyssa breathed.

"Don't know. Tossed a couple of rocks at the trunk, close as I could get without being seen from the house. Didn't hear anything in response."

"I wonder whose car it is," Drew asked. "Does he have help?"

"Don't think so," Liam answered. "Quinn called the

deputy who was at the school, he checked the plate for us and contacted the owner. Seems it's an unreported stolen, from an older lady who doesn't drive much anymore so didn't notice it was gone until he called. He'll be on his way here."

"So Luke could be in the house?" Drew asked.

"We haven't seen him yet. We need to know if Oliver's there before we make a move."

Cutter whined, clearly wanting out of the car.

"Easy, boy," Hayley called to him.

"The house the shed belongs to appears empty, no furniture or appliances," Liam continued. "Looks like it's been unoccupied for a while. We haven't gone inside yet."

Alyssa wanted to demand why, but didn't. And with a glance at her, Liam answered her unasked question. Perceptive bunch, these Foxworth people. Including Cutter.

"The deputy should be here for that. We try not to step on their toes, but we will if we have to," Liam assured her. "And we've checked it as best we can from a safe distance outside. I saw some blankets and food wrappers on the living room floor by the fireplace, and Rafe noticed the woodpile had been disturbed recently. We can't see into the shed, there's only a small window, and it's on the side facing the house, where we'd be seen."

"I just don't want him in Baird's hands one second longer than he has to be," Alyssa said, her voice tight with worry.

"That's what we're all about," Liam said. "Luke first, then we'll deal with Oliver. Or leave it to law enforcement."

"Or me," Drew said grimly.

Liam looked at him for a moment, and then nodded. "I don't think Quinn would be averse to letting you have a moment with the guy."

"Good."

Alyssa stared at him, a little stunned. Drew was strong, and tough, but he was also the most nonviolent man she'd ever known. But right now he looked more than capable of visiting mayhem on the hapless Baird Oliver.

And she realized with a little jolt that she might just enjoy that herself.

Cutter suddenly growled, audible even through the closed car. Simultaneously, a voice came through the speaker of the phone that was in its own pocket on Liam's vest.

"Movement in the shed. Still no visual."

They all froze. That had been the gravelly voice of Rafe Crawford, Alyssa thought. Immediately they heard Quinn's voice in response.

"Animal?"

"Gut says no."

"Good enough," Liam said. At Alyssa's look he added, "Rafe's gut is like a check that's cleared the bank."

Cutter growled again, even more fiercely this time.

"And he obviously agrees," Hayley said.

Liam nodded. "Cutter?" he said into the phone.

"Yes," Quinn said. "Bring him. But keep him close to you for now. Let me know when you're within range."

Hayley, who had clearly been expecting the order, hit the button on the key she had in her hand. The lift gate beeped and started to rise. The moment there was a foot of space Cutter squirmed through, clearly agitated.

"Cutter, stay with me."

The dog growled, looking down the road anxiously.

"I know," Hayley said, putting a steadying hand on his head, "but stay."

He did, but even Alyssa could see he wasn't liking it.

"You'll get your chance," Hayley told the dog. "But we need to be sure Luke doesn't get hurt."

As if she'd presented him with the only acceptable argument, the dog's growl subsided.

"His chance?" Drew asked as they took the easier path down the shoulder of the gravel road, avoiding the telltale gravel itself.

"Quinn may send Cutter in first," Liam said. "I mean, we're not one hundred percent certain Oliver or Luke is really here. He could have just abandoned the car like he did before."

"But this seems like a likely hiding place, doesn't it?"

"Yes. That's why we're assuming Luke's here and being held, until we prove different. We're approaching it on that basis."

Liam led them off the road and into the trees a few yards down the road. Cutter's posture changed once more, and Alyssa sensed the dog already knew where everyone was.

"We're on the east side, twenty feet into the trees," Liam said into his phone, quietly.

"Teague's still on his way from the other side. Send me Cutter," Quinn replied.

Hayley said softly, "Go to Quinn."

Cutter dove into the thick brush as if it weren't there, and in seconds it closed behind him. Hayley spoke into the phone.

"Cutter to you."

"Copy," Quinn's voice came back. "Going off speaker."

"Copy," Hayley returned. She changed something on the phone, then reached into her pocket and pulled out a small earpiece she put in her right ear. Liam did the same. Alyssa felt a qualm. Clearly she and Drew were now out of the loop, and it made her even more nervous.

The humans were forced to take a more zigzag route than Cutter had, along a path wide enough for them. The dog was already there when they met up with Quinn amid the thick trees that surrounded the house and shed. Alyssa looked around.

"I thought I heard Rafe."

"He's picking his spot," Quinn said.

"His spot?" she asked.

Before Quinn could answer, Drew, who got there quicker than she did, muttered, "He'd better be as good as you say."

"He is," Quinn said calmly.

And Alyssa belatedly realized that what Quinn had meant was that Rafe was picking his spot to shoot from. She stifled a tiny moan that held, she realized, the same anxious timbre that Cutter's growl had. The dog was now practically dancing with impatience, looking from Quinn to Hayley, as if awaiting the command that would cut him loose.

"Rafe is our insurance," Hayley said gently. "When the chips are down, or if things go sour, he's who makes sure the innocents—in this case Luke—don't get hurt."

She hadn't thought of it like that, and it made her feel better. And if the fact was unsettling—that having a man around with a sniper rifle was a comfort—it was only a sign of the chaos her life had fallen into in the last two weeks.

Oddly, it soothed Alyssa to look at them. She supposed it was the way of the world, that men who make ordinary people like her nervous were the ones they needed most at times like this.

But it was perhaps Hayley, with her reassuring air and utter confidence in the men of this team, who eased the strain most of all. She had complete faith in the man she loved and the team he'd put together, and it seemed to be catching.

Quinn put a hand to his ear, where Alyssa saw he also had one of the earpieces.

"Copy," he said, then looked at the others. "Rafe's in position. Go."

Without even a nod Liam went, moving silently through the trees, in the opposite direction, heading back toward the road. She guessed it was so he could cut Baird off, if he made it that far.

Before he was ten feet away Cutter's head came up sharply. He gave a short, sharp bark and took off at a head-down run through the trees.

"Damn," Quinn said. "So much for our tactical approach." He touched the earpiece and said "Cutter's incoming."

"I think he heard something," Hayley said.

"Looked like it," Quinn agreed.

"There's only one thing that would make him disobey like that," she said.

Quinn nodded, his jaw set.

"What?" Alyssa asked, although she thought she already knew the answer.

Hayley confirmed it.

"Luke."

"Yes, Cutter's taken the lead again," Quinn said, touching his earpiece, sounding only mildly acerbic as he updated the team. That there was apparently no complaint or even further comment said a lot about their acceptance of what some would find absurd, Alyssa thought.

"Let me go after him," Hayley said. "Oliver won't recognize me, I can be the neighbor chasing down her errant dog. I'm good at it because it's so often true."

Quinn was watching intently as Cutter headed on a beeline for the carport. Was he going for the car he knew was the same one that had taken Luke, or was it something else? Could that amazing nose tell, even from here, that the boy had been in the vehicle, maybe in the trunk? Alyssa felt another shiver go through her, fought it down. She would be no use to Luke at all if she panicked and fell apart now.

"Hayley," Quinn began, clearly about to say no.

"He'll try to bluff, pretend he belongs there, maybe that he just bought the place. I can get a look, see what he's nervous about, where he looks."

"What if he's seen us together?" Alyssa asked. "You've been to the house and we know he's been watching, we're only guessing he hasn't found the house yet."

"It'll still take him a minute to figure it out. And that's all they'll need."

"The shed," Quinn said suddenly.

Alyssa's head snapped around. She stared toward the small, ramshackle building. Cutter was there, along the far side, digging madly, as if he were trying to tunnel inside.

Odd, she thought, how he had chosen that side, where he couldn't be seen from the house. Or maybe not.

"That blows bluffing," Quinn said. "He'll be too paranoid now."

Then the dog's obvious urgency got through to her. "Luke," she exclaimed. "Do you think he's in there right now?"

"I can't think of another reason why he'd do this," Hayley said, her voice reflecting that urgency for the first time.

"Let me go," Alyssa said suddenly. "If Baird sees me he'll be so startled, it will take him off guard."

"Lyss," Drew protested, clearly not liking that idea.

"She has a point," Quinn said.

"And if Oliver's armed, she could get herself shot," Drew said.

"That's my decision," Alyssa said. "My risk to take."

"No," Drew said, his voice tight. "It's not just you you're risking. It's Luke, too. He can't lose his mother. I'll go."

"Baird will be afraid of you," she said. "So he might do something stupid."

"He's got my son, why would he be afraid of me?"

"Because people like Baird are always afraid of men like you."

"Truer words never spoken," Hayley said.

Quinn glanced at her, then back at Cutter. Then he spoke to the team. "Liam, Rafe, hold. I'm going to work around to where Cutter is."

"I'm going with you."

"Drew, no," Alyssa said.

"All due respect, you should stay here," Quinn said.

"I'm not standing here on the sidelines."

Quinn studied him for a moment.

"This is my son we're talking about."

"And he can't lose his father, either," Alyssa said.

For a moment Drew just looked at her, an odd sort of light in his eyes.

"Trust me," he said softly.

"I always trust you," she answered. And realized it was nothing less than the truth. She trusted this man, with her life and more, with Luke's.

Quinn, sounding regretful, ended the conversation. "We need to move. If we can get Luke out, maybe we can just leave Oliver to the hopefully not tender mercies of the sheriff."

"Not sure I want to be that merciful," Drew said grimly. But he was glad Quinn had decided not to fight him.

"I get that," Quinn said. Then, to Hayley, "I'll let you know. Both of you stay put unless you have to move."

She nodded, and Quinn turned and started through the trees. Drew followed. For a couple of big men, Alyssa thought, they moved with amazing quiet. But Quinn was trained, and Drew had grown up here. The branches they brushed past went back into place and they were gone, invisible even though they could only be a few feet away.

"I should be there," Alyssa said, staring at the shed where Cutter was twisted awkwardly, still digging, clearly trying to make room to wiggle through. She wondered what good getting underneath the shed would do, but if Luke was in there, maybe he just wanted to get closer.

"I understand," Hayley said, "But it's the nature of a warrior. They'll worry about you when they should be focused solely on Luke."

She looked at the other woman. She saw the sense of

her words, but couldn't help saying, "Warrior? Quinn, yes, and Rafe obviously, but Drew?"

Hayley met her gaze levelly. "Right now? Yes. Or Quinn wouldn't have let him go at all."

It seemed like eons, but Alyssa was sure it was probably only moments before Hayley put her hand up to her ear, then looked at them. "Quinn says Cutter found a rotted section of the shed floor. He might actually be able to get in. He'll help keep Luke calm. They're going to try and help him wiggle through without making so much noise it alerts Oliver."

Alyssa's breath stopped in her throat. The thought of Baird discovering them when they were this close to finding Luke terrified her. What would he do? He had to know he needed Luke alive to get paid, but if something went wrong...

She watched as a figure emerged from the trees and headed for Cutter. Her breath stopped yet again as she realized it wasn't Quinn, but Drew. Then Quinn emerged, and walked to the corner of the shed away from the house, weapon drawn and clearly ready to cover both Drew and Cutter.

Drew knelt beside the dog, who didn't even spare him a glance. He laid a hand on the dog's back, and Alyssa saw that he said something. Cutter backed out of the hole he'd made, but didn't look happy about it. Drew reached down into the hole the dog had dug, then laid down so he could reach further. Quinn leaned around the corner of the shed to look at the house, blocking her view of Drew and Cutter.

Alyssa waited, tension building until gritting her teeth was the only thing that kept her from screaming out her dread. Drew would keep him safe, she told herself. He would do whatever it took to keep Luke safe. He always had. He always would.

Then three things happened simultaneously.

Hayley touched her ear and said, "Cutter's in."

The back door of the house opened and Baird stepped out.

And she realized with a jolt that she loved her husband.

Chapter 31

He looked scruffy. Baird had never been the snappy dresser Doug had been, but then, he'd never had his charm and good looks to emphasize either. His jeans were ragged and droopy, his shirt looked dirty, and the green jacket was torn. Alyssa remembered the piece of fabric they'd found near Drew's office, and guessed they had the proof now it had been Baird that day.

He still had his hair buzzed, and it showed the oddly bumpy contours of his head. She'd told him once he should let it grow a little, it would be more attractive, and he'd made such a crude joke she'd barely spoken to him from then on.

He said she's the whiny, good-girl type. Good for sex, but not much else. He said I could do her, if I wanted.

The image of that video, the one that had shifted her perceptions of Doug so completely, hammered at her as she watched the man walk across the backyard of the house. Alone.

Toward the shed.

Toward Luke.

She was sure of it now. She wasn't certain when she'd come to trust Cutter's instincts so much, but she did. It was the only thing that made sense. Luke had to be in there, to make the dog so crazy. She looked at Hayley, who was listening intently.

"Rafe has him," she assured Alyssa. "He won't get to Luke."

"Will he shoot him?" To her surprise, she was almost hoping he would. Amazing how her aversion to violence vanished when her son was in danger.

"Not unless he has to." Hayley smiled encouragingly. "Rafe says he stays with Foxworth because we're so good he rarely has to." She stopped, clearly listening. "Quinn says Drew confirms someone's in the shed," she relayed. "He wants to go around to the door and break it down."

"But Baird would see him," Alyssa said.

"That's why Quinn said no. And don't forget, Cutter's inside," she reminded them. "Oliver's going to get a shock if he gets that far."

Baird stopped. He looked around. For an instant Alyssa was afraid to breathe again, afraid he'd heard them, or somehow sensed they were here. But he was looking up more than anything, and when he took a cell phone out of his jacket pocket, looked at it, then moved a few feet, she realized he must be looking for a spot with a stronger signal. Unfortunately, that put him even closer to them, and they froze in place. He was barely fifteen feet away now. Alyssa stared at him through the screen of branches as he tapped on the phone, then put it to his ear.

Her cell phone rang.

For an instant nothing happened. All four of them seemed frozen in shock. Then again, three things happened simultaneously.

She grabbed for her phone to silence it, even knowing it was too late.

Baird turned toward them, eliminating any hope he hadn't heard.

Alyssa did the only thing she could think of. She answered the phone.

"Baird?" she said.

His head snapped back around, as if he were totally confused. He'd never been the brightest bulb, so she pressed her advantage.

"I've been waiting for your call. I've got your money."

"What?"

He was looking around now, as if he was wondering if he'd imagined hearing that ring. Hayley had turned away, was whispering rapidly, clearly telling Quinn what had happened.

Telling him their client was an idiot who didn't even think to silence her phone when her own son's life was at stake.

"Your money," she said. "All one million of it."

That stopped him. She saw a tight little smile cross his face. "Good," he said, apparently distracted now.

"It's heavy, though, you're going to have to help me with it."

"Where are you?" He looked back toward the trees, as if he'd just remembered.

"I'm at Drew's office," she improvised. "You know where that is, don't you? You were there, after all."

"What the— Don't bullshit me, woman. You're here, aren't you? I heard a phone ring, right here."

She gave the best laugh she could. "Phones have changed a lot since you were in prison, Baird. Didn't you know you can hear the other person's ring on your speaker now?"

It was lame, but the best she could do.

"Keep him talking," Hayley whispered. "They're going in."

"Just listen, Baird," Alyssa said, trying to keep her voice level. "I've got the money, now you have to tell me where to bring it."

"Aren't you even gonna ask about your kid?" He sounded suspicious. It took everything she had to keep from screaming at him. The man was still looking in their direction, scanning the trees, clearly not convinced. She was grateful, now, because it meant he wasn't looking at the shed. But she was, and she saw Drew and Quinn at the door working at opening it.

She felt a surge of confidence. She looked back at the man who had gotten Doug killed, and who now was threatening to destroy her life all over again. He was not going to win. She wouldn't let him.

"Come on, Baird," she said. "I know you, remember? You're not stupid enough to hurt him. Or are you?" His intelligence—or lack thereof—had always been a sore spot with Baird, and if it would keep him diverted she had no aversion to jabbing at it.

Hayley touched her arm. Gestured toward the shed. They were in. They'd somehow managed to do it without drawing Baird's attention. Or she'd kept him just distracted enough.

"I'm not stupid," Baird said sharply, just as she'd expected.

"That's what I just said, isn't it?"

"Don't you forget it, either."

"You just want what's coming to you, right?" Alyssa said into the phone.

"All I ever wanted," he said, his voice taking on the self-righteous tone she remembered.

Hayley grabbed her arm. Alyssa looked at her. She was smiling. Widely. Nodding. Giving a delighted thumbs-up.

They had Luke.

Relief flooded her, making her weak in the knees.

"Baird," she said into the phone, "that's what you're going to get. Exactly what's coming to you."

Something in her voice must have warned him, because he looked over his shoulder at the shed. Just in time to see Drew stepping out, covered by Quinn, Cutter dancing at their side, looking up at the blanket-wrapped shape Drew held.

Held. Was Luke hurt? Worse? Her relief vanished, replaced by an impossible dread, which vanished when she saw Luke move, wiggling to look down at the delighted Cutter.

Her head snapped back around as Baird swore. He dropped the phone and reaching toward the small of his back with his left hand. Tugged at something, shoving his ripped green jacket out of the way until she saw what he was going for.

A gun.

Time stopped for an instant as she stared. The two people she loved most were out in the open, clear targets. She was the closest to the threat. Then he freed the weapon and she knew she had to do something. She was only vaguely aware of Hayley behind her, calling out "Gun!" to the others over the comlink.

Baird aimed the pistol toward the shed. Heedless of the danger Alyssa ran. She cleared the trees in the split-second before he fired. Terror filled her as, out of the corner of her eye she saw Drew hit the ground. The shot was still echoing as she shouted.

"Baird!"

The man turned, startled. And his hand, holding the small, black automatic, moved with him. In that split-second another shot rang out. Baird screamed. Dropped the gun. Grabbed at his left shoulder as he staggered back.

Alyssa heard a trumpeting bark she recognized, but she didn't look away from Baird, whose expression of surprise was now shifting to a contorted mask of pain and fury. He was clutching his shoulder, blood already dripping through his fingers.

Then, in an instant, everything changed. The fury in the man's face became fear. Alyssa turned her head.

Cutter.

The big dog was coming at a dead run, no longer barking. If she'd ever seen an animal intent on mayhem, this was him. He barreled into Baird before the man could move, knocking him down and snarling into his face with a ferocity that astonished Alyssa from the usually quiet or playful Cutter. She was so startled she barely thought to kick the weapon he'd dropped out of his reach.

"Don't move," Hayley said to Baird from behind her. "He'll rip your throat out. And I'll let him."

And then Quinn was there, bending to pick up the weapon Alyssa had kicked aside. "And if he doesn't, I may just shoot you for the sheer pleasure of it," he said.

Alyssa didn't wait, she ran to Drew, who was up on one elbow now. She went to her knees beside him, trembling.

"Drew!" She ran her hands over him, searching for blood.

"Lyss?" His voice sounded strained as he stared at her. Was he in pain? She couldn't find a wound. But he sounded so odd. She met his gaze then. His eyes looked strange. Different. Vulnerable.

"Please," she whispered. "You're okay?"

"Oliver?" he asked.

Then Quinn was back, crouching beside them.

"He's down," he said. "I let Rafe take the shot, he's better even at that distance. That shot Oliver got off hit you?"

"No. I'm fine. We need to get Luke."

"Luke!" Alyssa exclaimed, astonished at herself for having even momentarily let him slip out of her mind. "Where is he?"

"I told him to run into the woods when the shooting started," Drew said as he got to his feet.

"After you threw yourself on him, put yourself between him and the line of fire," Quinn said, but it was more admiring than critical.

"You're sure you're all right?" Alyssa asked, still not convinced.

"I'm fine," he repeated. And there was still a trace of that odd expression on his face when he looked at her. She couldn't help herself, she went to him, put her arms around him. After a second's hesitation he returned the embrace.

How on earth was she going to tell him? she wondered. Would he even believe, after all this time, that it was him she loved, not his brother?

Luke first, she told herself as Hayley arrived, Liam at her heels. Once she was assured no one was hurt, she spoke rapidly. "Teague's here. He and Cutter have Oliver."

"We need to find Luke. He'll be scared by now," Drew said. "I told him run as fast as he could, and not to come to anybody but one of us."

Quinn stood. Let out the piercing whistle they'd heard before. In mere seconds, they saw Cutter racing toward them from the road above the house.

"Liam, put on that tracking hat of yours."

"Yes, sir," he said as Cutter reached them. "Come on, boy. Let's find Luke."

Without hesitation the dog spun on his hindquarters and headed into the trees. Alyssa looked at Drew, who shook his head wonderingly. "Exactly the spot," he said.

"Why am I not surprised?" Alyssa asked, feeling remarkably calm now. Cutter would find Luke, she knew it.

And in just a couple of minutes, she was proven right. Quinn tilted his head as if listening, then smiled. "Copy that."

"He's fine," Quinn assured them. "Liam's got him. He's

a bit dirty and hungry, but fine. Consuming sugar, no doubt. You know Liam, he's always got a candy bar handy."

"I need to see him," Alyssa said.

"Of course," Hayley said. "You both do. Let's get the Kiley family back together again."

Chapter 32

"He told me he was a friend of my father's," Luke said. Drew watched the boy look up at Alyssa. "He said you wouldn't let him see me, even though he wanted to. That's why he grabbed me."

"He knew your father," she said, "but he wasn't his friend."

Luke smiled, then said earnestly, "I didn't believe him. He got mad, and tied me up and put me in that shed for the longest time, with tape on my mouth. I got really scared. But then Cutter was there, and I knew it would be okay," Luke said, petting the dog who was leaning against the couch where Alyssa sat with her son on her lap.

"You knew he'd save you, huh?" Drew asked, reaching out to scratch the dog's ear himself.

"No," Luke said, lifting his gaze to meet Drew's. "I knew you would."

Drew's breath caught in his throat. He stared at the boy he loved possibly more than if he'd been his own son.

"See," Luke said when he didn't speak, "I knew if Cutter was there, you were too. So I knew you'd save me."

"And he did," Alyssa said softly.

Something in her voice, in the way she raised her eyes to his made hope leap in his chest. He quashed it, fiercely. He'd had enough of this. He couldn't take it any longer. If nothing else, this nightmare had shown that to him. He just couldn't go on like this anymore. Hope then despair, it was more than he could take. He had to put an end to it.

Liam could take Luke outside, it was safe now. Rafe, after drily commenting that he'd damn near shot Alyssa by accident when she'd bolted into his field of fire, had gone off to wherever he went to unwind. Quinn and Teague were still at the scene with the sheriff's deputies, and Hayley was on the phone in the next room. This was his chance.

"Luke, you want to go out and play with Cutter?"

"Now?" the boy asked, looking happy but doubtful. His mother had refused to let go of him the entire time the sheriff's office had descended and made them go through it all time and again. Only Quinn's rapport with them, the respect they had for Foxworth, had let them leave when they did, to regroup here at the Foxworth building.

"We'll handle this end. You're going to need time to decompress, trust me," Quinn had told them. "Luke will be past this a lot sooner than you will."

"Yes," Drew said now. "Your mother and I need to talk."

Alyssa went very still, but Drew kept his gaze on Luke.

"Oh." The boy's nose wrinkled. "Okay."

"Come on, buddy," Liam said with a glance at Drew that said he understood they needed time alone. "We'll go see if we can find that big ol' raccoon we saw before."

Luke scrambled to the floor and followed the young Texan happily. Cutter got up more slowly, and paused at the door. He looked back over his shoulder, then back at Luke. Then, as if he'd reached a decision, he came back inside and sat at Alyssa's and Drew's feet once more.

Luke frowned, puzzled. "He's probably tired," Liam said. "He's had a busy day."

"Oh." The boy's expression cleared.

"You get too dirty, you're looking at another bath," Alyssa warned. She'd borrowed the bathroom here to clean the boy up once he'd been checked by medical personnel the sheriff's office had called in. They'd pronounced him, thankfully, uninjured, merely dirty and hungry, and not even particularly scared.

"He told us over and over he knew you would find him," the counselor who'd talked to him said when she released him. "You and...Cutter, is it?"

Drew had smiled as he lifted his son in his arms. "Yes, it is. A most remarkable dog."

And now he watched that remarkable dog forego the pleasure of a romp in the woods to stay with them. He didn't believe for an instant he was really tired, but was glad Liam had come up with an explanation Luke accepted. He wasn't at all sure what he himself thought.

"What do we need to talk about that you don't want Luke to hear?" Alyssa asked, sounding more apprehensive than angry.

Drew hesitated, then got up. He stared into the fireplace, at the flames that seemed cheerful compared to the thick, damp overcast outside. Finally he turned to look at her.

"A divorce," he said.

He'd expected her to be relieved, instead she just looked shocked. He hastened to reassure her.

"I'll see that you're taken care of, you won't have to worry. I'll support you and Luke. All I ask is you let me stay..." He stopped, swallowed tightly, made himself go on. "Let me stay in Luke's life."

"You want...a divorce?" She said it in a tiny, shaken voice, as if she'd heard nothing of his assurances.

"It's what you want, isn't it?" She opened her mouth as if to speak, and he cut her off. He wanted to get through this as fast as he could. "It's all right. I understand," he said. "It's my own fault. I should never have expected you to—"

He cut off his own words before he could say the one thing he could never take back.

"Your fault? What is your fault?"

That I fell in love with you, when you never wanted that.

He fought down the words and said instead, "I took advantage of your situation. I know that."

"I think that's called taking responsibility, not advantage. And that's all too rare these days." They both turned at the sound of Hayley's voice. She had come out of the other room, and for a moment stood looking at them from one to the other. "So you think he married you just to take care of Luke, and you think she still loves your brother. Want to know what I think?"

Given what Foxworth had just helped them through, Drew didn't feel he really had the right to say no, so he said nothing.

"I think," Hayley went on, "that people change, and you both need to question whether the reasons you began this marriage have changed. And admit if your feelings have changed." She eyed them almost warningly. "And don't blow it."

She started for the door, then stopped and looked back with a grin, "Oh, and I might caution you to be aware of who's at your feet. Somehow I don't think you're going to get past him until you work this all out."

They both glanced down at Cutter, who was alertly watching them both.

"Trust me," Hayley said with a laugh. "He's done this before. He knows what he thinks is right. So he'd better like your results, because you're not getting out of here until he does."

When she was gone, he turned back to find Alyssa watching him as intently as the dog was.

"Do you really believe I still love Doug?" she asked.

"Haven't you always?"

"I thought so." She stared at him. "But I was wrong. If nothing else, what happened these last two weeks showed me that the Doug I loved didn't really exist. Just as you always said."

"But at the end—"

"Yes, at the end he finally found…a tiny bit of his brother in him, and did the right thing." Drew sucked in a breath. He was afraid to speak, and after a moment she went on. "So we were both right, in a way."

"Lyss," he said, all he could manage.

"Let me say this," she pleaded, standing up, stepping past the watchful Cutter. "I owe it to you."

"You don't owe me anything," he snapped. She'd stayed with him this long because she thought she owed him, and he was done with that. It wasn't enough anymore.

Cutter got to his feet and moved to one side. Drew thought he was just getting out of the way as the tension grew, until he realized the animal had stationed himself between them and the door. He remembered Hayley's words, and wondered.

"Not for that reason," Alyssa said quickly, as if she'd read his thoughts. She crossed the short distance between them in a single stride. "I'm not sure exactly when my feelings changed. Maybe when I changed, when I finally grew up. Yes, at first I stayed because I felt I owed you, in the way you mean. But ever since this started I've been thinking about what my life would be like if something happened to you. I didn't even understand why it felt like the most horrible nightmare I could imagine. Now I do."

"You'd be all right. I told you that."

"No. No I would not be all right. Not without you." He heard her take in a deep breath before she said, steadily and with no small amount of force, "How could I be? I love you."

He really did stop breathing then. But every battered

emotion he'd felt in the last three years rose up to warn him, to tell him not to believe, not to hope again. But he couldn't seem to keep himself from reaching out to brush his fingers against her face.

"You're just saying that because today rattled you."

"I'm saying that," she said as she grabbed his hand, cupped it against her cheek, "because it's true. It has been for a long time, Drew, I just wouldn't admit it, for so many stupid reasons. I love you in a way I never could have loved your brother."

"Lyss," he breathed, stubborn hope rising again. He felt an odd sense of losing his balance, as though his world really was tilting on its axis. Then he realized it was Cutter, behind him, leaning into him as if trying to tip him into Alyssa's arms.

"All I could think about, when you were out there risking yourself for us without a second thought, was how awful my life would be if I lost you. How I'd never told you how I felt. That I love you," she said for the third time.

Drew stared at her for a moment that spun out in silence until he lost track of how long it had been. He'd denied his own feelings for so long that now that the gate was open, they still seemed to cower in a corner, uncertain. Cutter nudged him again. Then the dog came around and sat next to their feet, looking up at them. He made a sound that sounded astonishingly like "Well?" Drew was starting to feel outnumbered.

As maybe he was.

"Am I wrong, Drew?" Alyssa asked, her voice quivering in a way that shot straight through to that deep place where those feelings were cowering. "I thought... I had the feeling you felt the same way. After the other night... I realized you couldn't have made love to me like that, if you didn't care."

Memories of that night seared through his brain, shot fire into that dark place, bringing light to it all.

"Care? Alyssa Kiley, I have loved you since the day you colored those damned shoelaces for Luke."

She blinked, as if startled at that particular reason. "Really?"

"It wasn't just that Luke couldn't lose his mother that made me not want you to confront Oliver," he said. "It was that I couldn't lose you."

"And I can't lose you." She smiled at him, almost shyly. They had been married three years, yet it felt as if they were starting anew.

That smile undid him. He pulled her to him, lowered his head, and kissed her with every bit of the passion he'd concealed for so long. She went pliant in his arms but kissed him back with a fierce eagerness that blasted the last of his restraint to pieces.

For a moment Cutter watched, as if to be sure. He gave a short, satisfied sounding yip. And then, head and tail high, he trotted to the door, hit the automatic button and ran outside to find Luke and play.

Epilogue

"Dad, did you see? Cutter has on a bow tie!"

Luke's delighted giggle was the sweetest sound on earth, Alyssa thought.

She looked around the clearing, now amazingly decorated with ribbons and bows in a bright, clear royal blue and crisp white, row upon row of white chairs, and a pristine white carpet unrolled down the aisle between the sections of chairs. The sky itself was blue. Somehow the fates had conspired to gift the happy couple with one of those severely clear northwest winter days that Drew always said were worth ten days anywhere else.

They'd been prepared, Hayley had told her, to have the ceremony inside if necessary, and the big downstairs rooms had been decorated the same way just in case. But now the room was full of tables, chairs, and a gorgeous cake that Alyssa couldn't quite believe was real. Perfectly square, four stair-step layers tall, frosted in pure white with lattice work on the sides, and decorated with blue ribbons and blue roses, it was beautiful. The figures on top, man, woman and dog made everyone smile. Luke was already eyeing it with interest.

"Is that really a cake?"

"I think so," Alyssa said with a laugh.

"Cutter's on top."

"I saw that."

"Wonder what flavor it is."

"We'll find out," Drew said.

"Why do all the guys have on those funny suits?" Luke asked, looking around to where Teague and Liam were acting as ushers, seating guests in the rows of white chairs. Alyssa wondered which of the sizable crowd were friends and which were grateful former clients. Then decided they were likely all both, just as they themselves were. Or colleagues of a sort and friends, as the just-arrived Detective Dunbar was. Foxworth had that effect.

"The penguin suits, you mean?" Drew said to Luke.

"Don't make it worse, he'll repeat it."

"Fine," Drew said, grinning at her. "You know they're thinking it, too."

Alyssa laughed. She nearly got her fill of that grin these days. Nearly.

Her life had changed so much since that day everything had become so crystal clear to her. She'd come close, perilously close, to losing what she had before she'd realized how precious it was. She'd meant what she'd said to him, that she loved him in a way she had never loved his brother. A deeper way. A more complete way.

A forever way.

And once he'd been sure of her, Drew had opened the gates he'd kept closed for so long and let his love envelop her. From the day she'd come home to find he'd not only been to her parents and repossessed, as he called it, her artwork, but had hung her favorite—that night scene of a brightly lit ferry crossing dark water—she'd sensed how much things had changed. It was the most wonderful feeling she'd ever known.

And Luke had blossomed in the overflow. She felt a twinge of regret that they hadn't realized how much their relationship affected him, but now that it was nearly perfect, the difference was clear. And Drew had, of course, kept his word. He hadn't said another bad word about Doug, in fact had even managed to tell Luke a couple of funny stories from when Doug had been Luke's age. He'd seem surprised himself, as if he'd forgotten there had ever been fun times.

And she was confident enough now that it didn't even bother her when Drew said, "Wow," as a tall, strikingly beautiful brunette in an exquisitely cut blue silk dress that matched the wedding colors strode across the lawn.

"Indeed," she agreed.

"I just meant I wonder how she walks in those heels," Drew said. "On the grass and all."

"Uh-huh." She let a teasing note into her voice, not feeling a bit threatened by the beautiful maid of honor, whoever she was.

A man walked up to the woman in blue. Rafe, who was still a little taller than she was even in the heels. For a moment they didn't speak, although she guessed they had to have met each other before. Then they both nodded, the maid of honor and best man confirming their respective charges were ready.

And the ceremony began. She heard the sweet, mellow sound of a wooden Celtic flute, playing a slow, romantic tune that tugged at something deep inside. It was the only music there was, but in this setting, it was all that was needed. With the evergreens towering over the clearing, the blue sky above, it seemed perfect.

Alyssa felt her eyes begin to tear from the moment an obviously energized Quinn took his place in front of the festooned gazebo. Rafe, the limp barely visible today, stood beside him, his expression solemn. The woman in blue led the way, walking gracefully down the aisle between the two sections of seats. Smiles and a bit of applause broke out as Cutter followed, in his blue bow tie, gently carrying a blue satin bag by its strings.

"Do you think Texas could do that?" Luke asked.

Alyssa smiled at the thought of the black-and-white puppy who had nearly cost them so much, but who was now their son's beloved companion. They'd found out Baird had stolen the three from a backyard, using the first two to draw the attention of the other kids, and the last one to lure Luke off by himself by throwing it literally under a bus. The owners, upon hearing the story, had been horrified, and had gladly given the puppy to them when Luke had been loath to give him up.

And then the flute player changed to a gloriously triumphant flourish, and Hayley was there. Her dress gleamed white in the sun until she passed, and Alyssa could see the matching blue insert flowing down the back in a swath that seemed to pull everything together.

As Hayley herself so often did, Alyssa thought with a bit of whimsy.

"Wow," Drew said again.

"Indeed," Alyssa repeated. They smiled at each other. Drew took her hand. His fingers ran over her wedding band, and stilled there. She looked up at him.

"Marry me," he whispered.

She drew back, startled.

"You guys *are* married," Luke explained, distracted from the ceremony and watching Cutter walk perfectly down the aisle in front of one half of the couple he'd brought together.

"Marry me again," Drew said, never taking his gaze off her. "For real."

A tear welled up and over. "Yes," she whispered back. "Oh, yes."

Drew's fingers tightened around hers, and she thought she caught the gleam of moisture in his eyes as he turned back to the ceremony at hand.

The music faded, the bride and groom took their places, and Alyssa knew she'd never seen a couple more likely to make it through whatever life threw at them. She smiled when Cutter took his cue perfectly and presented the little bag that contained the rings to Rafe and the woman in blue. The dog that had begun it all then sat at their feet as if he were following every word of the vows his people then made.

And in that last moment, when they were introduced as man and wife, the entire gathering gasped as two bald eagles swooped into view, circled overhead, dived, rolled, soared again and then vanished into the trees.

"They mate for life, you know," Quinn said, looking at his wife, loud enough for all to hear.

"Yes, they do," Hayley said, looking at her husband.

Cutter barked. As if it were their own cue, the attendees as one stood up, cheering, applauding.

Whatever adventures awaited, the Foxworth family, all of them, would face it all together.

* * * * *

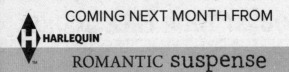

COMING NEXT MONTH FROM

ROMANTIC suspense

Available July 1, 2014

#1807 LONE WOLF STANDING
Men of Wolf Creek • by Carla Cassidy
Sheri Marcoli is searching for two things: her missing aunt and her fairy-tale prince. The damaged and fierce detective Jimmy Carmani is nothing like the man she envisions, but when the kidnapper sets his sights on her, it's Jimmy who rides to Sheri's rescue.

#1808 SECRET SERVICE RESCUE
The Adair Legacy • by Elle James
Secret service agent Daniel Henderson saves the rebellious secret heiress Shelby O'Hara from a cartel looking to pressure her grandmother to drop out of the political race. But when they're forced into hiding, sparks fly and Daniel realizes the biggest threat is to his heart.

#1809 HOT ON THE HUNT
ICE: Black Ops Defenders • by Melissa Cutler
Former black ops agents and ex-lovers Alicia and John are both on the hunt for the team member who betrayed them, but when the tables are turned, they must team up, trust each other and trust in the love they once shared.

#1810 THE MANHATTAN ENCOUNTER
House of Steele • by Addison Fox
When the commitment-phobic Liam Steele agrees to protect the shy research scientist Dr. Isabella Magnini, neither expects the explosive danger they find themselves in or the equally explosive attraction they feel for each other.

YOU CAN FIND MORE INFORMATION ON UPCOMING HARLEQUIN® TITLES, FREE EXCERPTS AND MORE AT WWW.HARLEQUIN.COM.

HRSCNM0614

REQUEST YOUR FREE BOOKS!
2 FREE NOVELS PLUS 2 FREE GIFTS!

ROMANTIC suspense

Sparked by danger, fueled by passion

YES! Please send me 2 FREE Harlequin® Romantic Suspense novels and my 2 FREE gifts (gifts are worth about $10). After receiving them, if I don't wish to receive any more books, I can return the shipping statement marked "cancel." If I don't cancel, I will receive 4 brand-new novels every month and be billed just $4.74 per book in the U.S. or $5.24 per book in Canada. That's a savings of at least 14% off the cover price! It's quite a bargain! Shipping and handling is just 50¢ per book in the U.S. and 75¢ per book in Canada.* I understand that accepting the 2 free books and gifts places me under no obligation to buy anything. I can always return a shipment and cancel at any time. Even if I never buy another book, the two free books and gifts are mine to keep forever.

240/340 HDN F45N

Name _____ (PLEASE PRINT) _____

Address _____ Apt. # _____

City _____ State/Prov. _____ Zip/Postal Code _____

Signature (if under 18, a parent or guardian must sign) _____

Mail to the **Harlequin® Reader Service:**
IN U.S.A.: P.O. Box 1867, Buffalo, NY 14240-1867
IN CANADA: P.O. Box 609, Fort Erie, Ontario L2A 5X3

Want to try two free books from another line?
Call 1-800-873-8635 or visit www.ReaderService.com.

* Terms and prices subject to change without notice. Prices do not include applicable taxes. Sales tax applicable in N.Y. Canadian residents will be charged applicable taxes. Offer not valid in Quebec. This offer is limited to one order per household. Not valid for current subscribers to Harlequin Romantic Suspense books. All orders subject to credit approval. Credit or debit balances in a customer's account(s) may be offset by any other outstanding balance owed by or to the customer. Please allow 4 to 6 weeks for delivery. Offer available while quantities last.

Your Privacy—The Harlequin® Reader Service is committed to protecting your privacy. Our Privacy Policy is available online at www.ReaderService.com or upon request from the Harlequin Reader Service.

We make a portion of our mailing list available to reputable third parties that offer products we believe may interest you. If you prefer that we not exchange your name with third parties, or if you wish to clarify or modify your communication preferences, please visit us at www.ReaderService.com/consumerchoice or write to us at Harlequin Reader Service Preference Service, P.O. Box 9062, Buffalo, NY 14269. Include your complete name and address.

HRS13R

Sheri Marcoli is searching for two things: her missing aunt and her fairy-tale prince. The damaged and fierce detective Jimmy Carmani is nothing like the man she envisions, but when the kidnapper sets his sights on her, it's Jimmy who rides to Sheri's rescue.

Read on for a sneak peek of

LONE WOLF STANDING

by *New York Times* bestselling author
Carla Cassidy,
available July 2014 from
Harlequin® Romantic Suspense.

"That's better than being poisoned, right?"

He was aware of the weight of her intense gaze on him as he pulled out of the animal clinic parking lot. "I'm no veterinarian, but I would think that definitely it's better to be tranquilized than poisoned." He shot a glance in her direction.

She frowned. "That man in the woods broke Highway's leg. I don't know how he managed to do it, but I know in my gut he probably broke the leg and then somehow injected him with something. Highway would never take anything to eat from anyone but me, no matter how tasty the food might look or smell. Jed and I trained him too well."

They drove for a few minutes in silence. "Sorry about the pizza plans," she finally said.

He flashed her a quick smile. "Nothing to apologize for.

I'm guessing you didn't plan for a man to attack your dog and then chase you in the woods tonight. I think I can forgive you for not meeting up with me for a slice of pizza."

"Thank God you came to find me." She wrapped her slender arms around her shoulders, as if chilled despite the warmth of the night. "If you hadn't shown up when you did, I think he would have caught me. I will tell you this, he seemed to know the woods as well as I did, so it has to be somebody local."

"We'll figure it out." He seemed to be saying that a lot lately. "Maybe in the daylight tomorrow we'll find a piece of his clothing snagged on a tree branch, or something he dropped while he was chasing you."

"I hope you all find something." Her voice was slightly husky with undisguised fear. "I felt his malevolence, Jimmy. I smelled his sweat."

"You're safe now, Sheri, and we're going to keep it that way. Highway is going to be fine and we're going to get to the bottom of this."

"So…so, what happens now?" she asked.

"Since we didn't get our friendly meeting for pizza, we're going to do something else I've heard that other friends do," he replied.

"And what's that?" she asked.

He flashed her a bright smile as he pulled in front of her cottage. "We're going to have a slumber party."

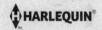

ROMANTIC suspense

HOT ON THE HUNT
by Melissa Cutler

ICE: Black Ops Defenders

**Lust and danger collide in the Caribbean in this
ICE: Black Ops Defenders title!**

Burned black-op ICE agent Alicia Troy spent years
plotting the perfect revenge on the man who left her for
dead...until her plan is foiled by her ex-teammate and
lover, who taught her the meaning of betrayal. She can't
trust John Witter...so why can't she stop wanting him?

Look for *HOT ON THE HUNT* from the
ICE: Black Ops Defenders miniseries by Melissa Cutler
in July 2014. Available wherever books and
ebooks are sold.

**Also from the *ICE: Black Ops Defenders* miniseries
by Melissa Cutler**

*SECRET AGENT SECRETARY
TEMPTED INTO DANGER*

Available wherever ebooks are sold.

Heart-racing romance, high-stakes suspense!

www.Harlequin.com

HRS27879

HARLEQUIN®

ROMANTIC suspense

THE MANHATTAN ENCOUNTER
by Addison Fox

House of Steele

"Men like Liam Steele didn't settle down."

When the commitment-phobic Liam Steele agrees to protect the shy research scientist Dr. Isabella Magnini, neither expects the explosive danger they find themselves in or the equally explosive attraction they feel for each other.

Look for *THE MANHATTAN ENCOUTER*
by Addison Fox in July 2014.

Don't miss other exciting titles in
The House of Steele miniseries by Addison Fox:

THE ROME AFFAIR
THE LONDON DECEPTION
THE PARIS ASSIGNMENT

Available wherever books and ebooks are sold.

Heart-racing romance, high-stakes suspense!

www.Harlequin.com

HRS27880